$90 MILLION MORE EXCITING THAN THE FRENCH CONNECTION

Brilliantly told by the author of the original FRENCH CONNECTION, from information that comes directly via the confidential files of the New York narcotics squad, this thrilling story of the biggest heroin heist in history emerges as a whirling typhoon of corruption that whips into the very heart of ambition and greed.

It all began that day in the offices of New York Prosecutor Nadjari, whose job it was to decide whether one dead cop was a suicide or a murder victim. It becomes the tale of how a bright young city policeman can be challenged to change into a vicious harbinger of the evil world to come; how a handsome, unmarried kid with sex on his mind can be strung out along a trail of high crime and —more dangerous than anything—*bad connections . . .*

Now, at last, this story can be told.

"THIS IS A SET UP, RIGHT?"

Sally Friedlander, the D.A., took her place in the big upholstered swivel chair behind the desk and spun around in it slowly, like a child playing in her father's office.

"They're just testing you out," she said. "They're pretty nervous about shoo flies these days."

The swivel chair tilted back to reveal a pink patch of thigh and a sudden flash of Pucci bikini. Palmer could even make out several golden curls of pubic hair peeking out from under the elastic.

Sally sat, her legs spread seemingly for balance, oscillating slowly on the swivel chair, her crotch swaying like a golden pendulum. She gave him a calculating look, her lips parting in a mocking smile.

"You don't *have* to play with us, Day," she said.

The Set Up

The Set Up

ROBIN MOORE
with
Milt Machlin

A Critic's Choice paperback
from Lorevan Publishing, Inc.
New York, New York

ISBN: 0-931773-01-6

First Critic's Choice edition: 1985

From LOREVAN PUBLISHING, INC.

Published in association with Interpub Communications, Inc.

Critic's Choice Paperbacks
31 E. 28th Street
New York, New York 10016

Manufactured in the United States of America

CHAPTER ONE

The black '66 Mustang rolled silently through the streets of the Barrio; like a rusted-out ghost—up Pleasant Avenue, across one of the side streets to Park, down Park to One Hundred and Third, across One Hundred and Third and up Madison. It cruised past the *cuchifrito* joints, past the travel agency marked *"Viajes,"* past the *botanicas* where you could buy monkey fists or frankincense or "chinese wash" to take off the hex some bitch *cura* had put on you.

Inside the car, two men talked a little and carefully watched the lonely three A.M. streets brightened only occasionally by a rare, still-open bar whose tinny jukebox sounds splashed eerily into the night.

The younger of the two men was driving. He was about twenty-eight, and tall. His head nearly touched the low roof of the Mustang. The other man was in his early forties, dark-skinned, good-looking with wavy black hair puffed into a little pompadour in the center. He held a Motorola Handie-Talkie portable radio unit in his hand which he flicked on and off occasionally, trying to make contact with base. The two men were Tactical Police Force officers in plain chothes. They were cruising the streets of New York's Puerto Rican community at the special request of the mayor relayed to them by their commander.

"The citizens want more coverage up in Spanish Harlem. Get your asses up there and make some good collars. If you have to roust a few citizens to do it; don't let it bother you."

So that's how Dayton "Day" Palmer and Sgt. Frank "Pancho" Navarro wound up in this foreign town in the middle of New York, rolling down one street and up another in Palmer's personal car.

The Mustang had been a high school graduation present from Palmer's father. Through the years he had modified it until it was as personal as his thumbprint. The original two-hundred-and-eighty-six-horsepower engine had been replaced with a '69 blown four-hundred-and-twenty-nine-cubic-inch mill fed by a four-barrel Holley carburetor. Slotted wheels with Pirelli radials on Cragar rims and a Hurst stick-shift transmission had been added. But the exterior was deceptively dull, covered with only a dead black primer-coat. Originally Palmer had planned to paint it fire-engine red. But later he enjoyed the reverse snobbism of sitting behind the wheel of an ancient shot-down looking wreck that could hit 100 miles an hour in forty seconds from a standing start.

"Fucking cheap outfit," Navarro said. "Can't even afford a two-way radio car. These goddamn Motorolas won't carry more than a few blocks if there's any obstructions around, and all these new housing projects block it out ninety percent of the time."

"Well, it won't be too much longer," Palmer said. He was blonde and thin-faced with a serious intense expression and looked more like the college basketball guard that he had been than a member of New York's tough elite police group. Navarro, his partner, looked like a cop—but a recruiting poster version. Sharp features, on the dark side, a smile that showed

6

straight shining teeth, a ready laugh. He looked like a fifties big-band singer with his slightly tousled black wavy hair, and he was almost as popular with women as a pop music star—or so locker room gossip had it.

Palmer, at the wheel of the Mustang, squinted at his watch in the light of the street lamp. "They told us if we don't see any action by four A.M., we should call in and get reassigned. It's after three now."

"Yeah," Navarro said, "not much chance for anything at this hour. Nothing but B and E's. Maybe some lush-rollers. No chance for any good narcotics collars. Too late. Maybe we'll run into some *cabron* hitting on his wife."

"Why did they give us this shit assignment, anyway?" Palmer asked. He was ambitious and resented the lack of action on that beat.

"Well, you speak that dumb high-school Spanish of yours," Navarro said. "And me, well, they don't call me Pancho for nothing, amigo." His great teeth flashed in quiet laughter.

"Are you a uh—P.R.?"

Navarro roared with laughter at this. "*Coño!* I'm not one of those Marine Tigers. I'm a Tex-Mex, boy! Remember the Alamo and all that shit. I had folks on both sides of the border but they figure I can handle these spics down here better than your average Paddy; and as for you, most of these scum bags on the force can't even talk English, let alone Spanish. So I guess you're all they got."

His smile showed that he was only kidding. In fact, the two men got along very well.

Day Palmer, after five years patrolling the eight-one on foot, had less than a year in the TPF but he had worked closely with Pancho most of that time.

Pancho had come to TPF from the Narcotics Squad, where he had made a fantastic record with very heavy collars. There was some occasional gossip around the station house attributing dark and mysterious motives to his transfer to TPF, which is a fairly straight-arrow gung-ho outfit, from the lucrative Narcotics Squad.

Some people said that Pancho was cutting too big a swath with the Narcs and the transfer was at his commander's request, even though TPF was supposed to be an all-volunteer outfit. Others said Pancho had sticky fingers. They called him a "ten percenter"—ten percent of any loot he confiscated was never turned in. Once, it was rumored he had ripped off half of a case of smuggled German guns.

Whatever the reason for his transfer, Day Palmer didn't care. Navarro was gutsy, dependable and had a good sense of humor and he was never boring to be with, although, sometimes Palmer was put off by Navarro's constant woman-chasing. It seemed to him heavy going for a man with a beautiful wife and a three-year-old daughter.

Palmer had actually never met the wife and daughter but he had seen their pictures displayed prominently in Navarro's wallet. He had to give Navarro credit for one thing—he never bullshitted his women. He always told them straight out that he was married and had a kid and was interested in only quick trips. So what the hell?

"What time did you say it was, kid?" Navarro asked.

"Just after three."

"I tell you what, do me a favor. There's an all night *bodega* on One Hundred and Third Street just east of Park Avenue. Let's roll over there. I promised the wife I'd pick her up some *refritos* and *chorizo*. She's crazy for that spic food."

Palmer wheeled the Mustang through the dark tunnel, frescoed with graffitti, that ran under the New York Central tracks. He drove south on the other side of the big dirty granite walls to One Hundred and Third Street, rolling past the *marketa* which was said to be the biggest supermarket in the city but which was silent now, its stalls of tropical fruits and magic herbs covered by dark canvases.

"The guy that runs the grocery store we're going to has a big *bolita* operation. Not as big a game as

8

the Harlem numbers thing. I guess they pull twenty-five, thirty-five million a year out of this little section. But I doubt that we can make any collar this time of night; besides I think he just got a kid watching the place, selling a little beer and some rice and beans—late suppers."

Day Palmer wheeled the Mustang smoothly around the corner at One Hundred and Third Street and pulled up in front of the little island of light, its windows a jumble of exotic fruits, sausages and cheeses. The window and food alike were liberally dotted with flyspecks.

He pulled the battered car to the curb behind a parked plumbing supply van—the only car in the street it seemed. Palmer could only guess that few people in this neighborhood had cars or didn't care to leave them out at night on the streets; or perhaps it was the fact that the street was marked "Tow Away Zone" on both sides. He wondered why the delivery van hadn't been towed away. Maybe there was a local pay-off.

Navarro turned to him. "Listen, kid, do me a favor. Practice your Spanish. Get in there and pick me up about a pound of *chorizos* and a couple of those big yellow cans of *refritos* and maybe five or six *platanos* too. You know what they are. They're those green banana-like things."

"Oh, yeah," Dave said. "They fry them, right?"

"Right, just like potato chips."

"How come you want *me* to go?"

"I'll tell you, I've been watching this place for a while," Frank said. "And I don't want them to get to know my face too good. You know what I mean? Like you're a new face. Keep your eyes open. Hang around there a little, look over the stuff. Maybe you can get a few ideas. We can make a good collar sometime. Take your time. You can write it in your book as a personal. I tell you what. Get a couple of containers of coffee while you're there, for us."

Dave looked at him skeptically. Navarro's story

didn't quite hang together as far as he was concerned; but what the fuck, maybe he was just tired.

Palmer got out of the car which was parked about twenty yards past the store and walked back toward the sound of an all-night rock station loud enough to echo off the brownstones across the street.

A dark pimply-faced kid who didn't look much over seventeen was lounging behind the counter reading a copy of *El Diario* and popping his fingers absently to the sounds of the *Led Zeppelin*. "Christ," Palmer thought to himself, "that kid looks more like a stick-up man than a store clerk."

He searched around on the self-service shelves and found the *refritos*. The black-flecked *platanos* were lying, along with a display of coconuts and mangos, in a stand on the left side of the store. He took them to the counter and asked the kid to cut off seven or eight links of *chorizo* and weigh them. The kid took the order, barely lifting his eyes from the paper and whistling through his teeth.

Palmer put down a five-dollar bill. The kid said, "That'll be five forty-two."

"Are you kidding?" Palmer said. "Just for a couple of sausages, some bananas and beans?"

"This ain't a supermarket," the kid said. "Besides, *chorizo* is a dollar eighty-nine a pound."

Grumbling, Palmer threw some coins down on the counter and left, forgetting entirely about the coffee.

When he got back to the car, Navarro was lying with his head thrown back against the seat, dead to the world.

"Shit," Palmer said, "that's probably why he sent me in. Wanted to take a snooze. No sense in waking him now, it's almost the end of the shift." He threw the paper sack into the back of the Mustang and started the car without waking his partner. As he turned south onto Lexington, Navarro suddenly slid down on the seat and then rolled clumsily against Palmer's arm.

10

"Hey, wake up, Frank. Wake up, Pancho!" he said. "I can't drive with you leaning on me like that."

Navarro didn't say anything. He just gave a little choking cough.

Palmer, glancing down in reaction to the sound, was shocked to see a broad stream of blood running from the corner of his partner's mouth. It wasn't till then that he noticed that Navarro's right hand was clutching his chest and even more blood was oozing through his fingers onto the floor of the car.

CHAPTER TWO

Palmer quickly pulled the Mustang to the curb on Lexington Avenue and tried to straighten up the stocky body, but it was completely limp. Palmer didn't need a medical degree to sense that he was dealing with a dead man. He reached for Navarro's pulse, but there wasn't a sign of a beat. The face was already going pale and grey.

The Motorola unit was on the floor. Next to it, near the door, was a silvery Walther PPK automatic. At least that's what it looked like in the dark, illuminated only by the courtesy light under the dashboard. Frantically, Palmer tried to raise a signal with the Motorola.

"Delta Mustang to Delta control. Delta Mustang to Delta control . . ."

Nothing. They must have been in another dead reception area. Palmer knew that whatever had happened here was well out of the range of his Police Academy first-aid course. In any event, they were only about five blocks from Flower Fifth Avenue

Hospital at One Hundred and Sixth and Fifth. It would be faster to get him to the emergency ward and call in from there.

Ignoring the one-way sign, Palmer wheeled right on One Hundred and Second Street, raced the four crosstown blocks and up Fifth to the emergency entrance of Flower, as the heavy limp form on the seat next to him bounced grotesquely and finally lurched over against the dashboard.

With one hand, Palmer tried to push his partner into a sitting position; but the body was too heavy and it seemed pointless to stop.

The interns, one a Turk who barely spoke English, the other a blonde kid who didn't look more than twenty, took a look at the gaping wound in Navarro's chest and shook their heads helplessly. "Sorry, this is a DOA, you'd better call the coroner and maybe Forensic. How did it happen?"

"Shit! Never *mind* how it happened! Do something! He *can't* be dead. He only got hit five minutes ago!"

"This guy's been *dead* for five to ten minutes, looks to me. Done a lot of bleeding and it looks like he took a shot right in the heart. I can't get any pulse beat and the heart's all torn up by the bullet. We'll put him in intensive care and shoot some adrenalin and blood into him, but I'm telling you now, you can just about forget it."

′ Palmer, who had been given to uncontrollable fits of crying in summer camp and at prep school, swallowed deeply, bit his lip and turned away from the interns. The last time Day Palmer had cried so anyone could see it was when they took his old man away to the federal pen in Danbury. He'd learned a lot of tricks by now to keep the tears out of his eyes, and fake the look of stoic indifference that was expected of a man among men. That's what his father had told him before he went away. He'd been angry. "I don't want you to cry, son. Act like a man. Pull yourself together and stop snivelling."

Those were the last words Day Palmer had heard

13

from his father. He died a few months later of a heart attack in the laundry room in Danbury.

Two attendants who looked like recent graduates from a school for the retarded, hoisted the detective's limp form onto a rolling stretcher. There was a small hole just below the lapel of Navarro's tweed sports jacket. It was surrounded by a wet puddle of blood the size of a dinner plate, which extended over the jacket and onto the yellow sport shirt. Palmer pushed the intern aside and leaned over the grey face of his partner.

"Pancho, you're okay, right, you're okay, aren't you?"

He thought there was the flutter of one eyelid.

"He's moving, you son-of-a-bitches!" he said to the interns. "He's not dead. Look, his eye just moved."

"That don't mean anything, kid. Take my word for it," the older intern said. "Just reflex or something. We'll do what we can."

They wheeled him off toward the intensive care unit. Palmer slumped into a plastic chair in the reception room. Next to him was a weeping Puerto Rican woman who sat rocking back and forth saying only *"mi hijo, mi hijo."* Across from him, a skinny black kid about fourteen, wearing a satin jacket in which the words "Savage Lords" were proudly traced in yellow flannel, sat holding up a knife-slashed hand patiently waiting his turn while the blood ran down his sleeve. In a corner, a grey-faced man, in a suit that matched his complexion, sat bent over in agony, groaning, "Can't somebody do something? I'm dying! God, this hurts."

Palmer watched it all dully, barely registering

How could it have happened? He hadn't been in the store more than five minutes, maybe ten. The streets were deserted. He'd heard nothing. Of course, that fucking radio would have drowned out the sound of any shots. It couldn't have been a rip-off, they would have taken the gun. Besides, there wasn't even time to have searched him. Was it just one of those

14

crazy cop killings? One of those *"off the pigs"* capers that had been so popular in the Eight One? An initiation stunt for some teenage street gang? It was senseless. Then another thought occurred to Palmer. Suppose Navarro had gone in for the sausage and beans. Would he himself had been the victim?

Detectives from the Two Three precinct were there in less than fifteen minutes. After talking to the interns, they approached Palmer, still slumped in his plastic chair in the reception room.

"You're partner's had it, kid," the older of the two precinct detectives said.

He was a tall, thin, grey-haired man. He looked more like a college professor than a cop. He put his hand on Palmer's shoulder.

"I'm sorry. We'd better call Manhattan North Homicide on this. Just take it easy for a while. Can I get you a cup of coffee, or a drink or anything?"

Palmer slumped over, his head between his hands.

"Nothing," he said. "I can't understand it. I can't understand how it happened."

In ten minutes, the car was there with the detectives from Manhattan Homicide North. The forensic team came shortly afterwards. They impounded the Mustang as evidence and did the usual swarming over the car, taking photographs and so on and dusting for prints. Detective First Grade Jules Myer took charge of the investigation for homicide. He was a stubby man, built like a fire plug with straight black hair, balding like a monk's tonsure in the back and what seemed to be a perpetual dead cigar clutched in his teeth. He took Palmer into a side room and questioned him briefly about the incident, but there wasn't much the young cop could say.

"We were cruising in the neighborhood. We didn't make any contacts at all. We just stopped to check out this *bodega*. I went inside, I was gone five minutes and when I came back he was . . . like that."

Myer took him over the ground two or three times,

but there was nothing to add to it. Palmer had heard no sounds, no shots, seen no one in the street.

"Do you think he could have met someone while you were in the store?" Myer asked.

Day shrugged, "Anything can happen. But it seemed to me we just suddenly decided to go there. I don't know who he could have met."

"Can I see your gun, Palmer?" Myer said quietly.

Palmer took the snubnose thirty-eight from his flip-on belt holster and handed it to the detective. The detective flipped the cylinder of the revolver open and smelled the barrel, then returned the gun.

"Just routine," he apologized.

About a quarter to five, Myer's partner Fred Klein came in looking grim.

"This is gonna look shitty for the department," he said disgustedly. "Navarro's definitely a suicide. The slug came from the Walther that was on the floor of the car."

"You're crazy," Palmer shouted. "Pancho didn't commit suicide. I just went in to get him some groceries to take home to his wife. Why the fuck would he commit suicide?"

"I thought you said you were checking the *bodega* out," Myer said.

"Sure I said that. I didn't want to say that I was on a shopping trip. Besides, I *was* checking it out, it's a *bolita* drop. But Pancho asked me to get beans and sausage for his wife. Does that sound like a guy who is gonna commit suicide?"

"Maybe he just wanted you out of the way."

"Listen, you guys are crazy," Palmer said. "A guy doesn't shoot himself in the belly when he commits suicide."

"It happens sometimes," Myer argued.

"Well, why would he use the Walther, lousy thirty-two caliber, when he had the thirty-eight service piece?"

"How do I know?" Myer said. "Maybe he was sentimental about his service gun."

16

"Well, what the fuck makes you say he was suicide? I don't get it."

"You got to believe it, kid, I'm sorry. The thing is, he left this note. It was on the seat next to him." Myer handed over a single sheet of typed paper. It said:

I AM SORRY FOR WHAT I AM DOING, BUT I CAN'T STAND IT ANYMORE. THE PROBLEMS ARE JUST GETTING TOO BIG. I CAN'T SEE ANY OTHER WAY OUT.

FRANCISCO P. NAVARRO

The signature was typed too.

Palmer read the note carefully three times before handing it back to the detective.

"Probably those broads he was seeing finally got to him," Myer said sympathetically.

Palmer turned to him angrily. "Who are you trying to bullshit? That note's a fake!"

CHAPTER THREE

Day Palmer lived in the Bailey Avenue section of the extreme northwest Bronx between Marble Hill and Riverdale. The house was a sagging wooden one-family structure, built in the boom times just after World War I. It needed paint, a new roof, new siding, new plumbing and new wiring. But Palmer had no intention of giving it all that attention. It had been left to him by his mother, who died only a year after his father's collapse, and had been listed with the local real estate agent ever since. Palmer was waiting only for the right price.

Once his parents died, Day Palmer had to drop out of Syracuse, where he had been playing guard on the basketball team and majoring in electronic engineering on the side. He joined the force. It was a way of getting even for all the rotten things they'd said about his father, a man who would walk a half mile to return the overpayment of a nickel in his grocery change.

Palmer planned to sell the house someday, marry,

and get out of the neighborhood. Meanwhile, he continued on in the old homestead, closing off his parents' bedroom and living in the large sunny room which had been his since childhood.

On the night of Navarro's death, the detectives impounded the Mustang as evidence and he was forced to take the Jerome-Woodlawn Lexington train to the Bronx and take a taxi from the Mosholu Parkway Station. It was a forty-five-minute ride. The train was empty at that time of day with all the passengers moving downtown to work. By the time he was actually on the train, it was almost nine o'clock in the morning.

He was exhausted from the emotional shock and the long hours. He would have welcomed the oblivion of sleep; but sleeping on the Jerome-Woodlawn or any other New York subway train was not a very good idea. The lush-rollers and stick-up men had no respect for hours; all they wanted was an empty subway car. In any event, Day Palmer would not have been able to sleep. There was too much on his mind.

Why had the detectives come so quickly to the conclusion of suicide? They'd barely given him a glimpse of the typed note. It was short and indefinite—simply claiming despair over "problems."

But Palmer had seen no sign of any such state of mind the four hours they had been together prior to Frank Navarro's death. The only thing odd about the evening that he could recall, even after much thought, was Navarro's asking Palmer to go into the *bodega*, and the request wasn't all *that* strange.

Certainly it seemed like an unusual time to select for suicide. Why would Pancho not have waited until he was alone? And then the Walther. It was unreliable for such a job. Too small-caliber, especially for a body shot, and with a tendency to jam. Wouldn't it have made more sense to use the heavier thirty-eight snubnose? Yet, the detectives had said that they found Frank's prints on the stock. Also, the automatic had been found on the floor near the door on the right hand side of the car. But Frank Navarro almost always shot with his left hand although he was ambidexterous.

When Day Palmer raised these questions to Detective Myer, the detective shrugged. "He didn't *always* shoot with his left hand, did he?"

"In practice he used both hands; but on the job he always used his left hand," Palmer insisted.

"Well, he *could* have used his right hand, couldn't he?"

"Yeah, but why?"

Myer shrugged. "Who knows? The guy was upset, right? Some broad probably. He was always after those broads, you know that."

"Yeah," Palmer said. "But he never got *involved* with any of them. They were all just one-night stands. Quick tricks."

"So maybe he *did* get involved. It says here in the note that he had problems, maybe they were *woman* problems."

"He was in *love* with his wife. He was getting her stuff for supper when he died."

"So what's *your* theory, Sherlock Holmes?"

"I think he was murdered."

"You mean some phantom just came out of the woodwork on that empty street, reached into the car and shot him for nothing?"

"Shit, how do I know? I'm not a detective," Palmer said. "But this whole thing smells bad to me."

Palmer had only a few hours to sleep when he got back to his house. They expected him in the precinct to answer more questions that afternoon but he couldn't still sleep. He wondered how Navarro's wife, Christina, would feel and the little dark-haired kid that he had seen in the picture. Had anyone told them yet, he wondered? They must have. He wondered if he should call her and decided that, perhaps, a letter would be better. After all, he had never actually met her.

How would she live? She'd make out all right, he

supposed with the pension. But then—no. The police department didn't pay pensions to suicides. And cops have the highest suicide rate of any profession.

It took only another day for the autopsy report. The coroner ruled that death had come from a gunshot wound with a thirty-two caliber bullet fired at close range. Just one shot. Through the heart. The bullet entered just to the right of the mid sternum line and descended through the heart at a downward angle toward the left, passing out of the body just below the rib cage, three inches to the left of the backbone. The bullet was found in the upholstery of Palmer's Mustang.

Not many people showed up for Pancho Navarro's funeral, which was held in Moriarty's funeral home in Long Island City, near the Sunnyside Gardens fight arena. Navarro's relatives all lived in Texas. He had lost track of them long ago.

Captain Handwerker, Pancho's commanding officer in the TPF, was there in civvies, as were Sam Shulman and Dave Cronin, a couple of other members of the force who apparently had worked with Navarro when he was on Narco. Day had never met either of them, but Captain Handwerker had told him who they were. There was nobody there in uniform. No police hero burial. No inspector's funeral. There were a couple of neighbors who had known the Navarros from church and various other communal activities. The priest who gave the eulogy was a young Jesuit who had also been a personal friend of Pancho.

After the service, the body was to be buried in a non-sectarian cemetery since there was no place for a suicide on Catholic holy ground. The young priest, looking pale and frightened—scattered childhood freckles still on his nose—spoke of the inhuman strain of police duty, of the great physical and mental toll it takes on the men who are sworn to protect the law.

Pancho Navarro's death, as he saw it, was as a victim of despair—the illness that must afflict every man with a conscience on whom the weight of so many

21

life-and-death decisions depends. Only a Jesuit could think that one up, Palmer thought.

Pancho Navarro's widow, Christina, sat in the front row of benches before the satin-draped coffin. Beside her, looking pale and uncomprehending, was her three-year-old daughter and holding the child's hand was a female relative or possibly a neighbor. Christina Navarro was dressed in a fitted black suit, a small hat and a veil. From the side, Palmer could see the bright glint of tears, but she held her shoulders steady and pressed her lips tightly together beneath the concealing texture of the black veil.

When the service was over, Palmer got up and approached her. As he drew near, he noticed she was quite tall. Maybe five-ten. The skin under the short veil was an attractive, dark olive tone. Probably a Mexican, also, Palmer thought. Her hair was black and hung to her shoulders. Running through its deep black texture was a streak, about an inch wide, of pure white and Palmer knew that no chemical had put it there. Christina Navarro just finished wiping her daughter Jennifer's nose when Palmer walked up to her. He put his hand on her shoulder.

"I'm Day Palmer," he said. "I was your husband's partner. I can only say I'm very, very sorry about what happened."

She looked up and her eyes seemed bright now with something more than tears. Was it anger?

"I'll *bet* you're sorry," she said bitterly. "You and Cronin and Shulman, you must be heartbroken. And I notice his pal, Eddie, didn't even show."

"What are you talking about?" Palmer protested. "I don't even *know* those guys."

"Look, the whole thing was a set-up and you know it. It smells worse than a two-day-old stiff and don't think I'm gonna let you guys get away with this. One of you did it and the rest of you are all covering up."

"Look," Palmer said urgently, "I want to talk to you about this. It smells rotten to me too. Can I come out and talk to you after all this is over?"

22

She gestured toward the coffin and the dwindling crowd.

"So you can shut me up, too," Christina said bitterly, her eyes flashing with hate. "Maybe you'd like to rub out little Jennifer also? I wouldn't put it past you guys."

"I'm coming to see you anyway," Palmer said firmly.

"Not if I see you first," Christina answered.

CHAPTER FOUR

Christina Navarro lived in an attractive frame clapboard house in Forest Hills, north of Queens Boulevard. It was in a row of older middle-class houses in one of the older sections, somewhat removed from the new housing developments—not far from Forest Hills High School. The houses were set back comfortably from the quiet, tree-lined street and each had a separate garage and garden behind it.

The day after the funeral, Day Palmer retrieved his Mustang from the custody of the property clerk and drove across the Triborough Bridge for his appointment with Pancho's widow.

She met him at the door dressed in faded blue Levis and a white, oxford, button-down shirt, open at the throat. Her long black hair was tied behind in a style that reminded Day of his high school days, and the strange white streak was now more clearly visible without hat and veil. It contrasted dramatically with her lustrous black hair. She looked smaller in the blue tennis shoes she wore, and much younger than Day had imagined.

When she saw who it was, she tried to slam the heavy white door on Palmer's foot.

"Get out of here you son-of-a-bitch!" she said. "I don't want to talk to any of you guys."

"Let me in, goddamn it," Palmer said patiently. "I have to talk to you."

Finally, after a brief tussle at the door, Christina shrugged and walked away, leaving him to let himself in.

"I'm not going to get into a wrestling match," she said, "but you won't get anything out of me. This whole thing is a rotten frame-up as far as I'm concerned."

Jennifer, the three-year-old, trotted out of her room in the rear of the house as Palmer entered, her face and hands smeared with bright yellow finger paints. In her fist was a large sheet of drawing paper. "Hi, Mister," she said before Christina could intervene. "Wanna see what I drew?" She held out the paper on which the only clear images were a huge yellow sun radiating spokes of light in all directions and several black stick-like figures along the bottom that might have been people or trees.

"That's a nice picture," Day said, examining it carefully. "What is it?"

"It's Miami Beach," the child said seriously. "See all the palm trees?"

"Yes, now that you point them out," Day said, politely. "It's very pretty."

Christina came and took the child roughly by the hand.

"Jennifer, go to your room. I don't want you talking to this man."

"But I wanted to show him . . ."

"Go to your *room!*"

Tearfully, the dark-haired three-year-old turned and trotted back toward the rear of the house. Christina stood facing the corner in the vestibule, her arms

25

folded across her chest. Behind her, he could see the living room, an attractive sunny place with an oriental rug, fireplace, and French doors leading into the yard. It was not what Palmer had envisioned. Somehow he pictured a giant crucifix and colored statues of Santos, but the only evidence of Navarro's Latin background was a large *charro* hat and lariat hanging on the wall behind the baby grand piano. Now that he could see Christina without the veil, it was apparent that she was a strikingly beautiful woman and anger had brought an attractive flush to her smooth olive cheeks. Her lips were full and sensual but she was holding them out in a tight-lipped expression of anger.

"What do you want from me now?" she said. "You killed Frank, isn't that enough? You fixed it so I didn't get any widow's pension. What are you after? Is there something he didn't tell you before you killed him?"

"You don't think I did it," Palmer said.

Christina shrugged impatiently.

"I don't know who actually did it and I don't care. It was *one* of you pigs anyway."

It was a hell of an expression for a cop's wife to use, Palmer thought. "Look if you'd shut up and stop attacking me . . .," he said.

She turned on her heel and walked away into the living room.

"Bug off," she said. "As far as I'm concerned, you and your whole mob of crooked cops can drop dead."

Now Palmer was really angry. He strode after her, grabbed her by a shoulder that was soft but surprisingly muscular, and spun her around to face him.

"Look, bitch," he said, "I am *trying* to help you."

He took her arm in his massive hand and led her to the couch and half flung her into a sitting position on it.

"Now you're gonna sit here and talk to me, and I'm gonna listen, and then I'm gonna talk to you."

"What about?" she said sullenly, rubbing her bruised arm.

"About who killed Frank and why they're framing it up to look like suicide?"

Her eyes, which had been flashing with anger and tears of pain, now held his in a cold speculative gaze. They were as black and cold as the bottom of a well. His question electrified the air between them and brought everything back to zero level.

"Are you trying to say that Pancho was murdered?"

"I know goddamn well he was," Palmer said. "Don't you?"

"He had a lot of faults. He played around with other women. He slapped me around a lot of times. He only told me half of what was going on in his life. But I know one goddamn thing," she said, "Pancho would never take his own life. He was too selfish."

CHAPTER FIVE

Now her expression had changed from one of anger to cool speculation.

"Are you going to try to help," she said, "or are you part of the problem?"

"You figure it out," Palmer said.

"What are you drinking?" she asked.

"Scotch with a splash of soda."

She held out her hand to the tall cop who was still standing truculently above her where he had thrown her on the sofa. He noticed a rock on her left fourth finger that must have gone three carats, and wondered if it was real.

"If you help me up, I'll fix us both one," she said. "I think we could use it."

As she led the way to the kitchen in the rear of the house, Palmer could not help notice the way the thin worn denim of her jeans clung to her firm, well-shaped buttocks and long tapering legs. It must have been quite a job, Palmer thought, to get *into* those pants in the first place. Come to think of it, he wouldn't have minded getting into them himself if only . . . if it weren't for Pancho.

Christina mixed the scotch and soda for Palmer and a Beefeater on the rocks for herself, and they sat at the yellow formica table in the bright, cheerful kitchen sipping their drinks.

"You've been with Frank less than a year, right?" she asked.

"That's right," Palmer answered. "I don't know how come I never met you."

"Because I told him never again to bring any of his cop friends around this house," Christina said bitterly. "It only meant trouble. Tell me how it happened."

Palmer went over his brief story again. It seemed he had told it a hundred times by now.

"Did you hear the shot?"

"No, the radio was playing very loud in the store."

"Did you see anyone in the street when you came in or when you went out?"

"No, in fact I noticed there was only one car. It was a delivery van."

He paused reflectively. "Come to think of it, the van wasn't there when I came out."

Chris seemed interested. "What kind of a van?"

"I'm trying to remember," Day said. "It was one of those Ford Econ-o-lines."

"Can you remember anything else about it?"

Day shrugged. "I wasn't paying that much attention. It was a plumbing supply van, I think; but I don't remember the name. I do remember it was like an Irish name. It wasn't one of these Spic names . . . I mean it wasn't a Latin name."

Chris permitted a tight smile at his blooper; but said nothing.

"What color?"

Day tried hard to remember. "I don't know. Dark. Something dark. Maybe dark brown or green. Maybe even grey. I'm not too good on colors. I wasn't really looking; it was dark in the street. We were parked just past the lamp pole."

There was a long pause. Christina seemed to be thinking about what he had said. Day waited for her next question. The feeling he got from her about Pancho's death was not so much grief as anger; that and a hard sense of determination.

She turned back to him now. "Day, I'm positive he didn't do it. And I'm not just talking out of a wife's natural reluctance to face the facts. I *know*."

"Have you told the homicide detectives?"

"Those idiots! All they could do was point to the note. They think it's *natural* that I would complain—the pension and everything."

"Yeah, I suppose they'd think that way. Who talked to you?"

"It was that Detective Myer. Do you know him?"

Day shook his head. "I never met him before last night. He's from homicide. Did he know Pancho?"

Chris ignored the question. "Do you know any of the men Frank worked with before?"

"No," Day said. "He was in Narcotics and I went directly into TPF from the precinct.

"Maybe you should talk to some of them. You saw them at the funeral—Shulman and Cronin."

"You think this has something to do with his work before he came to the Tactical Force?"

"It's possible. They had some rough guys over there in Narcotics," Christina said.

Day considered this. "Christina, you know something I don't know. Was he up to something in Narcotics? Why did he leave the squad?"

Christina looked at the pattern in the kitchen wallpaper behind him.

"He hardly talked about his work." She gestured toward the furnishings of the room. "We lived pretty well on a sergeant's pay. I didn't ask questions."

Day absorbed this information and registered the attitude, but he was not at all convinced that she was telling all she knew.

"Look," he said, "Pancho was my partner. We did a lot of bouncing around together. Maybe some of it

30

you wouldn't have liked. But as far as I'm concerned, he was a square shooter and he had plenty of—excuse me—balls. When we were first in the TPF, he must have saved my neck at least three times till I got the hang of how things were going. And now he's dead. Could have been *me* in that seat, but I don't know any reason anybody would want to kill *me*, except that I'm a cop. On the other hand, I don't know any reason anybody would want to kill *Pancho*, unless there's something you haven't told me . . ."

Christina favored him with a half-smile, revealing briefly a line of teeth like a fluoridated toothpaste commercial.

"I would say a *lot* of people could have wanted him dead. Sometimes even me."

It wasn't the kind of thing you joked about, involving a man whose name had so recently been carved in marble. Palmer finished his drink in silence and she watched him just as silently, her lips still curved in that sardonic smile, lifted about two more degrees at the corner than Mona Lisa's.

"Listen," he said, finishing the drink and putting the glass back down on the table, "I'm not letting this drop that easily, but there's a lot of angles here I don't understand."

"When you get so you understand them, you'll call me, won't you?" Christina said.

Day shook her hand and turned to go; but she held onto it for a moment longer.

"There's something else," she said. "If I were you, I wouldn't let anybody know that you're looking into this unless you're pretty damned certain of them; especially Cronin and Shulman."

CHAPTER SIX

Driving back up One Hundred and Eighth Street, Day thought he saw a brown Barracuda Hardtop that had been parked across the street from Navarro's house following him; but he lost it as he turned into the Long Island Expressway toward Manhattan.

He wondered if he wasn't getting in over his head. After all, he was not in homicide. Why didn't he just leave it to them? Why didn't Christina just go to the police? He had the feeling that she didn't trust anybody on the force, except maybe him. What did she know about Shulman and Cronin? He was sure that if he worked on the case a bit more, she would open up and tell what she knew.

There was the note, of course. But it was typewritten—on the precinct typewriter as it turned out. It could have been done by anybody. Even the signature was typed. The Walther had been checked out. It was an unregistered gun traced to a shipment hijacked off a Brooklyn pier; but that meant nothing one way or the other. A lot of guys carried pieces like that as "throw-aways." He himself carried a switch-blade knife that he'd taken off some Hell's Angel on Eighth Street and not turned in.

One of the first lectures he got from one of the old hair bags in the eight-one was to cover himself by carrying some kind of throw-away.

"You see, kid, if you get in a jam and have to blow somebody away, you could spend the next six months facing police hearings and you will even go up on Grand Jury charges. Why put up with all that bull-shit? You just carry the throw-away piece and if you gotta do the job, you throw the piece down and say he pulled it on you. It could be anything: a knife, a blackjack, a gun."

As far as the detectives were concerned, the Walther was just another black mark against Pancho, along with the disgrace of his suicide.

"Every time a cop commits suicide," Myer said, "it gives the public a chance to take a crack at us. They think we're psychos anyway. They figure a cop commits suicide, he's either crazy or he's up to no good—and Pancho wasn't crazy."

"I worked with him more than six months," Day said, "I didn't see anything crooked about him."

Myer's smile was very tight. "We know. We checked you out, kid. *You're* clean."

"And Pancho?"

"He has a clean record with the Tactical Police Force. But before that . . ."

"Listen," Day said heatedly, "you know goddamn well you had nothing on him. If you did, he would have been up on charges long ago; and he never would have made the Tactical."

Myer shrugged. "Pancho always had a good Rabbi working for him somewhere. He had the right kind of influence. He could make the moves he wanted."

"Look," Day said. "He's dead now without a pension. Why don't you lay off him?"

"Take it easy, kid," the detective said. "The case is closed. No sweat."

33

Now, driving home over the Cross-Bronx Expressway, Day Palmer tried to remember what he had heard about Pancho besides his prowess with women and his heroic exploits. There was something Christina had said about living well on a sergeant's salary—and that diamond, if it was real. Certainly, Pancho, off-duty, presented a dapper appearance. His suits from Saks Fifth Avenue had to go three hundred a piece. The watch he wore, Day remembered, was a Rolex with a solid gold band. But there was nothing really flashy in his way of life that would indicate that Pancho had a huge store of money. The dames, of course. Day didn't know about that. Women cost money.

What did Christina want from Day? Did she want him to prove that Pancho was murdered? That might mean uncovering a lot of dirt. Maybe she didn't care. After all, no matter how much dirt he uncovered, they couldn't bring Pancho up on charges now. And if murder could be proved—there'd be that pension for her. Twenty thousand a year for thirty-five or forty years—Christina couldn't be much older than her mid-twenties—that would amount to more than a half a million bucks! Worth fighting for. Even if a man's reputation was destroyed. But did he, Day Palmer, want to have anything to do with it?

His own father's reputation had been destroyed, he remembered. After twenty years as a trader in a Wall Street brokerage, a million dollars worth of stock turned up missing. According to the Feds, Willard Palmer was the only man who could have taken the certificates and the jury bought that story too. Day wondered—if he'd been a cop back then, would he have been able to clear up *that* case.

As to his father, he knew in his heart that Willard Palmer had never stolen those stocks; but in regard to Pancho . . . Well, Pancho wasn't his father.

He had been driving slowly across the Cross-Bronx Expressway as he tried to sort these thoughts out and now as he turned off the Henry Hudson on to Broadway and wheeled the Mustang toward home, he still didn't have the questions straight in his head. He pulled the Mustang off the street into the big, old, wooden garage that had once been one of the last stables in that area.

As he drove past the front porch, he thought he noticed a flash of white that looked like something attached to the door. Normally, he used the rear entrance through the kitchen, but now he parked the car and went around to the sagging porch that sheltered the front entrance to the building.

Attached to the door with a piece of scotch tape was a squarish white envelope. On the front, in a big almost childish handwriting, the name "Palmer" was written with a ball point pen. Puzzled, the young policeman opened the envelope and slid from it a cheap greeting card—a condolence card. On it was a drawing of some palm trees and a black wreath. Inside, in black script, were the words "Deepest sympathy."

On the bottom of the card, in the same childish scrawl that had appeared on the envelope was a simple message. "Watch your step! A friend."

CHAPTER SEVEN

As Day suspected, even after much discreet inquiry, he could uncover not a hint of anything irregular during Pancho Navarro's short stretch with the TPF; but a few of the older cops hinted that his history in Narcotics might be a bit more murky. Because of Pancho's background in Narcotics, he and Palmer had tended to make more dope collars than the rest of the squad. Often these arrests brought them into situations where they had to chase suspects out of their own territory and make arrests in other sectors. This brought extra paperwork and much embarrassment to the squad. Captain Handwerker had warned both of them several times to try to restrain themselves and not exceed their authority.

Day Palmer might have been inclined to drop his investigation if it had not been for the note on his door. Old-time cops knew that the fake condolence card was a common device used to give a warning. But why should anybody warn him to lay off if there wasn't a fire somewhere under all that smoke?

There was another aspect of the suicide that bothered Day also. Why had Pancho chosen to commit suicide by shooting himself in the chest? Wasn't he risking the possibility of not dying at all? The usual procedure was a pistol in the mouth. One of the old-timers felt that Pancho was so vain that he couldn't stand to ruin his face. It was one theory anyway; but it was a theory that Day Palmer wasn't completely ready to buy.

During the first week after the funeral, Day called Christina twice to inform her of his progress—or lack of progress. She thanked him warmly for his interest and before he hung up the second time, she said, "Please be careful, Day. I don't want you to get hurt."

Her concern left Day with an agreeable sense of warmth. It had been a long time since anyone had been worried about his welfare.

On Thursday, Captain Handwerker called him into his office. There was a letter in front of him, and he had a puzzled frown on his face.

"Have you been applying heat through some Rabbi at headquarters?" he asked.

Now it was Palmer's turn to be puzzled.

"I don't get you."

"I've got orders here from personnel, to transfer you to Group Two Narcotics. It says here it's in recognition of all your arrests—the ones you made with Pancho Navarro, but that don't make sense to me. I never had a request yet for a transfer *out* of TPF. This is an elite group. People fight to get *in* here. What's the story?"

Palmer was genuinely puzzled. "I don't know. I didn't make the request. I never even gave a thought to getting into Narcotics."

"Then why were you guys chasing all over the city after these dope fiends?"

"Hell," Palmer said. "Pancho was senior to me. He had a lot of experience in that field and I guess he just naturally stuck with it. We made some pretty good numbers for the squad, didn't we?"

37

"Good numbers, yeah," Handwerker said reluctantly. "But this isn't Narcotics and you guys were getting to be specialists."

He looked at the paper again.

"It says here that they've looked over your record, and find that you specialized in electronic engineering in college and have a knowledge of Spanish. They claim they need a man like you in Group Two."

"I say it's bullshit." Palmer was mystified. "Who made the request for the transfer?" he asked.

"That's confidential. But it was somebody pretty high up. You mean to say *you* don't *know* who it was?"

"I swear I don't."

Now the captain looked genuinely puzzled.

"This thing is fishier than Fulton Street," he said. "Until now, I had my suspicions about Pancho, but I figured you were a straight arrow. But if you go into that outfit, there's no way you can stay straight. That's a barrel that has nothin' but rotten apples in it. I'm signing this because the heat from upstairs is too much for me to refuse. But I can only say one thing to you, son. If you really don't know what this is all about, you better watch your ass when you get over there. That's a bunch of mean mothers. They would just as soon blow you away as look at you—if you cross them."

"I know," Palmer said.

"Okay, dismissed," the captain said. "Report to South Street in the morning."

Captain Andrew Kerr of the Narcotics Squad was a short, fierce, square-faced man with glinting blue eyes and an air of hard determination. He called Palmer in on the first day of his reassignment.

"We're trying to clean up this division, Palmer. If you're coming here for easy scores and shady deals, forget it. We're rebuilding this squad with new wood. That's why I was pleased to take you from Tactical. They're straight shooters over there and there's never been any trouble—if you know what I mean. You've got a good record and a college education. If you play ball with me, you can get ahead fast here. There's going to be a lot of changes in the near future."

"Yes, sir," Palmer said.

"If not," the captain drew a menacing finger across his Adam's apple, "you see what I mean?"

"Yes, sir," Palmer repeated.

"I understand," the captain said almost as an afterthought, "that you were Pancho Navarro's partner."

"That's right," Palmer said.

"Well, that was a goddamn shame what happened to him, but we all work under a lot of pressure. It's a policeman's lot, you might say."

"You might say that," Palmer said.

"You've been stirring up the woods a little bit about his suicide, I understand."

"Where did you hear that, sir?" Palmer asked.

"Never fucking mind," the captain said, and his voice had a hard edge now. Very different from the pal-style father-to-son tone he had adopted earlier.

"Now get this straight, Palmer. You've been transferred here to work on *narcotics*, and narcotics *only*. You leave the rest of that to homicide. As far as they're concerned, it's a closed case. It's bad enough a cop committing suicide, without you giving us all a bad name by stirring up a lot of scandals."

"But he didn't . . ."

"You've got my message?" The captain's hard voice overrode Palmer's objections. "Now get out there and learn something about the narcotics business. Keep your nose clean."

But if the captain had confidence in Day Palmer, certainly the men of the squad did not. They were suspicious of his sudden transfer and hesitant to trust a new man in any event.

He was given a variety of assignments at first; not working regularly with any partner—surveillance, monitoring legal taps and paper work in the bureau. None of it, in the beginning, giving him a chance to actually make any collars at all. Meanwhile, he thought that the men of the squad were probing him, feeling him out, testing him.

One of the first things he learned was that corner-cutting was the earmark of the Narcotics Squad. It was not unusual for officers to withhold small or even large quantities of captured dope to be used to buy information later on.

"They don't give us that much expense money," Barney Rogers, a veteran Narc, explained to him. "So we got to invent our own system. See what I mean?"

"I guess you do," Palmer said.

"Informants come high in this racket. You got a guy that's strung out and you offer him a little taste of smack and he's gonna lead you where you wanna go. Right?"

"Right," Palmer said.

"That don't look too good in the books, so you gotta bend the rules a little."

"I get it," Palmer assured him.

When he stood still for Rogers' speculations, it probably served as a signal that he wasn't about to rat to the authorities about minor infractions, at any rate.

He'd seen Cronin and Shulman going in and out of the First Precinct House in downtown Manhattan, where the squad was located, but had very little chance to talk to them.

Cronin was a heavy-set blonde man with straight thinning hair and pendulous jowls. He looked so much like a cop that Palmer wondered how he ever got close enough to a perpetrator to make a collar.

Shulman, on the other hand, was tall, dark and sallow with heavy black circles under his eyes and the worried look of a bloodhound. His arms hung loosely from his body and he had the relaxed movements of a born athlete. Squad room gossip had it that he'd been a star end at Stuyvesant High School in his teenage years.

Palmer guessed that both men were in their mid-forties; maybe a little older than Pancho. Their biggest claim to fame in connection with Pancho Navarro had been their involvement with the famous French Connection Case in which two hundred kilos of heroin being shipped from Marseilles to New York had been intercepted, and several important arrests had been made. But the leaders of the smuggling scheme had escaped and were still being sought.

It was not until his fourth week on the squad that Palmer really had a chance to work with Cronin and Shulman. They had discovered what promised to be a major heroin-cutting lab located in a paint and varnish factory on Stanton Street on the Lower East Side. Shulman, Cronin, Rogers, Palmer and two other men were issued shotguns to augment their normal armament and equipped with bullet-proof vests and assigned to assist in the raid.

As they assembled to pick up their special equipment, Palmer took the chance to say to Shulman, "This looks like a heavy one, doesn't it?"

"That's right, kid," Shulman said in his nasal Manhattan twang. "So just watch your step."

CHAPTER EIGHT

The paint warehouse where the suspected heroin lab was located was on Stanton between Essex and Orchard Streets in what had been the old Jewish Lower East Side. There were still plenty of signs of the Jewish presence there: Kosher delicatessens and restaurants, meat stores, clothing dealers and cut-rate optical houses. But there was also a new influence of Puerto Ricans evidenced by *lechonerias* with displays of golden crusty roast pork, street food stands where a passerby had a choice of sweet potatoes, tacos or garlic pickles.

The raid was scheduled for a Sunday which in any other part of town would have meant a day of quiet and no traffic. But not on the Lower East Side. Sunday, following the Jewish Sabbath when all the stores were closed, was the big market day. Orchard Street was filled with sidewalk stalls with hawkers and peddlers chanting the virtues of their merchandise in three languages: Yiddish, Spanish and English.

The six-man team tried to filter unobtrusively

through the milling crowd of bargain hunters. Those with shotguns carried them in long corrugated cardboard boxes, as though they were delivering merchandise to one of the local stores.

The warehouse had a rear entrance approachable through an alley way off Essex Street. The main entrance and loading platforms were on Stanton Street.

Palmer and Rogers were assigned to the rear entrance. Shulman and Cronin made it through the main doorway and Tommy D'Amico and John Sturges, the other two men in the squad, were assigned to cover the loading platform.

Advance information was that several black and Puerto Rican girls were being used to cut the pure heroin down into "nickel" bags, each containing two or three percent of the drug and ninety-seven or ninety-eight percent quinine and milk sugar.

At four P.M. the squad began to move in on the shabby old brownstone building. Rogers, a small, dark, wiry man with a narrow pimp's mustache, was a veteran of fifteen years on the Narcotics Squad. He briefed Palmer as they were approaching the rear entrance.

"Now just stay easy, kid, and watch me. Don't do anything without instructions. These kind of deals are very complicated."

"Right," Palmer said.

The rear entrance led them down a rancid alley heaped with garbage from a Chinese restaurant and a Kosher delicatessen which backed up on to it from one side, and left-over fabric trimming and rags from the small garment factory that lined the other side. The heroin "factory" was reported to be on the first floor. Opening onto the alley was a pair of double steel doors with tiny glass windows reinforced with hexagonal steel mesh.

There was a warrant for the raid and Rogers was carrying the three-foot pry bar and a bolt cutter under his bulky raincoat. Palmer had a riot gun in a cardboard box under his arm.

"Listen, kid," Rogers said, just before he attacked the steel doors with his pry bar. "Take it easy with that riot gun. Those things spray like crazy, you know. Don't shoot it if you don't have to."

At four-ten P.M. precisely, the agreed-upon time for the raid, Palmer cut the strings on the box he was carrying and removed the riot gun. Rogers hit the door with the pry bar and the reinforced steel lock gave way with a squeal and a sudden metallic snap.

The doors opened on a long corridor lined with cardboard chemical drums. At the end was a door with a frosted glass panel. Quickly the two narcotics agents ran down the corridor and kicked in the door. At the same time they could hear smashing noises from the far side of the room they were entering—the sounds of the coordinated attack, presumably of Shulman, Cronin, D'Amico and Sturges.

Rogers gave the inner door a sharp kick and Palmer jumped inside quickly with the riot gun ready; but the gesture was melodramatic and pointless because the only other people in the room were the four detectives they had come with.

It was a big room, about thirty by thirty feet. In the middle were several kitchen tables with ordinary folding bridge chairs grouped around them. One of the chairs was turned over as if someone had left in a hurry. On the table were piles of small glassine envelopes and several bags of white powder. Next to the table were drums containing more white powder. Also, left behind on the table were several gauze breathing masks used to prevent the lab technicians from getting an excessive "contact" high. But the perpetrators necessary for an arrest had obviously flown the coop. Whether they were tipped off or had somehow spotted the raiders before they arrived was a moot point.

Shulman and Cronin advanced on the tables and examined the material left there.

"Well, we got about a key between these two bags, anyway," Cronin said. "This must have been a pretty big operation. Look at all those glassine envelopes over there and these big drums."

Casually, he scooped up a bundle of nickel bags that had already apparently been prepared and stuffed them into the pocket of his coat. "I'll check these out. Now, you guys spread out and see if you see anybody that looks like they might have gotten out of here. Scatter through the building. You, Rogers and Palmer, check this stuff out. Don't forget there's two half key bags here. I want that stuff reported."

"Yes, sir," Palmer said.

"Blow it out your ass," Rogers retorted.

As the other detectives left, Rogers cursed under his breath.

"Those mother-fuckers want to cop themselves; but they don't leave any room for anybody else," he said spitting on the floor. "Still, all is not lost."

Rogers indicated the two half kilo bags on the tables.

"These bags ain't sealed anyway."

Approaching the table, the little man picked up the plastic bag of heroin, put a finger in and tasted the white powder and made a wry face.

"Good stuff, all right," he said.

Looking around, he found a couple of empty paper bags and hurriedly sifted about half of the contents of the plastic sacks of heroin into them. Then he picked the aluminum scoop out of the bag of milk sugar standing next to the table and sifted a half pound of the white substance into the bags that had held the heroin.

"There, now we mix this all up good, like this," he said, stirring the mixture. "And you got plenty of evidence to make the case. It'll pass the Marquis test with flying colors. Meanwhile, we got a half a key each to work with, right, kid?"

Palmer tried to suppress the startled look that rose to his face.

"Gotcha," he said, stuffing the paper sack into his pocket.

CHAPTER NINE

Palmer was uncertain how to handle the question of
the heroin Rogers had ripped off from the lab. He
had increasingly come to feel that Rogers, along with
Shulman and Cronin was mixed up in the death of
Pancho Navarro. All three had been cold, hostile and
uncooperative since he arrived on the squad, with the
possible exception of Rogers, who resorted to sly,
threatening innuendo rather than outright hostility.

Now he wondered why, on his first mission, such
temptation had been put in his way. Was it all a
frame? Were they trying to set him up? He knew that
such skimming of narcotics evidence was far from unusual on the squad, but why, after freezing him out
of all activities would Rogers suddenly turn gener-
ous? Palmer knew one thing. He was not walking out
of that loft with any half key of shit in a paper bag in
his pocket.

When they had almost finished listing the evidence,
Palmer pulled the sack out of his raincoat pocket and
handed it over to Rogers.

"I tell you what, Barney," he said, "why don't I list all the rest of this stuff and check it into the property clerk's office, then you can go back with the car and check in all this gear. Sign in my shotgun, too. That'll give you a chance to unload anything you ... might want to put away in a safe place. There's gonna be guys from the precinct and everything in here pretty soon."

"Gotcha," Barney said and gave him a wink. "You might turn out to be a savvy kid, after all. I'll have 'em send some precinct guys in to help you with all this stuff and they can send around a truck to tote it over to the property clerk on Broome Street."

Day Palmer pulled his black service notebook out of his pocket and began to jot down details concerning the evidence in the cutting lab. There was no way he was going to count that pile of glassine bags. He just estimated it at "several thousand." Two large drums of quinine and milk sugar respectively were listed after Day had tested them each by dipping a finger into the sweet white powder and the bitter one—the quinine.

There were several decks of playing cards on the table which were apparently used to scrape together the little piles of dope. Palmer dutifully listed those also, along with the scales and the masks left on the table. As he was finishing the listing, two uniformed men from the Fifth Precinct came in the front door and offered to be of assistance.

"You got a truck or something out there for this stuff? Seems like a bit much to go into the squad car."

"The sergeant radioed for one. It ought to be here pretty soon," one of the men said. "My name's Pringle and this here is Saracino. You from Narco?"

"Right," Palmer said. And he felt slightly embarrassed. These two old hair bags would probably be pounding a beat when he made captain.

"Listen," he said, "I've got this stuff listed. I'm just gonna look around here and see if there's anything else. So keep an eye on things till the truck comes."

"Right," Pringle said, looking around the room with interest.

Palmer suddenly remembered something that he'd seen on the way in the dark corridor outside. Several more drums resembling the ones that were standing next to the tables in the cutting lab. He went through the back door and into the long, dim corridor. There was no problem in identifying the cardboard drums of material. They were clearly labeled "lactose" in black stenciled letters with the name of a chemical provisioner who had provided them. All together, there were four more drums of milk sugar in the hall.

Conscientiously, Day Palmer took out his pencil and began to record the information in his notebook. As he did so, he was subliminally aware of a movement behind him. It wasn't so much a sound, as a variation of air pressure, a change in the draft. With a sure instinct for trouble that he had developed even in his short time in the field, Palmer swerved to the left and dropped to one hand just as a heavy pipe came arching down toward him from behind, striking him a painful but glancing blow on the shoulder. The impact knocked him to his knees and before he could get up, there was the sound of thudding feet as a figure hurdled over his prone body and ran for the door.

Day reached for his snubnose special and shouted, "Stop! Police!" But the man was out the door before he could get the gun out of the holster. Painfully, the young narcotics agent struggled to his feet and chased the fleeing figure out the back door. He had just time to catch a glimpse of a man in a plaid, double knit jacket, dark pants—a dark-skinned man sporting a wiry Afro, darting through the door on the other side of the alley leading to the street.

Unhesitating, Day Palmer took after the retreating subject who complicated the matter by knocking over several garbage cans to impede the policeman's way through the alley.

The black man in the plaid jacket shot out into Essex Street and ignoring the light, ran straight into traffic toward the Essex Market, dodging through the surprised crowds like a broken field runner on the Detroit Lions. Palmer burst out of the alley just in time to see a door swing shut behind a flash of plaid across the street. The door led into the Essex Street Municipal Market: a giant shed housing dozens of stalls which served as a sort of free-lance supermarket to the rest of the community.

By the time Day made the door of the market, the plaid jacket was ducking out another of the doors on the far side. His legs and arms pumping furiously, Day ran down the constricted aisles flooded with customers and purveyors of tin pans, shopping carts, meats, fruits and vegetables. In that crowd, there was no way he could risk a shot even if he could gain enough ground to take a crack.

By the time he got to the back door of the market through which the fleeing figure had bolted, there was no sign of the suspect. Day stood puffing for a minute, looking up and down the street and then on a hunch, jogged as quickly as he could through the still-heavy crowds south toward Delancey Street, the next corner. It was his hunch that the man would try to lose himself in the mob. The heaviest population was on Orchard Street. Palmer ran, twisting and turning, through the harried crowd, ignoring the insults that flew after him. *"Maricon!"* *"Cabron!"* *"Hijo de puta!"* *"Schmuck!"*

Once he got to Orchard Street, it was impossible to run. It was packed not only with the native population, but with hordes of uptown shoppers in fur coats who came on Sundays seeking bargains and local color. Day, at six feet two, was over the heads of most of the crowd. He could see almost to the end of the block. Sure enough, just as he turned into Orchard, there was another flash of the familiar plaid jacket and the wiry Afro turning left again on Stanton toward Allen Street, but looking at the wall-to-wall clutter of humanity before him, Day Palmer knew that the chase was hopeless. It took a good five minutes for him to get through the mass of protesting shoppers and by the time he reached the knish hawker and ice vendors on the corner, the suspect seemed to be permanently out of sight.

Disgustedly, Palmer continued up Orchard to Stanton, took a right and returned to the scene of the raid where the street had been barricaded and a number of police cars were on duty, including one NYPD panel truck.

Cronin was standing in front of the raided building, his face red with anger.

"Where the fuck did you go, shithead?"

Palmer looked at him coldly, "I was chasing a suspect. He went out the back door, down the alley and up Orchard Street, but I lost him on the corner."

"I thought I *told* you to do *nothin'* without instructions!"

Palmer was stunned. He said nothing.

Shulman came up, looking equally distressed.

"Yeah, I thought I told you to watch your step. You start fucking around too much on your own, sonny, you could get yourself in a *lot* of trouble!"

CHAPTER TEN

It took Palmer the rest of the day to get all the evidence moved out of the loft and over into the crowded property clerk's office several blocks north on Broome Street near Police Headquarters. Grudgingly, the property clerk made space on the shelves in the cluttered room, actually, a wired-in enclosure within a larger room where all sorts of evidence—radios, television sets, pistols, dope, jewelry—were checked in and out, just as they were in the parcel room in Grand Central Station. Only in this case, the detective or policeman in charge would check the material in and remove it as needed for trial.

What seemed to really bug the rubber-gun squad clerk (many of the clerical workers assigned to the property bureau had been relieved of their guns and assigned to less active duty because of psychological deficiencies or alcoholic tendencies—they were members of what was commonly called the rubber-gun or bow-and-arrow squad) was the sheer bulk of Day

Palmer's evidence which added even more clutter to the already jammed-up quarter.

"This stuff is too big," the clerk grumbled. "I shouldn't never even let you come in here with it."

"Well, it's here, so just give me a receipt and quit yapping," Palmer said, signing the property clerk's book.

By the time he got out of the property clerk's office, it was almost the end of the shift. There were no cars left to give him a lift, so Palmer took a subway down to the South Ferry Station which was nearest to the Narcotics Squad.

As he entered the busy squad room, he was surprised to see, draped over a chair in front of one of the cluttered desks, a plaid double-knit jacket which looked very familiar. It looked exactly, in fact, like the jacket on the suspect he had chased through the market only a couple of hours before. He approached Barney Rogers who was filling out his report on the raid.

"Hey, Barney, who belongs to that jacket there?"

Barney looked over without interest.

"I think that belongs to Easy Eddie Evans."

"Who's he?"

"He's a spade. Works undercover. Mainly out in Harlem. Come to think of it, he use to be pretty tight with your old friend, Pancho."

"What's he look like?"

Barney Rogers looked up with curiosity.

"What you wanna know for?"

"Nothing, I think I saw him someplace before."

"Well, he's around five ten, slim build."

"He got an Afro hairdo?" Palmer asked.

"Naw, he's got one of them shaved skulls. Like Kojak or more like Jack Johnson."

"Oh, I guess that's not the guy I was thinking of," Palmer said. But he was bothered. There was nothing distinctive about the jacket. On a good sale day in Kleins or Mays department store, they probably sold a hundred like it. But still, it was disturbing to see that same pattern again so soon after he had lost it in the chase on Orchard Street. He approached the chair and took another look and noticed that the armpits of the jacket were heavily darkened with sweat as though the wearer had had a heavy recent workout.

He was still looking at the jacket when Evans returned to his desk.

"Something I can help you with?" he said.

"Oh, no," Palmer said. "I'm Day Palmer. I understand you were a good friend of Pancho Navarro."

The man before him had smooth, light brown skin. His head had the glowing patina of the inside of a catcher's mitt. The man's age was hard to tell. Somewhere between thirty-five and forty-five. The features were sharp and aqualine and if he'd been so inclined, Easy Eddie Evans could probably have passed for white.

"Yeah, I knew Pancho," Evans said flashing a tight smile. "He was a good man. Too bad they moved him out."

"Wha'da you mean moved him out? I thought he volunteered for the Tactical Force?"

Evans smiled cynically. "You could say that, I guess. He volunteered the way a wild horse volunteers to be dog meat."

"You heard what happened to him, I suppose," Palmer said.

"Yeah." Easy Eddie was not big with words.

"What do you think?"

"What *should* I think?"

"You think he blew himself away?"

The black man shrugged. "What else?"

"I don't know," Palmer said.

"You got any other ideas? You think somebody offed him?"

"Well, if he didn't do it *himself*, then somebody else *must* have done it, right?"

"There's a certain cool logic to that," Easy Eddie said. "You got any *reasons* to suspect anything fishy about the case?"

Palmer shrugged. "Just a hunch and a feeling. We were on duty together all that night. He didn't seem uptight or upset or anything. Well, maybe a *little* uptight, like he was looking forward to something. I figured maybe he had a date later on. There was maybe something funny about the way he parked and sent me into the store, as though maybe he was keeping a meeting."

Easy Eddie showed some interest. "You think he met someone? You got any idea *who* he met?"

Palmer shrugged again. "Hell, I don't even know if he met *anybody*. It's more like a feeling. I do know that there was a truck there. Some kind of plumbing supply truck was parked in front of us when I went in. When I came back, it was gone. I'd swear it was gone. I've been thinking about that truck ... Whether he committed suicide or was shot, whoever drove that truck away must have heard or seen something."

"Hoo-ha, boy," Easy Eddie said. "We've got a regular Dick Tracy here. Why don't you just go up to homicide and tell them your theory?"

"Homicide, shit," Palmer said. "They bought that phony note and everything. They're not interested in stirring anything up. Are you?"

"Not really, I guess. But I hate to think of Christina going without that pension and I hate to think of people accusing Pancho of copping out like that. He wasn't that kind of guy. I guess he was sort of a hero to you," Eddie said, that cynical smile flashing on his face again.

"Kind of. Didn't you like him?"

"Oh, yeah," Eddie said. "We were like *that*." He held up two brown fingers crossed.

"Don't any of you guys think this thing smells bad?"

Eddie leaned back against the desk, his wiry arms folded across his chest.

"We have a deal. Homicide don't bust any happydust heroes, and we don't solve any murders. Dig?"

Palmer played past that.

"There's things that could *make* somebody open up the case, maybe. Like did ballistics run a test on the Walther slug? And, I been thinking. How about Pancho's jacket? If he offed himself then there ought to be powder burns on it, right? If there's no burns, there's no way he could have done a job on himself—unless he had very long arms."

The black narc sighed in exasperation.

"You been to college, Charlie. But you still got plenty to learn. You been hipped a hundred times. *Cool* it, man! The way you're playing this, you're begging for a one-way ticket to a marble ghetto, dig?"

"Hey, rookie," Barney Rogers called from his desk. "You can have the typewriter now. You wanna fill out your DD 19?"

"Oh, yeah, I guess so. See you around, Eddie."

"Later," the black detective said.

Barney Rogers offered the swivel seat he had occupied to Day Palmer with mock ceremony. "I see you were having a nice little cozy chat with Sam Spade over there."

"Yeah, we were talking about Pancho Navarro."

"Yeah, they use to call them the zebra patrol. You know, black and white. Only sometimes they called them the chameleon act."

"Why was that?" Palmer said, setting into the dilapidated office chair.

"Well, they were always going on stake-outs in these disguises. You know, the whole deal, funny clothes, face, hair, wigs, the whole thing."

Palmer looked up sharply.

"They wore a lot of wigs?"

"With a dome like that, wouldn't you?" Barney said, laughing.

"Did Easy Eddie ever use an Afro wig? A nice short Afro wig?"

"Sure, what else? Why do you ask?"

"Just trying to learn the detective business," Day Palmer said, beginning to type viciously.

Barney approached and leaned over his shoulder, as though to help with the report.

"Hey, kid, don't you want your piece of the skag?"

"Forget it," Day said. "It's yours."

Rogers looked surprised, even a little hurt. Finally he shrugged, "O.K., kid. It's your funeral."

CHAPTER ELEVEN

Day Palmer needed time to think. When his shift was over, he headed for Barry's Shamrock Grill which was on South Street, a block or so from the First Precinct. A couple of guys on the squad were in the front having drinks. Palmer waved at them and continued to the back of the bar collecting a scoop of Rheingold from Polasky, the bartender. He grabbed a handful of pretzels from the bowl on the bar and settled into a dark corner at a table to work things out.

If Easy Eddie was a crooked cop, it certainly would indicate that Pancho, also, was in on the take; and from the things said around the squad, it seemed more likely than not. Why should Pancho be an exception? But what had Eddie been doing on the site of the raid? Was he there to warn the heroin dealers of the upcoming bust? Was that why so little dope was found with so much adulterant?

Certainly it was obvious that the lab was set up to handle some really big pieces of dope. Probably, in excess of a hundred pounds at a time. Were the two half kilo bags left behind simply to sweeten the pot and make the collar look good? Or could he have been mistaken; was it somebody else—not Easy Eddie—who clobbered him? He would have liked to quiz a couple of the guys on the squad. He was sure the answer was there but he was afraid that asking questions too openly would get him into more trouble than it would be worth.

Finally, he went to the bar, got change for a quarter from Polasky and made a call from the booth near the door. From his wallet he extracted a small slip of yellow paper on which he had written Christina's number. It was a Boulevard exchange. She answered after five rings.

"Hello, Christina," Day said. "This is Day Palmer. Can I talk on the phone?"

"I don't advise it," Christina said cautiously. "Maybe you'd better come out here. I'd like to see you again, anyway."

Something in her tone of voice made Day's face flush with pleasure.

"O.K., tonight all right?"

"Sure," she said. "Come on out anytime. You had anything to eat?"

"No, I just got off work."

"Well, come on out here and grab a bite with me. It gets lonesome eating all alone anyway, and I can't very well eat my dinner at five o'clock the way Jennifer does."

Feeling unaccountably happy, Day jumped into the Mustang and headed north toward the Williamsburg Bridge leading to Forest Hills. As he turned right on Delancey for the bridge, he noticed a little *bodega* on one of the narrow streets that angled off toward the lower part of the East Side. The neon sign in the window flashed a yellow signal *"Comidas Crillos."* In the other window the sign said *"Groceria."* He turned off into the side street, pulled up in front of the store and bought two pounds of *chorizos,* a bag of yellow rice with the saffron already added and a couple of cans of *refritos.* At the last minute, he added six bottles of San Miguel beer.

As though she had read his mind, Christina appeared at the door in a crisp white embroidered cotton Mexican dress which made her olive skin appear even darker but with a golden hue coming through that gave it a luminous quality. She was wearing her hair loose now, down to her shoulders, the fullness of it around her face minimized the contrast of the white streak.

"*Buenas noches,*" Day said, presenting the paper sack.

Christina laughed. "What's this? You didn't have to bring anything."

"It's something I know you like and I was passing through the neighborhood," Day explained.

He followed her through the living room into the sparkling and immaculate kitchen where she deposited the bag on the counter and unloaded its contents.

"*Chorizos! Refritos! Arroz!* And San Miguel. You must be a mind reader."

She turned and with surprising swiftness embraced him lightly and rewarded him with a peck on the cheek. Her lips felt soft and warm and Day had the impression there was more intimacy in the contact than was absolutely necessary for courtesy—not that he minded.

"Well," she said, "I was going to make pork chops but this might be more fun. I can take care of the cooking later. Now, how about a drink? The usual? A short scotch and soda?"

She had a good memory, Day thought.

"That will be great."

"With all this stuff, we probably should have Tequila," she giggled. "But it's a bit strong for me. I'll have the same as you. Why don't you make them?"

She indicated the bottle of Grant's standing on the shelf near the sink. Next to it was an ice bucket in a stars and stripes pattern. It apparently had been filled in advance. A bottle of soda stood next to it.

As Day Palmer mixed the drinks, Christina drew up a stool beside him. Her voice was serious now.

"Anything happening?"

Day dropped a couple of cubes into the tall blue tumblers that she had put in front of him.

"You know anything about Easy Eddie Evans?"

"Sure, he was Pancho's partner sometimes. They paled around together."

"Do you think he was straight?"

"What do you mean?" Christina seemed puzzled.

"I mean did he take? Was he crooked?"

She shrugged.

"They didn't let me in on stuff like that. But I know that he keeps a girlfriend up in Lennox Terrace in Harlem, and that isn't exactly a lower income housing development. I don't see how he can do that on first-grade detective's pay and keep a family and a house in Corona at the same time. Why do you ask?"

"I'd rather not talk about it until I have more to go on. Do you have any idea of his girlfriend's name?"

"I think it was Cheryl Brown," she said. "I've got the number anyway. At least I have it as an alternate number to call Eddie at. Pancho had it in his telephone book. I'll get it for you."

She rummaged around in one of the drawers in the kitchen near the white wall-telephone and came up with one of the small blue personal phone directories the telephone company sometimes distributed. Cheryl's number was an Audubon exchange.

Day copied it into his notebook and then on second thought asked, "Do you use this book too, or is it just Pancho's?"

"No, I have my own," Christina said.

"Then, can I borrow it?"

"Sure, why not?"

Day slipped the blue book into his jacket pocket. Christina opened the sack of yellow rice and poured it into a Revere saucepan.

"Do you want to go into the living room and watch TV while I get this stuff ready?"

"No," Day said. "I'll squat on the stool here and watch you work and talk. I'm not too big on TV."

"This is kind of fun," Christina said, slicing up the sausages and putting them into a cast iron skillet. "There isn't any place to buy this around here and I haven't had much of it since Pancho . . ."

Day cut her off before the conversation could get too heavy.

"I used to eat a lot of that stuff when I worked in the Ninth Precinct over on the Lower East Side. I really dig it."

He sat for a while sipping his drink and saying nothing, watching the smooth movements of her tall, lithe figure as she reached up the cabinets for dishes and condiments.

"You move like a dancer," he said. His words were matter of fact, not meant particularly as a compliment.

"I did some of it in my day," Christina said.

"Professionally?"

Christina grinned deprecatingly, revealing an unsuspected dimple in her right cheek.

"I studied with Pearl Primus, but I don't think I really had the gift."

The name meant nothing to Day Palmer, but he assumed it was someone he should have heard of. He shifted the subject.

"About Cronin and Shulman—why did you warn me to be on my guard against them?"

Christina was sprinkling *cilantro* into the rice. She stopped for a moment and looked at him, seriously and thoughtfully.

"I'm not sure," she said. "They were up to something—something very big with Pancho. I know that Pancho was afraid of them and he wasn't a man easily frightened. Are you?"

It was a double-edged question. Day Palmer sipped his Scotch and said nothing.

61

CHAPTER TWELVE

Palmer put his Japanned tool box on a bench in the brightly-lit cellar of Building D in Lennox Terrace Apartments and surveyed the large, modern phone switch box before him. He knew he was taking a chance but he had thought it out carefully.

Any cop that was heavily on the take would not be using his home phone for communications. Day was certain of that. Besides, Easy Eddie's house in Corona was a one-family attached duplex. It would have been almost impossible to put a tap on it without being noticed by a leery cop or members of his family. Any funny business that was going down with Easy Eddie would logically have been worked out of his girlfriend's apartment. It was obvious from the fact that he had listed this as an alternate number with Pancho. Now was the chance for Day Palmer's early electronics training, courses in surveillance techniques, to pay off.

He attached a handset to the bottom of the switching box and dialed the Audubon number of

Cheryl Brown. Letting the phone ring, he wet his finger and quickly ran them down the pairs of brass screws, each attached to one of the phones in the big housing development.

In the middle of the second row he felt the tingling at the end of his fingers that told him he had the right pair. From the box, he got a set of thin, almost transparent lead-in wires. He attached one to each screw and began to tape the wires up inside the box to where he could run them out unobtrusively to a listening post. He thought a janitor's closet around the corner from the telephone box would serve if he didn't use it too often. He'd just have to take his time and hope that he could pick up something useful.

Actually, he felt guilty about it. If Easy Eddie was *not* the guy who tried to slug him, it didn't seem right to listen in on his private phone calls. But considering what was at stake, Day Palmer felt he could afford to finesse a few scruples.

Getting into the building itself had been no trouble. A five-dollar bill and a flash of the tin had contented the doorman. From a work clothes supply store, he acquired a pair of brown slacks and a brown Eisenhower jacket with the word "maintenance" across the pocket. He hoped that the uniform would explain his presence in the cellar. He had already figured out that if anybody alerted the cops, he would tell them that he was on the job.

The day before, he had pulled Cheryl Brown's yellow sheet. There wasn't much on it. She had had two arrests for prostitution, one for possession of a couple of joints of marijuana, and one for suspicion of heroin conspiracy. The other charges had been dismissed. But with that record, he could probably make a pretty good case out of justifying surveillance of Cheryl Brown's apartment.

The problem was, he didn't have a warrant to put a legal tap on the phone and he knew he couldn't get one. Still, they'd have to catch him at the actual tapping, and if it were somebody from the Narcotics

63

Squad or even the Precinct, they'd probably be willing to wink an eye. Certainly, it wasn't all that unusual to slip an occasional illegal wire tap on somebody's phone.

He took a chair out of the laundry room across the way from the wall box and pulled it up to the box in order to draw the lead-out wire through the top. As he climbed on the chair, he heard a quiet voice behind him.

"Just freeze right where you are, mister. Get down off that chair and lean against the wall."

The voice had the unmistakable ring of police authority.

"Take it easy, man. I'm on the job," Day said tensely.

"That's o.k.," the voice said. "Just get off the chair and lean against the wall. I'll find out what you're up to soon enough."

Day did as he was told, casting a rapid glance behind him as he descended from his chair.

There were three serious-faced men, each holding a snubnose revolver. They were all in plain clothes; but their faces could have been blue serge with brass buttons. They had that look.

He felt hands patting up his trouser leg now, removing the service revolver from the shoulder holster he had put it in because of the shortness of the uniform jacket. They also removed the throw-away switchblade from his side pocket. In his rear pocket they found his leather case with the police department shield.

"O.K., mister, you can put your hands down now. What's this all about? You got a warrant for this tap?"

Palmer reddened and gulped.

"Not exactly. But I plan to get one. I've had this woman under surveillance."

"Don't bullshit a bullshitter, son," the man in front of him said. He was the same height, or maybe a little taller than Day, about six three, broad-shouldered with a hook nose, a ruddy, coarse, veined face—a little reminiscent of John Wayne in his late years—and a paunch to match. He must have been quite a piece of work when he was younger.

The other two consisted of a medium-height, dark-faced guy who looked like he might have been an Arab or Italian with short, curly, dark hair and a stubby guy with a round pink face and an idiotic smile.

"Who you working with, mister?" the big man said.

"Narcotics Squad. Manhattan South."

"What are you doing up here?"

"Well, I worked on the raid on the cutting lab thing on the Lower East Side. And we didn't find all of the junk that we should have. My informant tipped me off that this girl, Cheryl Brown, might have a lead."

"I see. So you decided you'd be Super cop and come up and do the job yourself. Come on, officer, you trying to say that you don't *know* that you're supposed to have a warrant to run a tap like this?"

"I hoped to get one, but I had to move fast."

"Well, you better have a very nice story for the D.A.," the big man said.

He pulled out an ID card and flashed it.

"We're from the Internal Affairs Division. The fact that you're on the Narcotics Squad only makes things a lot more hairy for you. Now, pick up your dolls and dishes and let's get going."

CHAPTER THIRTEEN

"Give him his rights," the big man with the John Wayne face said to the round-faced one.

"Hey, wait a minute," Day Palmer said. "You're not going to book me on this are you? O.K., so it *was* an illegal tap, but I'm trying to bust somebody on a narcotics case. It's not as though I was . . ."

"Kid," the big man said. "You are in one hell of a lot of trouble. Before Watergate, maybe you could pull that kind of stuff, but guys are going to jail for this kind of thing every day now. You've got not only a state rap against you, but a federal charge. Give him his rights, Charlie."

Charlie took the familiar rumpled card from his pocket and began to read from it to Day.

"You are hereby advised of your right to remain silent and you do not have to say anything unless you choose to do so. Do you understand? Answer yes or no."

"Yeah, I understand," Day said sullenly.

"Anything you say may be used against you in a court of law. Do you understand?"

"Sure, sure."

"You have the right to have an attorney present with you during any questioning now or in the future. Do you have an attorney?"

Day shrugged.

"If you cannot afford an attorney, the court will appoint one to represent you. Do you understand?"

"Yeah," Day said.

"If you do not have an attorney presently available, you have the right to remain silent or the opportunity to consult one. Do you understand?"

"Yeah, I understand," Day said.

"Sign your name here."

The pudgy man held out a sheet which he took from his inside pocket. It had been pre-typed for such an occasion. Reluctantly, Day signed.

"How come you're giving me my rights here? Couldn't you wait till we got to the station house?"

"No, we're going to go down and talk to the Feds now. Charlie here is attached to the U.S. Attorney's Office."

At least they did Palmer the courtesy of not cuffing him as they rode downtown in the federal unmarked car. They crossed over One Hundred and Twenty-Fifth Street and went down the East River Drive all the way to the Brooklyn Bridge and Foley Square where they parked outside the Federal Court House.

Day was taken in the elevator to a U.S. attorney's office on the second floor where he waited for more than an hour while a team was assembled to interrogate him.

All the way down in the car, Day had sat silent and the three men, the guys from the Internal Affairs Division and the Fed had studiously kept the conversation away from the subject matter at hand. His mind was still numb with shock. Running the pairs in the phone box certainly hadn't seemed like a crime to him although he knew it technically was. Still, it was possible to believe that a good cop's life could be ruined and he might even be sent to jail for *this*.

He knew that if he'd been able to sit on that phone for two or three hours a day for a week or so, that he would be picking up some good leads, not only on the case of Navarro, but possibly on some very high up crooked dope dealing in the police department. It didn't seem the sort of thing a man should be punished for. A lot of cops had been busted since the appointment of the Knapp Commission and of Nadjari as special prosecutor, but damn few had gone to jail.

Still, it wasn't a question of that. If he were kicked off the force with prejudice, what would he do? Where would he get a job? Even a suspended sentence would effectively ruin his life.

Now Day felt that somehow God had it in mind to zing his whole family. First his father on that trumped-up stolen stock charge and now him. He felt glad at that moment that his parents were both dead. There'd be nobody he had to explain this to, except maybe Christina. It would be a blow to her and it certainly would mean the end of any hope of finding out what actually happened to Pancho Navarro.

In the old days, Day knew, a collar like this could be fixed for five bills—five hundred dollars; but those days were gone and besides, there was a Fed on this and they were much harder to get to, and the IAD was known for being incorruptible.

The big guy, the IAD lieutenant, had a face like the avenging angel himself—if the avenging angel had been punched in the nose a few times in his early youth.

They left him alone to commune with his dark thoughts for more than an hour. Then the frosted door on the side of the U.S. Attorney's office behind the oak rail barrier, was opened, and pudgy Charlie led him in through the swinging gate to a conference room where four men waited for him—and one woman.

Basically, it was the three men who had arrested

him, plus a young hippy-looking guy with a reddish-blonde beard and hair almost down to his shoulders.

The woman was tall—almost as tall as Christina, with well-brushed shiny blonde hair, sharp grey eyes, a long, thin nose like Lauren Bacall, and a mouth that seemed to be curved in a perpetual grin of sardonic amusement. She was wearing a striped jersey dress which faithfully followed every curve, dent, and dimple of her beautifully assembled body.

Probaby a stenographer to take my statement, Day thought. The Feds did things up in style.

The lieutenant from IAD stood up as he came in.

"These two men you know," he said indicating the pair that had been in on the arrest. "Jerry Fiorini there is from DEA and this is Sally Friedlander, deputy U.S. attorney. The lieutenant gestured toward the well-stacked blonde. "Take a seat here." The big man indicated a chair at the head of the table placed so that he was in the center of the group of law enforcement officers.

"How long have you been with Narcotics?" the lieutenant asked him casually, offering him a Marlboro from a soft pack he pulled from his pocket.

Palmer waved it away.

"Only a few months," he said.

"You were a partner of Pancho Navarro's?"

"That's right."

"How well did you know him?"

"Pretty well. We were partners in the TPF for about six months."

"Was he a straight cop?"

"As long as I knew him," Day said.

There was a pencil and pad before him—a large yellow legal-ruled pad. He picked up the pencil and began to doodle zig zag nervous lines on it as he spoke.

The lieutenant's eyes were ice blue, and cold as a popsicle. The DEA man pulled a Kaywoody from his tweed jacket pocket and lit it from a bag of aromatic rum and maple.

Day had a feeling about people who smoked pipes. Every time you asked the pipe-smoker a question, he would take four or five puffs, rub the pipe on his nose, and cough once or twice before answering. It was a terrific dodge, if a man wanted to lie. It gave him lots of time to think up answers, but in this case it was Day who was doing the answering.

"You hear anything about Navarro while you were in the Narcotics Bureau?"

"Just that he was a good cop," Day said. "What's this got to do with my illegal tap?"

"Take it easy and you'll find out," the lieutenant said.

The blonde U.S. attorney, Sally Friedlander, was looking him over as though he were a frog in a high school biology class. Her mouth might have been smiling. The eyes were shrewd and calculating.

"You got a pretty good record until you got in this jam here," the lieutenant said, changing the subject. "How did it happen?"

Day sighed and then thought, What the hell! he might as well lay the whole package out in front of them.

He told them about his suspicions concerning Navarro's suicide and the reason why he was tapping Cheryl Brown's phone.

"You understand," he said, "that I have nothing definite on Eddie Evans—yet, but I know that he was the guy that slugged me and there has to be some reason behind that—for all the good it'll do me now to know it."

"Did you give the stuff you picked up in the raid on the East Side a Marquis test?"

The question came from the hippy with the blonde beard and the pipe, Fiorini, the DEA man.

"No, my partner, Rogers, brought it in."

"Then you have no idea of the purity of the heroin that you captured?"

"Nope."

The DEA man just nodded and blew a couple of streams of rich, sweet smoke from his narrow nostrils.

"Do you know that Navarro was scheduled to undergo questioning in this office next week?"

"He never told me that," Day said. He was genuinely surprised. "About what?"

The big man ignored his question. Sally Friedlander had a question.

"Did Navarro seem upset or disturbed that night?"

"No, he seemed, maybe a little ... distracted, as though he had something else on his mind besides the work."

"I'd like to tell you a story," Sally Friedlander said.

Palmer said nothing but he knew the story was not going to be Snow White and the Seven Dwarfs.

"Once upon a time," Sally Friedlander said, a sardonic smile still on her well-shaped lips, "there was a very big, very beautiful, very bad and very crooked narcotics cop. This cop's name was Pancho Navarro ..."

CHAPTER FOURTEEN

Day Palmer heard the introduction to Sally Friedlander's story with only the slightest sense of shock. His ears wanted urgently to believe that Pancho was a straight arrow but everything—the comments of the guys on the Narcotics Squad, Pancho's style of life, the house in Forest Hills, and the little child's drawing of Miami Beach, that Palmer felt sure was done from memory, added up to "wrong."

Sally Friedlander continued with her story.

"This Pancho, one day, was caught with his hand in the cookie jar and before he could open his hand there were a lot of very big cookies found in it—not all the cookies—but a lot. Now, Pancho was in trouble, but the big blue federal fairy godmother gave him three choices: One, he could face trial for theft of the magic cookies, for these were very magic cookies (and they were worth a lot of money). Two, he could escape from scandal and jail by blowing himself away; or three, he could keep his status as a law enforcement officer by joining the Joint Federal-City

Task Force, which basically consists of the elements you see here: the U.S. Attorney's office, the DEA, the Treasury Department and the New York Police Department.

"If he took choice number three, his job would be to find *all* the rest of the cookies which were now missing, and get evidence against the men who set up their theft—men we have reason to believe are largely connected with the New York Police Department Narcotics Bureau. This story I'm telling you has a very unhappy ending. Pancho was not pleased with the choices we gave him. We were positive that he was going to take choice number three. He told us he would, but then it seems the day before he was to report to us, he took choice number two."

"Did he?" Day Palmer said. It was his turn to flash the sardonic grin. "Maybe nobody gave him a *chance* to pick *any* of the three choices."

Sally Friedlander smiled back at him. "Those were the only three choices we had to offer him, but you're right, some bad people might have given him some other alternatives."

"Could we stop the Sesame Street routine now and give me some idea of what we're talking about?"

"You have no idea?"

"Not a clue."

"You ever hear of the French Connection?"

"Sure."

"Well, as you probably know, a little while ago, Pancho Navarro was a member of the team that helped to make the biggest narcotics bust we ever had in this city—two hundred kilos of pure Marseilles heroin."

"That I know," Day Palmer said.

"It hasn't been made public, yet," the big man from IAD said, "but we have known for some time that almost all of the evidence seized at the time of the French Connection has been smuggled out of the Property Clerk's office and replaced with milk sugar. The stuff was signed out on nine different occasions

73

in the name of Detective Frank Navarro. Among the other detectives who are involved in the French Connection bust for the New York Narcotics Bureau were Detectives Shulman, Cronin, Rogers and Evans. I believe you know them all."

"I do," Day Palmer said.

The DEA man, Fiorini, said, "Sally Friedlander was scheduled to try the case but it's going to be very hard to make a case with all of that evidence missing."

"Where do I fit into this?" Palmer said.

"Remember the three wishes we gave to Pancho Navarro? We're giving you the same choice. Do you think there was something fishy in Navarro's death? We're giving you the chance to clean it up, clear your name and set up one of the most important collars ever made by the Narcotics Bureau or the Joint Task Force."

"Of course," Sally Friedlander said with a smile, tapping her gold Dunhill pencil on the legal pad before her, "if anybody finds out what you're up to on the Narcotics Squad, you will wind up deader than Pancho Navarro."

CHAPTER FIFTEEN

Day Palmer didn't need any warning from a blonde U.S. attorney to tell him the kind of danger that would be involved in becoming a shoo fly. Serpico tried it and wound up with a bullet in the face. Whether it was from a narcotics addict or a cop, nobody was ever quite sure.

Phillips tried it and wound up going up for murder One on the testimony of other cops; but these were only the public cases. Police work was a dangerous business and sudden death was commonplace. If they were out to get you, Day Palmer knew, they would get you.

The whole thing went against the grain. The guys in the Narcotics Squad were not exactly his pals and, in fact, gave the impression of being a bunch of scum bags in general, but it was one thing to know that—even to know that they were as crooked as a spiral staircase—and another thing to turn them in to the Task Force, ruin their lives, take away their pensions, leave them without support for their families. This hadn't been Day Palmer's plan when he was transferred to Narcotics. He'd only been trying to find out if somebody got Navarro.

From what he had heard recently, he wasn't even sure that Navarro was *worth* saving; but unfortunately, they now had his neck on a block.

This joint force played a tough game, a rotten game, and a dangerous one. Palmer wanted no part of it.

"Get yourself another boy," he said. "I'm not turning fink."

"You sure you know what you're doing?" the IAD lieutenant asked.

Palmer shrugged, "What's to know? You got me on a wire tapping rap, or maybe it's *attempted* wire tapping since I never did listen in on any conversations. So I get a lawyer and we go to trial, and I cop a plea. And then I go out and get a job in a hi fi shop repairing quadrophonic systems. Maybe I go back to college and get that degree, nights."

"That's a very nice plan," Sally Friedlander said. And there was no sardonic smile now. "Only that's not the scenario that *we're* writing. In the first place, they'll be no plea copping. That has to be done with our collusion. We're gonna recommend a maximum sentence on this, and the judge usually listens to our recommendations. It's one-to-three on the federal rap.

"In the second place, when we go to trial and we leak that you were trying to pin the death of Pancho Navarro on Evans, Rogers and Shulman, I don't think your life will be much fun after that.

"I want to tell you something," Sally went on, "we had another guy before Pancho, who was working on those guys. He was a dealer that had paid them off and he was ready to talk. We offered him protection but he refused it. Before we ever got to an arraignment, he was found in a vacant lot on Staten Island with a bullet through his eye.

"And how do you think it'll be when you go to the federal pen? How do you think those guys up there are gonna feel about an ex-cop and an ex-narc? If you ever escape from that bunch down on South Street, you'll never live through the one-to-three in the federal pokey."

There was silence for a long time. He had the horrible feeling that he belonged to a generation of losers. What a family legacy. The second generation to kick off in Danbury, and a frame-up both times at that.

Thinking as reasonably as he could with his back to the wall, Palmer had to accept the fact that it made sense at least to hear what the plan was. He leaned back in his chair and crossed his arms belligerently.

"What do I have to do?" he said.

"The first thing you have to do, is tell us what you know up to now. You haven't told the whole thing, have you?"

Day Palmer doodled more savagely than ever on a yellow page which was now black with nervous scrawl. It had to be Rogers they were talking about and the missing key of heroin from the Lower East Side raid. But how did they know it? Did they run a full test on the stuff that Rogers turned in, or was Rogers working for the IAD himself, or some other shoo fly outfit?

The big lieutenant heaved an exasperated sigh. "Sonny, I want to tell you something. We're not fooling around. You just heard what kind of rap the Feds have for wire tapping; in this state it's a class E felony that gets you up to four years. So think hard before you hold back anything."

Day Palmer was thinking very hard. There was a long pause while he debated with himself what loyalty he had to Rogers in the first place or to cops in general. One thing he was sure of, he wasn't going to the joint in order to save Rogers.

"O.K.," he said releasing a breath through his pursed lips. "There were these two half keys in the lab on Stanton Street . . ."

He told the story about Rogers cutting the two

keys in half and checking them in for lab analysis after stashing the rest of the stuff somewhere.

"You were planning to split the stuff with him, right?" the lieutenant said sharply. "You know what that stuff is worth?"

Palmer shrugged. He knew damn well what it was worth.

"A cool half million on the street, right?"

"I guess so," Palmer said.

"Ten, maybe twenty thousand wholesale. Are you with me?"

"That's the figure, all right, but I wasn't planning to split it. That's why I didn't take my half right then."

"What *were* you planning to do?" the lieutenant asked sharply.

Day shook his head in exasperation.

"I don't know. I honestly don't know. The thing was opening up faster than I could plan and I just kept getting in deeper and deeper."

"Well, you're in it up to your eyebrows, now, son. Don't make waves."

Sally Friedlander was monitoring the proceedings with seeming amused curiosity. She took an occasional note but did not seem to want to take part in the actual questioning.

Even in the midst of all this pressure, Palmer couldn't help noticing the way her high rounded breast pressed against the striped jersey of her dress as she reached across the table to stub out a cigarette. What a time to be thinking about sex, but at least it showed he was still alive.

"What am I going to have to do?" he asked finally. "I mean, how do I go about this?"

The lieutenant laid it out carefully. "You go to work every day, the same as before. You put in a full shift. If anything is offered to you, you take it. You'll be wearing a wire."

"A wire! You know what happens to me if they catch me with that on?"

"Well, you'll just have to see to it that you don't get caught. That's part of the job, isn't it?"

"Holy mackerel!" Palmer said in disgust. "What do I do with the stuff I get—with the money, the loot?"

"You just voucher it to us and keep working. At the end of the day, you have to try to shake any tails that are on you and I'll give you a number where you can reach us. You call that number and we'll set up a meet, whenever necessary. That'll be almost every day."

"What makes you think I'll have tails?"

"They're already watching you, sonny, like a hawk. You aren't the best candidate we could find for this job, but right now you're the only man we *have* on that squad, so we got to go with you and just hope you last long enough to be useful."

Day stood up and stretched his legs.

"Is that it?"

"We're drawing up an indictment on you," Sally Friedlander said, "a federal indictment to keep it out of the hands of any city politicians. But we won't move it, as long as you play ball with us."

Even now, despite the cold threat implied in her voice, there was warmth and humour in her eyes and Day Palmer resisted the impulse to take up the straight line she had handed him.

"You can go now," she said. "Somebody will be in touch with you tomorrow."

"Yeah," Palmer said stretching his arms wide. He suddenly realized that his neck and back were tied up in little knots from tension, and had been growing more and more cramped by the hour.

"I'd better be going," he said. "I've got a long day ahead of me—if I live through it."

CHAPTER SIXTEEN

Day Palmer had never felt so totally alone in his life. First there had been the blow of losing his father, then his mother, then when he joined the force he gradually lost more of his old friends. It wasn't so much that they hated cops, but rather that his life pattern no longer fit with theirs. He hadn't made that many close friends on the force, and the only one he *had* made was now overlooking the traffic on the Long Island Expressway from a grave in Calvary cemetery—his guts stitched back into his belly after the autopsy, the holes closed neatly, his hands folded on his chest.

That first day back on duty there wasn't too much to do; a lot of paper work and reports to wrap up about the Stanton Street raid, conferences with the district attorney's office on the preparation of the case. Nobody was aware of the events of the night before because they had taken place during his off-duty time; that is unless somebody had been watching him, which he doubted. Before he went up to Lennox Terrace, he'd taken a lot of precautions to make sure he was not followed.

Nobody could say that Day Palmer couldn't take a hint.

Before he went off duty that day, he called Christina from the detectives' squad room. The phone buzzed once but before she answered, he slammed the receiver down. It would be hard to keep it a secret but there was no sense in advertising the fact that he was seeing Pancho Navarro's widow.

He left the Mustang parked in the street, jumped into the South Ferry Lexington Avenue local, hopped off the train and on it a few times, changed to the express, got off at Grand Central Station, went up into the station, and doubled back enough times to make sure he was clean. Then from one of the booths in the station, he called the Forest Hills number.

Jennifer, the tiny, curly-haired heiress to Pancho Navarro's estate, was still up when he arrived, padding about in flannel Doctor Dentons dragging a Yogi Bear doll with her. In the dark curls and the piercing straight gaze, Palmer could see an uncomfortable resemblance to his dead partner. He wanted to take the kid on his knee and hold her, talk to her, but there were too many other affairs clouding his mind for him to express tenderness at that moment.

Chris started to mix his usual drink, a short Grant's and soda.

"Make that a double. A big double," Palmer said.

"Tough day?"

"Murderous," Day said sinking back in the soft cushions of the couch.

"You want to play with me and Yogi?" Jennifer asked seriously, looking at the tall form sprawled out before her.

"I promise I will, some other time, honey, but tonight is not the night."

"That's what Daddy always said," the little girl answered with a pout.

Day was stuck for an answer. The girl held his eyes with a dark, serious gaze.

"Are you going to go away, too?"

"No, I'll be around, honey—I hope," he said gently, forcing his voice to be tender.

Chris appeared from the kitchen with the drinks. She was wearing a pair of grey flannel slacks that fit tightly over her firm well packed rump and descended in loose folds around her ankles. On top she wore a soft, white sweater with a V-neck and a little shirt collar. Under it, as far as Day Palmer could tell, she wore nothing. But her body was so firm that it was hard to tell for sure.

She set out a tray with two drinks on it and a basket of Fritos. Next to it was a little ceramic bowl with a greenish sauce, the consistency of mayonnaise in it.

"*Guacamole,*" she said. "Dip in, it goes good with the drinks."

Turning to her daughter who stood there still on the verge of tears, she said, "Run along, honey. Sesame Street is on now. You know it's your favorite program."

"I will," she said. "But I'm coming back," and stalked off in indignation.

Chris sat down on the couch next to him at such an angle that her knees grazed his slightly. Day pretended not to notice the contact. She picked up her glass and clicked it gently against his.

"*Salud,*" she said.

"*Amor y dinero,*" Palmer said completing the toast.

They both took a sip from their drinks. Christina's eyes held his in a serious gaze, not unlike that of her daughter. It was a look of expectancy. But what was she *expecting?*

"Do you have something?" she said. "You sounded very serious on the phone."

Day sighed painfully. "I have something all right—trouble."

He had been lounging back on the soft cushions of the couch. Now he sat up suddenly, his back erect,

82

his eyes looking back into hers. He took her hand in his and pressed it seriously.

"Chris, I've got to talk to somebody and I'm afraid you're the only one. I hate to lay this on you . . ."

Chris placed her warm brown hand over his.

"Day, I need somebody to talk to as badly as you do. There's things I can't talk to anybody else about. Now, what's happened with you?"

Day bit his lip, subconsciously trying to hold back.

"I got caught by the IAD tapping Cheryl Brown's phone. They threatened me with a federal and a state rap and they got some narcotics business on me too. I didn't know what I was getting into. The narcotics, I mean. The whole thing."

"Why were you tapping Cheryl Brown's phone? Isn't that that girlfriend of Eddie Evans?"

Palmer bit his lip in frustration.

"Shit! I was positive that I spotted Eddie Evans during a raid we made down on Stanton Street on the East Side. Frankly, I was getting a hunch that Pancho and Eddie were up to something between them and that they were crossing the other three. I think that may be the reason that Pancho got it."

He turned earnestly to the dark-haired widow on the couch beside him, and took both her hands in his.

"I really hate to say this. You know that nobody loved or respected Pancho more than me. But Pancho was in this deal—the narcotics rip-off from the French Connection loot—up to his neck. And today I had it confirmed by the Feds. I really didn't want to tell you about that . . ."

Christina smiled grimly, her lips pressed firmly together.

"After five years of being married to Pancho, there weren't too many surprises left for me. But I tell you, I could never have made it on a detective's income. You don't think we have this, the house, the trips to Florida in the summer, the color TV, Pancho's clothes, my fur coat, this diamond just on his department salary? I had to know that the money was coming from *somewhere*. Maybe in some ways I'm as guilty as he is. I sure never put up a squawk."

Day couldn't accept this. He pressed her hands even tighter now.

"Chris, don't say that, it's not your fault. It's Pancho. Maybe he was poor too long as a kid down in that Chicano ghetto in Texas. Who the hell knows why guys do these things? It's just that heroin is worth so much, and it's right there—so easy to dip your hand in. A man shouldn't be asked to face that kind of temptation. The first time I went out on a job, I got offered a half a key of skag by Rogers and that wasn't so long ago. Do you know what it's worth? About twelve five on today's market—more if I break it up and retail it. Over a hundred grand that way. How can they expect a man to stay straight with that kind of stuff passed under his nose every day?"

"Yes," Christina said softly. "Pancho could resist anything except temptation. It didn't take much of a push to put Pancho over the line in business or in pleasure."

Day looked up sharply.

"You *knew* about . . ."

"The women," Christina laughed with no humour. "I'd have to be simple to believe all those stories about working late and bouncing around with the guys, and besides, there's one thing a man never thinks about—the smells. A woman could always tell where a man's been by the smells on his clothes. If he's been in a bar all night, the clothes smell from smoke and sweat. But if he's been with a woman, there's always some special smell—some scent—perfume, talcum powder, and maybe sweat too, but a different kind. Hell, I could even tell *who* he'd been with by the different smells he came home with."

"You'd brace him with it?"

Christina lifted her shoulders in a hopeless gesture.

"We probably would have had it out some day. We had dish-smashing, pot-throwing go-downs several times, and I'll have to admit, as far as I was con-

84

'cerned, the bloom was off the rose with Pancho a long time ago. But there was Jennifer ..."

"Did you know that they had the goods on him, the IAD and the Feds? Do you know the kind of choice they gave him?"

"I had an idea," Christina said softly.

"Well, it's the same show all over again. I suppose in a way, I'm taking Pancho's place."

He felt the tears rising in his eyes now and fought them back.

"Hell, Christina, I don't know what to do," he said, his voice choking up now.

He took her by the shoulders and buried his face in her neck as much to conceal his weakness from her as anything else. Her hair, brushing against his nose now, had the cool, fresh smell of cut roses. It was not so much a perfume. It was almost as though she were actually *wearing* the flowers. Christina leaned forward in sympathy and put her slim muscular arms around him, patting his back in a vain gesture of compassion. Now he put his face up to hers and they were only inches away. Those two broad lips were before him like a pair of warm, soft, moist, comforting cushions. Slowly, very conscious of what they were doing, they moved together and he touched his lips to hers. They were moist and so hot they seemed almost feverish, and her tongue now suddenly thrusting into his mouth was sweet and warm and penetrating.

Now it seemed that the heat of their contact, the fusing of their flesh could erase all of the dark images. There was no dead Mexican detective, there was no bust by the IAD, there was no rolling over for the Feds. There was only their bodies entwined, their legs gripped tight together, their tongues penetrating deep into one another's mouths. After about five minutes of this urgent contact, Christina pulled back and looked deep into Day Palmer's eyes. Her face was flushed and her breathing was deep.

"I'm sorry," Day said, "I ..."

"Don't be dumb." Christina rose with a single lithe movement from the couch. "I'll be back in a minute. I have to see about Jennifer."

Day had completely forgotten about the kid. It would have been beautiful if the child had walked out while they were gripped together like that—really *beautiful!*

While he was waiting for her return, and to calm his quivering muscles, Palmer took the blue telephone address book from his inner jacket pocket. At first, he was so agitated that the notations blurred. Then despite himself, he began to be interested in what he was reading. Most of the names in it were cryptic, except for those he recognized as police numbers: but there were others that had either initials only or first names combined with initials. Sometimes there were only what seemed to be last names.

The names of Shulman, Cronin, Rogers and Evans were there, as well as Cheryl Brown who was listed as C. Brown. Day had been originally able to trace her because her number matched that given for Evans. The numbers of various precincts were there, as well as the property clerk's and a lot of last names that Day assumed were those of girlfriends.

In the back of the book were some pages provided for memoranda which were largely blank. One of the pages was marked with some doodles, some memoranda that had been scratched out, a few notations on what seemed to be appointments such as: *Rogers—lunch, twelve* P.M., *Barry's.* Day recognized that as an abbreviation for the bar near the precinct. Another said: *Eddie—Big Nig, Small's, 3* P.M., *Wednesday.* Palmer wondered whether the number of appointments that had been scratched out were those that had already been kept and still in the book were Pancho's unkept dates. One notation said: *SF, 10* P.M., *Americana* and in parentheses the word "flowers." Another said: *Potatoes—ABBC, Wednesday, 7* P.M. Underneath was the name Gennaro with an arrow pointing to the initials ABBC.

There were at least a half a dozen entries for the initials SF with other hotels after them—The Hilton, The New Yorker, The St. Regis, The Americana, again, and the Abbey Victoria. One of them, the second notation, was marked with a small asterisk.

"You must be bored, to be reading the phone book."

Christina's voice startled him. He placed the address book in his pocket.

"No, just seeing what I can dope out." He noticed that Christina was now wearing a long brown robe, trimmed with pale beige lace. She took him by the hand and half pulled him to his feet. Day was sure that she was sending him home. Certainly a woman lonesome, isolated in her grief, was vulnerable, but Day thought he had taken unfair advantage.

"Jennifer is asleep," she said. "Come on, we can go upstairs."

CHAPTER SEVENTEEN

At lunch time the next day, he called the U.S. attorney's private number. Sally Friedlander answered.

"Where are you calling from?" she asked.

"I'm at the Ferry Terminal, in a booth. There's nobody near me."

"O.K., that's good. Can you meet me at Charlie Brown's at 7 P.M.—the place in the Pan Am Building?"

"Right."

"O.K. See you."

Charlie Brown's was a good choice for the meeting, Day felt. It was packed with men and women from the huge office building and the surrounding areas who met there for cocktails and personal contact. The bar would be jammed. He remembered from previous visits that the dining room in the back had booths where a reasonable amount of privacy could be insured and would not begin to fill up with dinner people until eight or nine o'clock.

He was wearing a brown tweed jacket that day and

brown slacks. In his pocket he carried a wide, solid brown knit tie which didn't wrinkle when carried that way. He usually took it along with him when wearing a sport shirt in case he was called on to drop into a restaurant which required a tie.

The bar was crowded with young executives on the make and somewhat younger secretaries, clerks and executive assistants with similar inclinations. Some were coupled off and some were still cruising.

Day pushed through to the rear, grabbed a booth for two and indicated that he would be waiting at the bar. That area, however, was so packed, that he was still standing there trying to attract the attention of the bartender when he saw Sally Friedlander approaching from the escalator leading down to Grand Central Station.

She was wearing a yellow linen dress with a wide belt that looked like burlap fastened by heavy brass clasps, probably adapted from some sort of horse harness. She was carrying a huge shoulder bag with similar hardware. Day wondered if there was a tape recorder in it.

As she entered the bar, at least five would-be stars in grey flannel suits made a mental note of her as target for tonight. Her hair was buttery yellow and covered by a jaunty wide-brimmed straw hat. A close observer might have guessed that she was not just one of the girls in the building. Everything looked too expensive. But Day Palmer doubted that anybody would spot her for a U.S. attorney.

He waved to her and she ran to him with a smile and kissed him lightly on the cheek as though he were a date. Day had to admit that it was a lot better than dealing with Whitney North Seymour.

"Crowded, isn't it?" she said.

"I have a table reserved in the back."

"Oh, how sweet."

He led the way back and the guy in the red jacket that had taken his reservation, showed them to a booth decorated in mock-English pub style like the rest of the place.

"Dinner?" he asked. Day looked at Sally Friedlander inquiringly.

She nodded.

"Right," he said. "What will you have to drink?"

"Martini, extra dry on the rocks with a twist, Tanqueray gin."

This was a girl who knew her own mind.

"I'll have a bullshot," Day said. "Heavy on the Tabasco."

"Have a nice day, dear?" Sally said, flashing a brilliant smile.

Day had no way of knowing whether it was for the benefit of any possible observers or simply part of the act.

"Bloody wonderful," he said.

"Marvy! And now I've got a wonderful day planned for you tomorrow."

"That's nice. I was beginning to be afraid that you'd forgotten me."

"Forgotten *you*, Bubbeleh? But I've barely gotten to *know* you. I surely *hope* we'll be seeing a lot of each other from now on."

All this was delivered with Sally Friedlander's habitual sardonic smile, so that it was impossible to know how much was real and how much put-on. Anyway, Day thought, if she wanted to play house, he'd like to be asked to play daddy.

"You're going out to Long Beach on the Island."

"Kinda chilly there this time of year, isn't it?" Day said. It was already September.

"It'll be plenty hot when you get there. You'll be joining Shulman, Cronin and Rogers in a raid on the home of Tommy De Angelo. Tommy is very well connected with the Gambino family. We have reason to believe that there may be a very important cache of smack somewhere on the premises."

"What am I suppose to do?"

"Just make yourself useful like a good rookie Narc and wear a wire."

The waiter arrived with the two drinks as she finished her sentence.

"You got a lot of balls to drink one of those," Day said. "I mean . . ."

Sally Friedlander said, "I never have more than one, when I'm on duty. After that, it's club soda."

"And after work?" Palmer said, stirring his brown bouillon and vodka.

"That depends on how I feel and who I'm with," the blonde U.S. attorney replied.

CHAPTER EIGHTEEN

The big lieutenant from IAD who looked like John Wayne, was named Hack Diendorfer. His closest friends called him Lieutenant Diendorfer. The pudgy, round-faced Fed was named Charles De Groot. His friends called him "Dutch." The two men met with Day Palmer in a riding stable on the south side of Van Cortland Park about an hour and a half before he was due to report on duty at South Street. The lieutenant was carrying an attaché case. He led Palmer into a tack room in a corner of the manure-smelling stable which seemed at the time to be deserted. Day was sure that that had been arranged in advance.

In the tack room, the lieutenant took from the attaché case a soiled white girdle belt. It was about six inches wide; just about the width of the belt that Sally Friedlander had worn the night before. But this one had pouches inside of it for batteries. Each of them was about the size and shape of a pack of Marlboros. The transmitter was flat and about the thickness of an Irving Wallace paperback. Running

from it were wires which served as antenna and microphone wires.

"Strip," the lieutenant ordered him, "to the waist."

"Why *lieutenant!*" Palmer protested.

"Come on, don't fuck around. We got to tape these
wires to your body."

"Jesus, do you think we can get away with this?
That transmitter's pretty big, isn't it?"

"If it were any smaller we wouldn't be able to hear
you more than ten feet away."

"I hope that thing is bullet proof, because those
guys are gonna plug me the minute I show up."

De Groot laughed. "Don't worry, by the time we
get it stashed on you, it won't be so noticeable. We've
done it hundreds of times. Leave it to us."

"Where have I heard that before?" Palmer said disgustedly.

Palmer strapped on the girdle and battery pack
and had trouble refastening his pants. De Groot
leaned against the wall laughing. The lieutenant,
working quickly but efficiently, attached two grey
wires to Palmer's freckled skin. On the end of one
was a small clip-on microphone. The tape ran right
across the patch of sparse ginger-colored hair on Day
Palmer's chest.

"That's gonna be a son-of-a-bitch when I pull it
off," Palmer grumbled.

"Let's hope that's the worst pain you feel before
you're finished with this job," De Groot said. It did
nothing to sooth Day Palmer's feelings.

When he was all wired up, the lieutenant helped
him put his jacket on and Palmer walked around
modeling the transmitter.

"Can't see a thing," the lieutenant said. "Now
remember you can only transmit on this job. You
can't receive. We'll follow along and you transmit in
the hope we're picking up, if you get in any trouble.
Stay away from jukeboxes and air conditioners and
radios and things like that. It knocks hell out of the
transmission. We'll try to be in earshot at all times

but we don't want you to take any action, at all. If there's anything funny going down, you just go along with it. See if you can get some identification of the various people speaking on the transmission. You got it?"

"Got it," Palmer said.

The lieutenant put a hand on his shoulder. "And listen, kid, you're playing in a very high stakes game, so watch your fucking step."

Some days, it seemed to Palmer that *everybody* was telling him to watch his step.

The raid was on a sprawling brick, colonial ranch house out in Long Beach on the Island. There was nothing remarkable about the house, just one of a row of houses built after the war and occupied largely by Jews and Italians with large families.

The four-man team: Shulman, Cronin, Rogers and Palmer went out in two unmarked cars equipped with two-way radios. Shulman was running the operation.

"There's an alley in back of this row of houses," he said, "where they got the garages and they put out the garbage. Cronin and I will hit the house from that side. You two pull up in front and make sure nobody busts out. We've had the house under surveillance for a week now and there's nobody in it this time of day. Potatoes is probably on Mulberry Street drinking Anisette, picking up the latest scam from his wise-guy buddies."

The name flashed a signal in Day Palmer's mind. "Who's Potatoes?" he said.

"*Potatoes*, you fucking idiot—that's Tommy De Angelo. The guy whose house we're busting. After we get in, if you don't hear any action, we'll give you the signal and you can come in through the front door. If there's any cars parked out front, check 'em. See if there's anybody in them, and take a good look around the street. You got it?"

"Got it," Rogers said.

"And you, kid," Shulman said, "just play follow the leader. Let Rogers handle things. Right?"

Palmer could feel the pressure of the transmitter in his back and wondered how well these words were going down and where the federal cars were. They couldn't be too far away because the transmitter didn't put out that far. There were only a few cars parked in the street as Rogers and Palmer pulled their unmarked Plymouth Barracuda up in front of Tommy De Angelo's house. The reason there were so few cars, Palmer reasoned, was because of the row of garages behind the house and, also, because at midday—it was about 11:30—most of the people who lived in these houses were probably at work, in school or shopping.

Rogers, who was riding shotgun, instructed Palmer to pull up in front of the De Angelo house, which was surrounded by a low brick wall and a garden fringed with evergreens.

"We'll wait in the car, till we get a signal," Rogers said. "Get your gun ready in case anything happens, which I doubt."

Palmer pulled his police thirty-eight from its belt holster. He had to be careful at the same time not to disturb the battery pack that pressed hard against the holster from beneath.

They sat in the car watching the De Angelo house for a good fifteen minutes.

"Do you think there's anything wrong? It's been a long time," Palmer said.

"Just stay cool. There's nothing wrong. If there was, we would have heard something."

"How do we know they didn't get the drop on those guys?"

"Look, kid, you're not paid to worry. Right? I tell you what. We don't get a signal in another fifteen minutes, we'll go in."

Palmer had to smell a rat. It seemed like a very odd way to carry out a raid but then he'd been tipped there *was* a rat on the premises or perhaps three of them. Another five minutes passed and the door opened. Shulman's lanky frame emerged and he signaled to Rogers to come in.

"Bring a crowbar," he yelled.

Rogers got out, opened the trunk and took from it a pinch bar and a claw hammer.

"All right, kid, keep covering the front entrance. I'll go in and see if I can help."

"You don't want me to come in?"

"I *told* you. Cover the front entrance. I don't know who the fuck assigned *you* on this detail, anyway. Just keep your gun ready in case there's any action."

Rogers took the tools, walked up the concrete path and disappeared behind the white front door. Palmer snapped open the cylinder of his thirty-eight to check that there were shells in the chambers and snapped it back. He hoped the Feds weren't disappointed. Finally, feeling a bit foolish talking into thin air, he said, "The three of them are in the house now. I don't know what they're doing, but they sure as hell don't want me in there."

A white Eldorado turned the corner from the direction of Park Avenue and cruised past the house. It's windows were all made of tinted glass and it was not easy to get a look inside, but there seemed to be two men in the big car. Day wondered whether that was the Feds or the bad guys. There was really no way for him to know.

"A car just went by," he said into thin air again. "I hope it was you guys. Anyway, I'm going to use it as an excuse to go in or at least get a peek at what's going on."

Palmer replaced his pistol quickly in its holster, fastening it down, went up the concrete walkway and rung the bell.

Shulman's face, sweaty and dusty, appeared in the viewing window. The door opened a few inches.

"What the fuck do you want? I thought you were supposed to lay chickie."

"I just want to tell you I saw a big car go by. I think they might be casing the place."

Palmer peered around the detective's bulky shoulders and saw that the three men with pinch bars, sledge hammers and axes, had demolished the place. Walls were broken open in sections. Panels were hanging down from the ceiling. Upholstery had been ripped up and was scattered around the floor. Floorboards were pried up and the sound of further demolition was emerging from what Day presumed was the attic.

"Find anything?" he said innocently.

"Sure," Shulman said sarcastically. "We found a carload of shit. If we found it, dummy, do you think we'd still be tearing this joint apart?"

Day shrugged.

At this point, Cronin came down from the upper story, a crow bar in his hand, his moon face and dark suit covered with white plaster dust.

"They had to be tipped off. There's not a fucking thing here."

"Shit, it's *got* to be here," Shulman said anxiously.

"Well, it ain't," Cronin looked suspiciously at Palmer. "What about him?" he said.

"Well, fuck it, if it ain't here, what's the difference?"

Palmer hoped the Feds had heard that one.

"Well, there sure isn't any *big* piece here. That's certain. Let's spread out and see if we can find anything. We got to make *some* kind of collar to justify this mess. You can look, too, kid," he said.

Nobody told Palmer what he was supposed to be looking for. The three detectives seemed to be concentrating on wallboards, floor and ceilings. It was obvious that what they were looking for was something bigger than a monkey's fist.

Palmer roamed aimlessly around the big house, opening closet doors (the inside of most of the closets had been ripped out also and the clothes scattered on the floor) and opening and closing drawers.

In the master bedroom, which looked out on a barbeque area in the backyard, there were twin beds with matching eighteenth-century bisque figures and little frilled lamp shades. There were night tables next to each bed.

On one end table was a five-by-seven color print of a family group in a leather frame. It showed an enormously fat man lounging in a beach chair. A lady, almost as fat as he, was standing in a bathing suit beside him. The fat man was holding a toy poodle. The setting appeared to be some sort of beach club or cabana.

There was a telephone on the night table nearest the door. Aimlessly, Day pulled out the little drawer under the table. The first thing he saw was a big blue Luger. There was an extra magazine in the drawer, a couple of ball point pencils, a pack of De Nobile Italian cigars, a couple of crumpled Kleenex, a nail clipper, a rosary, a St. Christopher's medal on a silver chain and a key with a worn brass tag attached to it. On the key was stamped the letters ABBC and underneath, C-43. The capitalized letters had a familiar look. They were the letters he had seen next to Potatoes' name in Pancho's book!

Day risked a fast look around him to make sure there was nobody behind him and slipped the key into his pocket. Then he shouted for the others.

"Hey, Shulman, Cronin! I think we got something here we can make a collar on." He left the drawer open with the Luger in it.

CHAPTER NINETEEN

Day Palmer met Lieutenant Diendorfer and Dutch De Groot, the pudgy Fed under the elevated highway on West Street just above the Market Diner. He had long since stripped off the irksome weight of the transmitter and handed it to them in a brown paper bag.

"Well, how do you like show business?" the lieutenant said.

"I'm afraid I haven't got my act together, right?"

The lieutenant gave him a quizzical grin. It was obvious that he wasn't all that unhappy with the day's transmission.

"We didn't get exactly what we want," he said, "but the stuff is there. Those guys knew what they were looking for and whatever it was, it was big, except I don't think they had any intention of handing it over to the powers that be."

"I figured that," Day said. "They were pretty careful to keep me out of there in the early part of the search; but I don't see how I can get anything on the wire if they don't trust me."

The lieutenant shrugged.

"Right now you're the only act we've got. I'd rather have the wire on Rogers or Cronin but I don't think they'd sit still for it. If we could find a room where they would be together, we might be able to get a bug in, but those guys are very antsy."

Day felt no compulsion at all to tell Diendorfer about the key. Later he drove out to Forest Hills and showed it to Christina. On the way, he stopped and bought a pound of play dough at a kiddie supply shop on Twenty-third Street for Jennifer. It seemed to make her happy, and it was a lot less messy than the finger paints.

Christina greeted him with a warm open-mouthed kiss. It was like coming home.

"I don't suppose we could go upstairs right now," he whispered to her.

"Everything in its own time and place. At least until after Sesame Street," Christina said smiling.

They sat on the living room couch and drank bloody bulls. Christina had bought the bouillon and tomato juice in the supermarket that afternoon.

"That's really nourishment," Day said savoring the drink. "Throw in some meatballs and some noodles and you've got dinner."

He put the drink down on the straw coaster she had provided.

"Can you make anything out of this? Those letters ABBC mean anything to you or the numbers C-43?"

"Well, it's not a house key. It's not made like it. It seems to be stamped out of metal instead of being a machined piece of brass," Christina said. "It's got to be some kind of a locker key."

"Yeah, I figured that. But what locker? It's not one of those jobs they have in Grand Central or at the airport. Those have yellow keys and no tags. It might be the key to a padlock on a storage bin. Some of those keys are made like that."

"Yeah," Christina said, "but cellar storage bin keys don't have letters die-stamped on them like that. I figure that the letters ABBC stand for some kind of club. It's a locker in a club, I figure," Christina said. "The number underneath is the number of the locker."

"That figures. But there's a lot of clubs in town."

"Not so many," Christina said, "if you figure they'd be the kind of clubs that have lockers."

"What kind of clubs have lockers?" Day said. "Athletic clubs, tennis clubs, squash clubs, gymnasiums, you know, like the New York Athletic Club."

"I don't think Potatoes De Angelo would belong to an athletic club," Christina said.

"Suppose we find this locker," Day said. "What do you think is in it?"

Christina put down her drink and turned to him seriously.

"I *know* what's in it, or I have a pretty good guess. You know the French Connection dope that was ripped off from the property clerk's office?"

"I heard about it," Day said.

"What did you hear?"

"I heard that it was all checked out of the property clerk's office, in nine loads, by Pancho, or at least he signed the slips."

"Right," Christina said.

". . . and then they replaced most of the heroin with milk sugar, leaving enough to pass the Marquis test in case the stuff was checked out at the lab again."

"That's about it," Christina said. "And I'm not clear, exactly who was involved or how it was done, but I got the impression that it was Pancho and Easy Eddie that signed the stuff out and that Rogers, Shulman and Cronin only got into the deal later. Maybe they found out that Pancho had turned the stuff back to the Mafia and then decided to go after it themselves.

"You have to realize, I'm piecing it together from what I heard. Pancho didn't tell me too much of anything—anyway, that's got to be what's in the locker. Two hundred keys of pure heroin, according to what they said in the papers."

Day whistled. "That's a big piece of junk. At $25,000 a kilo, that would go on the wholesale market for four or five million. I guess that's worth a lot of anybody's time."

"That's right," Christina said. "Even if it's wacked up into four or five shares."

Day did some mental calculations.

"Right now," he said, "there's kind of a heroin famine on. The stuff is going for pretty near $25,000 a key wholesale. If you figure the stash was only 400 pounds, actually there's another two-tenths of a pound in every key, but I can't figure that in my head, anyway, it comes to a cool five million dollars."

Christina's eyes glistened with excitement. Or was it greed?

"A person could buy a lot of happiness for that kind of money."

"Yeah," Palmer said, "or a lot of grief. People don't give that kind of stuff up easy."

"Back a few years ago, when we were closer ..." Christina said wistfully, "Pancho used to daydream about making a big score. He even had a villa picked out in Zihuatenejo. That's a resort town near Acapulco. We'd use that as a base, we figured, and we'd have a big ocean-going yacht. We could travel any place in the world we wanted and live on it. We could even send it through the canal to London, or Paris, or fly over later to pick it up."

"Not bad," Day said entering into the dream. "Pancho had style all right."

"The trouble was," Christina said, "that he couldn't sit back and wait for the big one. He kept scoring a thousand here, for letting a guy go after a bust, or five thousand, or else he'd hold back some of the dope when he made a good collar and sell it off to his informers. And if he had a good one, there'd be a ring like this one," she indicated the diamond on her finger, "or a fur coat. All he'd tell me about it was that he'd just gotten a 'bonus' from the department. I suppose he realized that I know they don't give bonuses like that, but it was an easy way to explain the sudden money. We usually made enough for a trip to Miami every year and sometimes Vegas."

"Did you *ask* him about all that?"

Christina shrugged.

"Look, honey, I enjoyed it. If he were still in uniform, even if he made lieutenant, we'd probably be living in some dump in Elmhurst or some place like that, driving a five-year-old car, taking our holidays at Jones' Beach or up in the Catskills. I'd be wearing a cloth coat, last year's fashions, and costume jewelry, instead of the real thing. I didn't have any kick coming, except that he never made the big score."

"O.K.," Palmer said. "What if I *do* find the stuff in that locker?"

Christina put her hand on Palmer's knee and looked at him from very close. Her dark eyes burned into his, delivering some message. But all she *said* was, "You're a big boy now, Day, and you've got a lot of trouble to work your way out of ... one way or the other ..."

After the TV show was over, Jennifer came in and showed them a lopsided airplane made out of the play dough.

"A seven forty seven," she said, "with a trap door for bombs."

"She must have been watching something besides Sesame Street," Day said.

"Will you come along with me while I put her to bed?" Christina asked.

Day accompanied her into the little bedroom off the kitchen that had obviously once been a maid's room. The walls were hung with various amorphous scrawls in multi-colored crayon. In the corner was a wooden crib with a giant panda doll inside of it.

Jennifer crawled, with surprising docility, into the crib, and clutched the panda to her as she curled up

103

on the mattress to sleep. Christina tucked the pink flannel blanket around her shoulders and kissed her gently.

"Isn't Day going to kiss me?" Jennifer said.

Day leaned over and gave her a noisy, smacking kiss.

"Here, how's that, little one?"

"Nice, nice," Jennifer said. "Now read me a story."

"Oh, no," Christina said, "that's enough tonight. We'll read a story some other time. We've got our own stories to think about right now. Now, go to sleep."

She turned out the light and led Day by the hand back into the living room.

"We can go up later," she whispered to him and Day realized that she assumed he would stay with her again. It was not something to which he had any serious objections.

"I was thinking in there," he said. "There was a picture on that night table of Potatoes sitting in a big beach chair and he was in front of some kind of a cabaña. I think that the 'BBC' on that tag must stand for bath or beach club or something like that, but what does the 'A' stand for?"

"I think you're right," Christina said seriously, "that's the kind of tag they have on those beach club lockers. Besides that really narrows it down. If he has a home on the South Shore, we have to assume that the beach club is on the South Shore, probably in Nassau County and as a matter of fact, we've got a Nassau County phone book right here and it's my bet that the A on the tag stands for Atlantic or America, probably Atlantic. It's worth a try anyway."

Day opened the pages of the Nassau County phone book which was only about a half inch thick, and ran his finger down the numerous listings under the word Atlantic ... Atlantic Auto Service, Atlantic Bakers and there it was—first crack out of the box, Atlantic Bath and Beach Club, Long Beach, Long Island, right in old Potatoes' backyard.

"I wonder if they're still open for business this time of year."

"I doubt it," Christina said. "Those things usually close on Labor Day."

Day closed the phone book after jotting down the address, on Park Avenue, at Beach Twenty-first Street.

He took Christina's shoulders and looked into her eyes.

"Last night, honey, I didn't think I could ever walk out on you, but I'm afraid I'm going to have to do it tonight."

Christina looked concerned.

"Is anything wrong?"

"No, but with the time schedule they've got me on, double timing between the Narcotics Bureau and the IAD, about the only time I have for burglary is in the middle of the night.

CHAPTER TWENTY

"Was Pancho any kind of a handy man?" Day Palmer asked. "Did he have a tool shop or anything like that?"

"He usually was too busy to do much of anything around the house but he had a workbench in the cellar. Do you want to look at it?"

"Yeah."

From Pancho's tool collection, Day selected a small bolt cutter with handles about eighteen inches long, a vise-grip pliers, a hack saw, a pinch bar, a three-pound sledge and some cold chisels, a length of quarter-inch Manila rope and a pair of cotton work gloves. In a corner with some garden tools, he found a pile of gunny sacks apparently used to wrap the backyard trees in. He selected six of these and put the tools in one of them.

In a corner closet he found a pair of Air Force surplus dark blue coveralls which he put on. They were short for him and his hands and feet stuck out awkwardly from the sleeves and legs of the garment but it was cut full and there was plenty of room for his torso inside. On the back it said: Fifth Air

Force, Ninetieth Bomb Group—a nice nostalgic touch.

With Christina's help he was able to load the tools into the car in one trip. Fortunately, it was dark and at that time of night, there was nobody on the street to observe their movements.

Palmer returned to the house for a last slow passionate kiss.

"Do you need anything else?" Christina asked as he prepared to leave.

"I sure do, honey, but I can't stop for *that* now. On second thought, there *is* something else. Have you got a pair of dark stretch socks upstairs somewhere?"

Christina looked puzzled. "I don't think I get the idea, but I'll find a pair."

She dashed up to the bedroom and returned with two man's black nylon socks.

"Will these do?"

"They'll do fine," Day said, slipping them into the pocket of the coveralls.

"Must you do this tonight?"

"Honey, these guys were some upset when they didn't find anything in Potatoes' house. They're going to be ripping apart everything in sight and there's a chance they'll pick up on a clue just as well as I did. Besides that, the IAD is trying to find out what happened to that stuff, also. The time to move is *now.*"

"What'll you do when you find it?"

"I'll jump off that bridge when I come to it," Day said with a final reluctant peck at Christina's warm brown cheek.

It was a cool breezy night and at that hour, the streets were almost deserted. After consulting a map, Day decided that the best way to avoid the toll bridge at Atlantic Beach was to take the Van Wyck Expressway to Sunrise Highway and turn right on Route One, Long Beach Road, which had a non-toll bridge. There was no point in being identified by any more witnesses than necessary.

At Park Avenue in Long Beach, he took a left, past the Long Beach Memorial Hospital.

The club itself was located about a half mile west of the toll bridge leading off the east end of Long Beach Island on the ocean side near Jones Inlet.

Day Palmer cruised past the long, low, white buildings—the tennis court, the swimming pool and the main building (which presumably contained the bar and other entertainment facilities) and a few outlying maintenance huts. There was a big sign over a white-painted wooden gate with the words "Atlantic Bath and Beach Club, Members Only." There were no lights and no signs of any guard dog or electronic protection. After all, what was there to guard in a beach club?

The whole area was surrounded by an eight-foot-high galvanized chain link fence, topped by several strands of barbed wire, a token attempt at security. It was an almost sure thing that the Long Beach cops came by there on patrol at least once or twice an hour. But they probably wouldn't give the place too close a look.

Day pulled his Mustang around to a sandy stretch of dune road that ran down to the beach along the east side of the club enclosure. He pulled the nylon socks from his pocket and fitted one on either side of the license plate. If there was any kind of chase, there was no sense in making things easy by having them get his license number.

From the glove compartment he took a small chromium pen light which he tucked into the narrow pencil pocket on the sleeve of the coveralls.

Breaking in was a simple job, really, the sort of thing teenage kids did every day and got away with. But if a teenager pulled the job, he'd probably get off with a reprimand or a suspended sentence. If Day Palmer got caught doing this job, he would probably never make it to trial, unless it was the IAD that caught him, in which case he could look forward to twenty years in the slammer.

When he reached the corner of the fence facing the beach and out of sight of the road, he extracted the bolt cutter from his bag of tools and quickly snipped the chain link up to a height of about four feet and an equal width along the bottom so that he could peel back the corner and duck in without leaving any noticeable entrance. He pulled back the stiff fence wire, crawled through and pulled through the burlap bag of tools after him.

Pancho's tools had obviously been bought several years before and were not the sort to carry serial numbers or other identifying marks. Day was reasonably certain that if he really got into a jam and had to run for it, he could leave them behind without fear they would be traced.

There was a three-quarter moon that night and Day was able to proceed on the silent grounds without needing the pen light.

He skirted the pool and entered an area shielded by canvas awnings. Swatches of fabric that had torn loose during the summer, made a slapping noise in the breeze that startled him at first. Day stood motionless for a full minute, his ears alert for any sounds of human activity. Then he heard it, a scraping, rasping sound, rhythmic, like a frightened person breathing—or a child. It was coming from behind the bamboo and palm-thatched bar in a corner of the enclosure covered by the awning.

Crouching low, Day reached in the pocket of the coveralls where he had placed his thirty-eight and took a quick sweep of the area with the pen light. If it was a guard, he knew he was making a target of himself but a guard would have had plenty of chance already to get the drop on Day. Was it someone watching, waiting to get the goods on him? Someone who knew the stuff was *somewhere* in the beach club but not *where*? Or was it just another burglar interrupted in the course of his work?

Carefully keeping below the line of sight that might have made him visible to anyone peering over the bar, Day crawled around to the end of the bamboo counter and paused listening. He still heard the breathing, light and regular. Now it sounded to him like a man who was either in hysteria or really sick, the breath was coming so rapidly. Cautiously, he edged around the corner of the bar, and finally he flipped the light on, rapidly shining it behind the bar and holding his pistol ready.

"O.K., freeze!" he said.

Day was a dog-lover. He would have hated to shoot the animal. For a moment, the two of them each held their ground—the dog snarling in the low, deep grumbling fashion that meant business, Day staring straight ahead of him, waiting for the dog to make his move. The dog was still lying on its belly and then Day saw there was something between its paws—a giant ham shank bone. The dog wasn't protecting the cabana, only the bone!

"It's o.k., Rover," Day said quietly. "I won't take your bone. Calm down."

He switched off the light and backed away slowly from the bar area and he could hear the dog's growl subsiding and then the gnawing sound of a contented canine.

Lighting his way with the pen light, he went back to where he had dropped the burlap bag, picked it up and went through the archway leading to the cabanas and lockers. To the right of it was a sign that said: "Members Turn in Your Towels." There was the smell of damp sand, wet bathing gear and salt. Underneath the rubber soles of his shoes scraped gently on the granules of crystalline sea-sand left behind by the bare feet of the members.

There were rows of green-painted doors, open at the top and bottom with numbers on them and the stencilled letters ABBC. Many of the doors swung open on their hinges and revealed steel lockers, abandoned beach towels, rubber sneakers and tin sand pails, the residue of the summer.

The others were closed with dime-store padlocks, presumably to guard the left-over terry cloth bathrobes, bathing suits and air mattresses for the following summer.

Day could see that row C was the third down in the ranks of green painted wooden dressing rooms. C-43 was about half way down the row. The door was fastened with a heavy, expensive combination lock but Day knew that, if necessary, he could simply rip the door apart with his pinch bar or cut off the hasp with the bolt cutter. However, there was a good foot of space between the concrete floor and the bottom of the locker door and there was no sense in calling attention to the burglary, if anyone should accidentally inspect the premises.

Day dropped to his belly, thankful that he had worn the blue overalls, shoved the gunny sack full of tools ahead of him and eased his thin frame under the door with inches to spare. Inside, he flicked on the pen light and its round beam immediately picked out a tall, steel, green painted locker—more of a closet. In this case, the doors were fastened with a heavy laminated lock of what was obviously case-hardened steel. Day suspected that the hasp was of a similar material.

He had time, if he had to, to hacksaw his way through. But then that wasn't necessary since he had the key attached to a brass check in his pocket. Day was surprised to see that his hands were actually trembling as he started to insert it in the heavy padlock.

At first, the lock offered metallic resistance to the entry of the saw-tooth key blade until Day realized in his nervousness, he was holding it in reverse position.

He turned it over and felt the satisfying snap as the lock hasp swung open. Nervously, he pulled the lock from the holes that held the door together and pulled out the steel door by its handle. There was an alarming squeak of hinges—and then a buffeting avalanche of white plastic bags descended from the packed locker. The steel enclosure was stacked from top to bottom with skag!

111

CHAPTER TWENTY-ONE

Day Palmer was able to move the huge collection of half kilogram bags in four gunny sacks, each requiring a separate trip. As he reached the loose flap in the chain link fence with the fourth bag, he was forced to flatten himself to the ground and wait nervously as the Long Beach patrol car cruised slowly down Park Avenue to the end of the line.

Palmer knew it was only a few miles before the road ended in the cutoff leading to Meadow Brook Parkway and bridge but he decided not to chance the possibility that one of the men in the patrol car had noticed his parked car and might decide to come back and check it. Hurriedly he threw the last bag of dope into the trunk, threw the tools after it, slammed the lid and jumped into the car. He checked only for an instant to make sure the cruiser was not already returning, then turned the key, praying for a fast start.

The big Boss 429 engine caught and began to turn over noisily. Palmer slid the Hurst shifter into first gear and moved forward very slowly, being careful to avoid spinning his wheels in the loose sand. The last thing he wanted at that moment was to get his tires sunk in a sand rut. He was glad then for the mag wheels with extra wide radial tires he had stuck on the car in his more enthusiastic youthful days.

The Mustang rolled smoothly out to the highway. Day paused to look both ways, particularly to the right where the patrol car was probably making its turn-around already.

And indeed in the distance appeared the approaching pin points of two distant headlights. Without turning his own lights on, he eased the car on to the highway and accelerated rapidly to sixty. A town like that probably had only one cruise car out in the middle of the night, so he wasn't afraid now of being stopped for speeding. What was important was to get off the Long Beach Island before there was time to send a radio message blocking the only three roads leading to it.

The four-barrel Holley carburetor made a considerable noise—a sound much admired in the hot rod set but not too useful at this time of night. Day Palmer roared through the deserted shopping center of the town, out on to Route One and on to the mainland of the Island.

When he reached the turn-off onto Sunrise Highway and was certain no one was behind him, Day stopped and removed the socks from the license plate. At this point their value would have been negative. The loose flap of fence at the beach club might not be noticed for days. In any event, it would only be a sign of forced entry and even if it *were* noticed, it was doubtful that anybody would check all those lockers. He had carefully restored the lock in room C-43 and left, as far as he could tell, no signs of his presence.

Two miles down Sunrise Highway, Day pulled over to a phone booth at a closed gas station and called Christina's number. She answered so quickly that he was positive she had been waiting for the call. It was a calculated risk. There was a good chance that there was a tap on Christina's phone, but nobody could know, yet, what the import of his message was. When he heard her voice, he said only, "This is me. I know you weren't feeling well a little while ago, so I just called to see if you were all right."

"I'm all right," she said. Her voice was tense. "How are you?"

"Oh, I'm fine," he said. He thickened his voice into a rough approximation of rummy hoarseness. "Just bouncing around a little. Having a few with a couple of friends. I've been out most of the night and I got to worrying about you. I guess I'd better get to sleep, tomorrow's a work day."

"Yeah, I guess you'd better," Christina said. "Goodnight." Her voice was tender and he was sure she got the message.

"Good night," he said and hung up.

It seemed a melodramatic precaution but there was a lot at stake here and a number of people interested in that load of skag. If they'd been listening to the phone during the past few days, they would have known that something was going on between Day and Christina. But even if he might be getting information from her, there would be nothing to alert anyone tapping the phone to the activities of this particular night—not *yet*, anyway.

Day circled Christina's block three times to be certain he was not being followed and that there were no stakeouts on Sixty-fifth Road. There were only a few cars parked in the street and he made sure there was nobody in any of them. The houses all were private and while it might have been possible to arrange a stakeout in one of them, officially or unofficially, with the use of a police "tin," it would *not* have been easy without risking a leak. Day was reasonably sure Christina's house was not watched, at that particular moment, anyway. To be doubly sure, he parked the car on Yellowstone Boulevard and walked back to

Christina's house. He felt more than a little nervous leaving five million dollars worth of stuff in his trunk but it was a quiet and peaceful neighborhood and his battered car was not likely to attract the attention of any wandering strippers. His eight-track stereo deck had been ripped off long ago, so *that* temptation was gone.

There was a light burning in the upper story of the Navarro house as he approached it. By the time he got up the narrow front walk, Christina had apparently spotted him. The door opened silently before he could even ring. She stood there in a long, white, heavy silk nightgown. In the darkness it seemed almost luminous in vivid contrast to her dark flesh.

Without saying anything, she gestured for him to come in and closed the door, then threw her arms impulsively around his neck, and pressed herself to him. He could feel the tall body trembling underneath the smooth texture of the gown.

"You're cold," he said, "you'd better put something on."

"It's not cold that's making me shake like that. It's fear and maybe excitement. Let's go to bed where we can talk."

"O.K.," he said, "but I don't think I better stay tonight. There's just too much at stake."

Before going upstairs, he slipped out of the air force coveralls and dropped them into the clothes hamper in the downstairs bathroom.

Intuitively Christina went to the kitchen and poured them each about two fingers of straight scotch in short glasses. She returned as he was leaving the bathroom and handed him the glass.

"Here, take this. I think you can use it."

Quietly, they went upstairs, sat on the edge of the bed and Christina took his hand eagerly.

"What happened? Did everything go all right? Was it *there?*"

Day nodded his head slowly.

"The whole big piece. It was all there."

115

"Beautiful!" she said, her eyes shining as though lit from behind by a pair of hi-intensity bulbs.

"Was there any trouble?"

"No, I had a few close calls, got scared by a dog and ducked a patrol car, but everything went so smooth, it almost scares me. Do you realize what people would *do* for that load of skag?"

She nodded her head seriously. "What about you? What do *you* figure on doing with it?"

Day put his head in his hands. Up till now, he had not seriously faced the question.

"I don't know, Chris. I *should* turn it in to Lieutenant Diendorfer. I could explain that I had been afraid to tip my mitt until I was certain of what I had. I doubt that he'd *believe* that. But if I turned it in, he'd be pretty glad to make the bust. The trouble is that he still would not have anything on the guys who ripped the stuff off.

"I figure maybe after Pancho ripped the stuff off from the property clerk's office, he and Eddie Evans turned it over to Potatoes for a split. It would have been tough for them to unload that much stuff themselves."

"Then what happened to the money?" Christina said. "He never showed up with that kind of a score around here."

"Potatoes wouldn't have given him the money until he unloaded the stuff himself, and I don't think he had time to do that yet. Somewhere along the line, as I said, Rogers, Cronin and Shulman got into the act. They found out somehow about the dope being out of the property clerk's office and about the deal with Potatoes and they decided to snag the stuff for themselves. It gets really complicated in here, and I haven't got the picture clear in my mind. I figure Rogers, Cronin and Shulman are all working together, at least until they get the stuff. Then maybe there'll be trouble. But Eddie was working with Pancho and maybe for himself also. I haven't figured out where he fits in on the deal, but I'm pretty sure that the others were not including him in anything that they were doing."

"O.K.," Christina said. "But what's your move now?"

Palmer noticed that a vein in the smooth column of her throat was pulsing visibly with excitement. He took her by those satiny, bare shoulders and looked deeply into her eyes.

"A lot depends on you," he said. "When I got into all this, I didn't think it would wind up this way for the two of us. When I met you, it was as though I'd been marking time since my folks died, just living mechanically. Going to work, coming home to that shack in the Bronx, waiting for my promotions, doing the job. Being with you, and Jennifer too, seems to light up my whole life, even with all this trouble, there's a new reality and excitement to everything. Shit," he said, "I'm not good at explaining this sort of thing."

"You're coming across o.k. so far," Christina said softly.

"What I mean is, it all started out to clear Pancho's name and get you the pension. Now it looks like that's out of the question. I mean Pancho was murdered all right. The suicide was a frame. But there's about a million guys trying to cover it up, that's for sure, and for just as many reasons. There may be some things that we don't even *know* about, but the fact is, if we open up that can of worms, there'll be enough stuff coming out on Pancho so that he probably wouldn't get the pension anyway. And when the press gets a hold of it ..."

"That part of it's over now," Christina interrupted. "We've got other things to think about."

"I know. Look, they gave me the same three choices they gave Pancho and they forced me to roll over. But now I've got something to offer *them*. I think if I give them all the stuff, they'll let me roll back, you might say, and everything will be the way it was before."

"Big deal!" Christina said, scornfully. "You're giving up *five million dollars* for a lousy police pension? Where does *that* leave me and Jennifer?"

"With me, of course . . . I hope."

Christina was silent for a few minutes. She stood up and began to pace about the carpeted bedroom in her bare feet. The light from the bedroom lamp, piercing the thin tissue of her gown every time she crossed the beam of the bedroom light, defined the shape of her body like an X-ray.

"Day, as far as I'm concerned, I love you more than I ever did Pancho. At least more than I have in the last years. I love you more than any man I've known. It hasn't been long, but because of all this pressure, I think we've come to know each other better than we ever would in such a short time. But you have to understand *me*. I don't want to go into my background right now, but I grew up *poor, real* poor, in the beginning anyway until Daddy got a good job. If we had meat once a week, it was a big deal. I'm just not amused by poverty any more. And as for *this* life," she gestured at the room around her, "it's better, yes, but you still have to count pennies, figure out what you're gonna pay for a new fridge, how much you could afford per tile for the bathroom, and whether it's worth the money to lay it down yourself rather than hire somebody."

She had been standing with her back to him, looking out the window. Now she turned.

"Day, I'm not *interested* in moving back to a ghetto, and to me, even this police thing is a ghetto. All you do is see other policemen, live with other policemen and talk about your cheap little scores. I don't mean you, of course, but I've been through it all. It would get you eventually, just like it did Pancho."

"What are you getting at?" Palmer said.

"I *want* to be with you, Day, but *not* as a cop's wife. Not sweating out every little scandal and investigation and promotion for a few lousy bucks. You've got your hands on something big now. Something that can change our entire life. Pancho and I weren't that close, but I wanted what he wanted. I want that villa in Zihuantenejo or wherever. I want the fur coats, the jewelry and the foreign cars and the trips to Europe ..."

"And if I turn the stuff in, that's all out, right? Well, isn't it?"

Palmer sighed and buried his face in his hands trying to think his way through the implications of what Christina had said.

"If I turn the stuff in, get immunity, and go straight, it's no deal, right?"

"It's no life," Christina said.

Palmer felt very tired and now he was conscious of a stabbing headache pressing up toward the top of his vertebra into the base of his skull—like a dull knife pressing into his brain. "My father ... died in the federal prison in Danbury. I've always been sure he was framed; but then I was sure that Pancho was innocent too. Still, I think that's one of the main reasons I joined the force. Sort of to square the beef for my family. I know how it is with most of the other guys. I've been on the force long enough. But I was never on the take. I never went for those easy scores. Even cruising with Pancho, sometimes I had to close my eyes. But I never went in on those deals with him."

"And what did it get you?" Christina asked bitterly. "A knife in the back from the department and a chance to roll over and play dead. And believe me it could happen again no matter how straight you play the game. There's always some ambitious prosecutor like Nadjari around looking to ace you, or some other cop after your skin."

She moved closer to him, looking into his eyes, an urgency creeping into her voice.

"You know damn well, if you try to go straight, they'll get you somehow. So why bother? Do you realize what you're trading in for that piece of tin you carry around in your pocket? Think about *five million dollars* for a while. If you sock it in some Mexican bank at ten percent, you've got a cool half a million a year to live on. That's big rich back where I come from. That's never having to worry about the laundry, or going to the supermarket or mopping the floors, or having your kid ripped off or raped in the schoolyard."

"Yeah," Day said softly, "And it's also having to look over your shoulder for the rest of your life, waiting for the time they come and get you. Waiting for the rat who'll squeal on you and turn you in. Always thinking about them slamming those big steel gates on you. I don't want to die in the pen like my father."

"Don't be dumb," Christina said stepping back from him. "The hard part is over. How often does a man get his hands on that much stuff? Never. It will never happen again that an opportunity like this will come to you. And don't forget, I'm part of the package. I'm worth something, aren't I?"

She held her hands out like a dancer and twirled slowly on one bare foot. Her body seemed actually to shine through the cloth outlined by the light from behind. Palmer tried to think past the headache that was spreading now through his upper shoulders, knotting the muscles like hard pieces of Manila rope. Finally, he stood up and grasped her by both naked tawny shoulders. He stared deeply into her large dark eyes.

"I really want to get this straight now," he said. "You're saying that if I take the skag and turn it back to the department, it's all over between us, right?" His voice was urgent and demanding.

Christina didn't answer for a moment, and then softly, she said: "Yes. Right. I don't want it to sound that way, but ..."

"No, no," Palmer said. "You *want* it to sound that way. You just don't like to *say* the words right out, like that ... And if I *keep* the skag and split it with

120

you, then you're mine, right? I get you *and* the skag, or the money, whatever?"

She moved a step closer and put both her soft smooth arms around his neck, which by now, was slightly damp with sweat.

"That's right, honey," she said. "You get me—all of me."

His movement was quick, almost involuntary. With one hand, Palmer pushed the clinging form of the woman from him. And with the other, moving in a short arc, he slapped her once—hard, across the high cheekbones. The force of the blow sent her reeling back against the couch, where she sprawled, her legs awkwardly akimbo.

"Bitch!" Palmer said, breathing heavily. "You really *are* the bitch of all times, aren't you?"

Christina lay there on the couch, unmoving, her jaws set and stoic, her eyes glittering with hatred—or passion—or both. She said nothing.

"No way, baby!" Palmer said. "I never paid for it before, and I'm not starting now! Especially not at these prices."

Christina still lay on the couch, motionless, her eyes watching him, bright as a hawk's. She was breathing deeply now, her lips half closed, her teeth shining out of the darkness like tiny neon lights. The side of her face, where he had slapped her, was now turning red and splotchy. There were no words for several seconds. Finally Christina sat up, took a cigarette from the box on the coffee table in front of her and lit it.

Day stood opposite her, poised to go, yet unable to leave without hearing what she had to say.

"O.K." Christina said finally, in a slow quiet voice. "I've been slugged before—plenty of times—by Pancho. That doesn't solve anything for you. Maybe you get a kick out of it. Maybe that's your number . . ."

It was Palmer's turn to remain silent.

Christina blew a long cloud of smoke through her nostrils, and stubbed out the cigarette still almost unsmoked. It was as though the action of dealing with the smoke distracted her from more serious thought.

"Who do you think you're kidding, Palmer? You might as well have punched *yourself* in the jaw. Because that's what you *were* doing. You were taking out all your self-hate on me. It's not *me* making the decision. It's you. And you already made it. I'm just laying it on the line for you, so you can see clearly what you're doing. You know damn well that there's no way you're going to turn that stuff back. You made that decision when you let me in on the deal in the first place. O.K. Let's think about it *your* way. You turn the stuff back, right? You think you're gonna come out clean? They'll have you marked for a wrongo anyway. And they'll get you—someday. You'll never live long enough to make that pension. The next time a big score comes along, you'll realize what a jerk you've been and you'll grab it—and you'll be right back where you started from. Because it's *got* to get to you someday, handling that stuff."

She stared at him with a question in her eyes. But Palmer remained icy, his hands hanging limply by his side, his feet poised, as though ready to go. Christina continued.

"You just go back to that lonely grubby pad in the Bronx, or whatever, and you'll know that I know. You'll never feel safe again in your life. What are you going to do? Rub me out? Put me out of the way? Get rid of the kid, too? I don't think you're that kind of guy."

Palmer crossed the width of the living room, and threw himself into a wing chair in the corner near the piano. He rubbed his face in a scrubbing motion with both hands. Suddenly his skin felt hot and heavy and his eyes were burning with fatigue. She was really getting to him, because he knew in his heart she was right. But there was something else too. He knew he could never be happy back in that shack in the Bronx now. He knew that he could never give up that warm tan body, and those soft probing lips.

He stood up, stretched, and leaned on the piano staring at the *charro* hat hanging on the wall, its round eye staring at him, a grim reminder of it's previous owner—and Christina's.

"O.K.," he sighed finally, "let's think about *your* way. If we move that stuff, we have to move it fast. Too many people know it exists. Ultimately, it has to attract trouble. That stuff is white hot. We have to unload it somewhere and I don't think it would be safe to try to go the retail route. Too many people to see. Too many deals to make. We have to go somewhere where we could dump the stuff without getting in trouble. Maybe somewhere where the cops are even crookeder than they are here."

"Where did you have in mind?"

"I was thinking, maybe, Mexico. You know the territory down there, I guess, your folks and all ... I know the language, too, well enough to get along. Maybe we could make a connection to unload this stuff. If we made the move fast enough, I think we could just drive across the border without being caught. They're not going to be searching cars going *into* Mexico. The stuff all flows the other way."

"You've been saying 'we', Day. That means you and me and Jennifer, right?"

"That's right," Day said, "the three of us ... for good, as far as I'm concerned."

Christina put her smooth brown arms around his neck and very slowly and deliberately pressed her open mouth to his. There were a few minutes when all the plans and all the danger were forgotten. Day Palmer felt himself sinking into a warm cushion of living flesh. But then Christina pulled away.

"You know that I have no folks in Mexico, don't you, and that Pancho's are long since gone? We'd have to go it alone.

"I didn't know that," Palmer said, "I thought ..."

"You thought I was Mexican?"

"Yes."

"There's something you ought to know," Christina

said. She got up from the couch and went to a small antique desk on the other side of the room where she rummaged in the drawers for a few minutes and came back with a small leather-framed easel shot.

"Take a look at this," she said.

It was a family group, a smiling man was holding up an infant in a white trailing gown. Next to him stood a buxom round-faced woman in a dress that came half way down between her knees and her ankles. They were standing in front of a nineteen fifty Buick. The woman in the black and white photo appeared to be dark complected. She had full lips, dark eyes, almost slanted, and dark hair which she wore in a bun. The tall man holding up the child was beaming. His white teeth brilliantly displayed against his dark skin, his short kinky black hair, clearly silhouetted against the sky.

"That's my baby picture. It was taken in Philadelphia. Those are my parents," Christina said. "Daddy was a Pullman Porter."

CHAPTER TWENTY-TWO

Day sat on the couch looking at the leather-framed family portrait.

"You're telling me that you're black?" he asked.

"I *used* to be black," Christina said with a bitter smile. "Now I'm Mrs. Middle Class Whitey. You know Pancho was always very particular that people knew he was Mexican. He couldn't *stand* the idea of being taken for a Puerto Rican. That would be lower than being black, as far as he was concerned."

"Pancho hated blacks? Did he know about you?"

"He knew about me, sweetie, but as long as the *world* didn't know about me, he didn't care. Except, when we were alone he kept calling Jennifer 'the picaninny.' At the beginning he was really afraid that she'd have kinky hair. You know, when she was born, her hair was dark blonde. It only turned black in the last year."

"But you don't *look* black," Palmer protested.

"Listen, thanks to your slave owners, there *aren't* any real blacks left in this country. Every American

Black has got, probably, anywhere from one-eighth to three-quarters white blood in them and it's always the fashion to marry light. Everybody wanted to marry somebody lighter than he is. That used to be a status thing among us blacks. Besides, light slaves brought higher prices, right? So who knows what percentage of black blood I have in me, really? A sixteenth, maybe, an eighth? They didn't keep records of how many times Whitey inpregnated slave women, so it's a little hard to know."

Day sat silently, still looking at the picture.

"Kinda makes you think, doesn't it?" Christina said. "Kinda shakes you up?"

"So now I'm buying *you* for five million dollars, right?" Palmer said.

"If you want to think of it that way."

He put the picture down on the end table and turned to Christina. Taking her by both shoulders, he examined her face carefully from the peak of her white streaked long black hair to the smooth brown forehead to her serious dark-lashed hazel eyes, to her straight nose with the flaring nostrils, to the full, swelling, pink lips (now devoid of make-up), her teeth straighter and whiter than a pearl-handled pistol grip) to the neck, smooth and tawny without a horizontal line of wrinkles to mar it, to the collar bone, sweet and tender as chicken wings.

He bent down and pressed his lips tenderly to the joint where the neck reached the collar bone (it smelled like fresh cut roses). Then he took the white, heavy silk hem of the nightgown and raised it slowly to her hips, revealing the smooth tan column of her legs and the dark mass of curls where they joined.

"If you don't lift your ass, sweetheart, how am I going to get this thing off?" he said to her tenderly.

Now it was Christina's turn. She took his cheeks, now slightly stubbled with patches of blonde beard, between her tan hands and looked very deeply into Day Palmer's blue-green eyes. Without taking her gaze from him, her hands ran down the outside of his arm and finally reached for his bulky brass belt buckle. There were no words as she helped him out of his trousers, rolled down his socks, slipped them off his feet and completed undressing him. Christina waited until the last minute before reaching over her head and pulling the silk nightgown from her smooth, tan body. Her breasts were high and tight and rounded like twin halves of a Persian melon with big brown areolas around the small, pink nipples. Day Palmer buried his head in her breasts and kissed her gently in the valley between them. Then suddenly, without further foreplay, he was inside of her and they were together in a peak of writhing ecstasy, unlike anything they had known together. It was both the shortest and the longest climax either had ever felt.

Afterwards, he lay breathing heavily on top of her, holding her close as his pulse beat slowed to near normal. They must have lain there for twenty minutes before either said anything and then finally Christina murmured, "Do you have your answer?"

"About what, sweetness?"

"About you and me. Am I worth it?"

Now her voice assumed a down-home drawl that was ninety percent put-on.

"Shee-t, honeh, evvabody likes some black slave pussy once in a while; you ain't seen *nothin'* yet."

Palmer pushed up on his elbows. His eyes were angry.

"Don't ever put me on like that, Chris. That's a lot of shit and you know it. I don't care if you are brown, black or yellow. We're together now, and we're staying that way. Now what about the stuff? You think we can get rid of it south of the border? If we're gonna do this, we got to start moving fast."

Christina lay back on the pillow, her arms behind her head, her eyes still languorous with subsiding passion.

"I'll stay with you forever, sweetie, but your plan is the lousiest one I ever heard."

CHAPTER TWENTY-THREE

They were in the kitchen now, sipping hot, black espresso and munching on animal crackers.

"Sorry about the cookies. That's all I've got in the house right now."

"It's o.k.," Day said, "they always were my favorites. Now, let's go over this again. What is it that you don't like about my plan?"

Christina put her hand over his. "Honey," she said, "I have not been a cop's wife for five years for nothing. The deals I have heard going down or *overheard,* would make your eyes boggle. Even a cop's wife gets a certain amount of street savvy. You're new in narcotics and you don't know that much about the business, but I want to tell you one thing. You wouldn't have a chance of unloading this amount of stuff in Mexico without getting caught. It's true their cops may be crookeder than ours, but there is no way they would give you your split. If you're found by a straight cop, you'd wind up burning your ass in one of the worst jails on this continent. And if you're found by a crooked cop, which is more likely, you'll never make it to jail. You'll be in the bottom of some *arroyo* with five tons of boulders on top of you, or getting picked over by buzzards in the High Sierra. They've had a stepped-up campaign on this stuff over there you wouldn't believe. And they got plenty of our DEA guys riding their ass to make sure they stay in action.

"It's not that I'd mind living down there—once we had the money. But the minute you leave town, they're gonna have word out on you in every state of the union. You'd never even *make* it to Mexico. You don't think IAD wouldn't notice if you were missing for one *day*, let alone those hard noses in Narcotics? And believe me, they could put two and two together—if they haven't already. It might take a few days, but when word gets out that all that smack is missing from the locker, there's going to be a lot of frantic searching around and there's nobody that won't get a close looking over, if not something worse."

"O.K., what's your idea? You can't very well push this stuff back to the Mafia. They'd soon figure out where it came from and have me fitted up for a cement leisure suit. That's if they even gave a hoot where it came from. Chances are they'd knock me off anyway, just for the hell of it—and the profit."

"You know, when we were lying there in bed, nice and warm and close together, I was thinking."

"Bitch," Day Palmer said smiling bitterly. "How could you be thinking about money at such a time?"

She refilled his coffee cup and laughed.

"You *know* women are more practical than men. Besides, I was thinking about us."

She broke the head off a cookie tiger and crunched it in those ivory-white teeth—actually, they were whiter than ivory with its yellowish cast. They were more like Ivory *Soap* it seemed to Day.

"You know the pattern's been changing a lot in this city. There's new forces coming up, new mobs, new combinations—Cubans, Puerto Ricans—and Blacks.

129

You know who shoots up ninety percent of the skag in this city? It ain't Mr. Grey."

"You're talking about moving the stuff in Harlem?"

"Only place. You can't be parcelling this stuff out in nickel bags the rest of your life. You got to move once and for all and then clear out. They got some big ambitious men up there looking for heavy scores—looking to move in on the combinations."

"You got a connection?"

"No, but I got a connection *to* a connection."

"Meaning?"

Her eyes, dark as the espresso, were shiny with excitement now. "I know that Pancho was moving into the Black world with Easy Eddie Evans; but we can't use those connections. However, there's somebody I want to introduce you to. Do you play tennis?"

"Do I play tennis? What kind of dumb question is that? Yeah, I play tennis. Pretty good, as a matter of fact."

"Cool. I want you to go to the Astoria Courts, just over the Queensboro Bridge, tomorrow right after work."

"That's if IAD doesn't have a little chore for me to do."

"Right. The guy I want you to meet, he's there every night. His name is Frazer T. Arnold. A good-looking black dude in his thirties. He's deputy controller of the City of New York.

"For Christ's sake, you gonna tell *him* what's up?"

Christina laughed. "No way! I'll just tell him there's a member of the force that wants to make some good contacts on a top level. I'll tell him you're a friend of Pancho's. He used to play with Pancho on Saturdays. They were good friends."

"Look, even if I don't tell him everything, how do I know I can trust this guy? He's with the city, right? How do I know he won't spill to the D.A. or something?"

"He won't spill. He's my half brother."

CHAPTER TWENTY-FOUR

It was six A.M. by the time Palmer left the Navarro house in Forest Hills. It had been a long night and he was feeling dragged-out. But the stimulation and excitement of what was going on kept him from being really drowsy. He walked three blocks to One Hundred and Eighth Street whistling aimlessly a Calypso number that crept into his mind from his college trips to the islands.

The streets were still deserted and Palmer's Mustang sat by the curb undisturbed as far as he could see. There were four other cars parked in the block. He took his service thirty-eight from the holster and put it into his side pocket and walked down the row of cars, looking carefully into each one, to be sure there was nobody waiting for him. It was highly unlikely, but he was beginning to feel that in a high stakes game like this, all precautions had to be taken. The cars were empty.

Palmer got into the Mustang, turned into Yellowstone Boulevard and doubled around three or four blocks to be sure there was no tail on him. When he was positive he wasn't followed, he parked on a quiet side street, hopped out briefly, opened the trunk and made sure the gunny sacks were still safely stowed in the rear—all five million dollars' worth. Then he slammed the lid and jumped back into the car. But as he started down Queens Boulevard toward Manhattan, he began to think that he would have to stash those two hundred kilos *someplace* and his broken-down family shack in the Bronx was definitely *not* the place to put it. As long as nobody actually had their hands on the stuff, he felt, his own life was fairly safe.

But where could you hide four hundred pounds of flaky white dream dust? He'd have to leave it in the car, at least overnight, until he could work up a plan. But he was even hesitant to take the car home. It was too easy to spot for those who knew him.

When he reached the Brooklyn-Queens Expressway, Day Palmer turned south and then right, over the Williamsburgh Bridge to New York's Lower East Side. He drove straight across Delancey, to Essex Street. Between Stanton and Rivington there was a four-story municipal parking lot. It was semi-automated. You drove in, a big yellow arm blocked your way until you pulled the ticket from the machine and then the arm rose up and you could wind your way up successive tiers to a parking space and then walk out, unseen by human eyes. The only time anybody would actually see you was when you picked up your car and paid the fee at the exit gate.

Palmer was able to find a space at the second tier. At that hour, the only cars in the place were those of merchants who had arrived early to open stores, owners of pushcart stands or employees at the Municipal Market across the street. He parked the Mustang, double checked the lock and went downstairs unnoticed. At the corner he descended into the Independent Subway, caught a D train for the Bronx and home.

He arrived at Bailey Avenue by seven-thirty, showered, changed, bolted down two scalding cups of strong, black instant coffee, called in to the squad and told them he'd be late and managed to hop the downtown Broadway Express by eight-fifteen. He was at South Street less than an hour later.

Easy Eddie and Rogers were playing gin in the squad room.

"Been bouncing around a little, son?" Rogers asked sardonically.

"Just overslept, I guess," Palmer muttered, pouring a coffee from a Silex in the corner. His eyes felt as though they'd been dipped into Tabasco and his hands shook with fatigue as he poured the sugar into the styrofoam cup, spilling half on the table top. The phone rang and Rogers knocked with six points, catching Easy Eddie with two kings and an ace.

"I'll take the squeal," he said picking up the phone.

Day Palmer slid into a chair beside the black detective whose head was shining brightly in the beams of morning sun; so much so that the glare caused Day Palmer to blink and turn his eyes away.

"Listen, Eddie, you got an upper somewhere? I'm bushed."

"Chasing the foxes all night, eh?"

"I didn't say that."

"You ain't no speed freak, are you?"

"Come on, Eddie. Are you kidding?" Palmer said. "I just need something to get through the day, otherwise I'm going to go right out on my face."

"Take it easy, kid," Evans said. He opened a drawer in his battered oak desk and took out a police department envelope from it. Inside were three or four triangular-shaped Dexamyls.

"These ain't as potent as the Dexidrine, but they'll keep you going and they won't charge you up too much," Evans said, handing him two tablets.

"You want to be in pretty good shape. You know there's a preliminary hearing coming up this afternoon on that dope lab you busted on Stanton Street."

"Christ!" Palmer said, "I forgot all about that."

"You better pick up lab reports and everything on all that stuff you found to answer questions. Shulman and Cronin are handling the collar for the lab bust itself, but there was that other stuff you found outside. You're going to have to testify on that."

Palmer looked sharply at the bald, tawny-skinned detective, but Evans' face was as dead as yesterday's news. Was it possible that it *wasn't* Evans that had tried to clobber him at the Stanton Street lab? Or did Evans know something about the tap up in Lennox Terrace and the bust by IAD? Day wondered whether Evans was a shoo fly himself. *I bet that son-of-a-bitch would know where to unload all that skag,* Palmer said to himself. He palmed the two triangular pills, threw them to the back of his throat and washed them down with the tepid squad room coffee.

He had completely forgotten about the pre-trial hearings. But now, as he thought about the two huge drums of milk sugar, a plan began to form in his mind.

CHAPTER TWENTY-FIVE

When Rogers returned after taking the squeal, which was from a mother complaining about barbituates being sold in the schoolyard of PS 41, Day Palmer questioned him about the court appointment of the day.

"I didn't make any collar when we busted that lab. How come I have to go down for a preliminary hearing? Who *was* collared anyway?"

"We know the guy that leased the loft, a guy by the name of Gaetano "Puggy" Zicarelli. He's connected to the Genovese Family. We're going to try to bring him up on maintaining the premises for sales and distribution of narcotics, maybe conspiracy to sell. I don't know if we can make it stick but we'll shake him up all right."

"But what about me? Do I have to show up in court?"

"Naw, I think the D.A. wants to talk to you, ask you a few questions about that stuff you found. But you don't have to go to court. Actually, it's some young A.D.A. named Gillman. Just routine."

"What about that raid out in Long Beach?" Day said. "You got any clues to what was going on out there?"

Rogers held Day's eyes in a steely gaze. "No, have you?"

Day turned away as casually as possible. "Hell, I didn't know what it was about in the first place. Remember, you didn't let me in the door till it was all over?"

He started to move away.

"Hey, Palmer," Rogers called, "you aren't messing with any shoo flies or anything are you?"

Palmer looked surprised. "Who?"

"You know, we all work together in this department. It's dangerous work, you can get hurt any time, shot by suspects, unknown perpetrators, sometimes you can even get hit by *accident* in a mix-up on a raid."

"What is that, a threat?" Palmer said.

Rogers looked surprised. "Why would I threaten you? I was just saying that being a shoo fly is dangerous work, so I wouldn't get into that if I were you. I was just saying it for your own good."

"Thanks," Palmer said dryly and left the squad room for the precinct desk downstairs.

He had a plan in mind that he'd been thinking about all morning, ever since they told him in the squad room that the raid on Stanton Street was coming up for review. He had been frantic all night about what to do with those gunny sacks full of happy-dust. He knew he couldn't risk leaving them in the Municipal Garage for very long. Access to the cars parked there was just too easy. But now he thought he saw a way to cope perfectly with the mess of smack, to stow it safely without calling attention to himself or endangering Christina.

From the precinct motor pool he requested an unmarked station wagon for transporting evidence. The best they could do was a '69 Chevy Nova wagon with a hundred thousand miles on it.

"I hope you ain't taking this thing too far," the sergeant said as Day signed it out.

"Naw, I'm just going to the property clerk's office and over to the court and back. I guess I'll be safe for that distance.

At the property clerk's office, Day stood patiently in line waiting his turn to sign out the four drums of milk sugar. When he had signed them out, they had him go around to the rear entrance where there was a loading ramp for bulky material. Day wrestled the four drums into the back of the wagon, closed the tail gate and headed downtown for the D.A.'s office.

Next to him on the seat was a clipboard with the lab report on the contents—one hundred percent lactose milk sugar.

He waited only a few minutes before being buzzed into Gillman's office. There to his surprise, he found the blonde U.S. attorney, Sally Friedlander.

"Hi, how's cases?" he said.

"Great," Friedlander answered, "and I hope you're getting along with your work all right. I haven't heard from you in a few days. Everything's going great with me. I suppose you young cops go bouncing around and have your fun."

"No, mostly I just keep my nose to the grindstone," he said modestly. He turned to Gillman, a serious-looking guy of about thirty-eight with horn-rimmed glasses and a slight cast in one eye, which made him seem to be looking out the window or at the ceiling when he was talking to you.

"I believe you have copies of these lab reports," Day said. "Is that what you wanted to see me about? I brought the stuff over anyway if you want to look at it."

"Look at it?" Gillman said, "What the Christ for? I've got the report here."

"Well, I didn't know what you wanted. It seemed an unusual request to see me."

"Oh, yeah," he said. "Well, actually, Miss Friedlander here would like to talk to you also. I'll be back in a minute. I got an appointment with a couple of detectives from the Two Five."

When Gillman had left, Day turned to the blonde U.S. attorney. "This is a set up, right?"

She shrugged. "As good a place to meet as any, although not as entertaining as Charlie Brown's. Gillman's an old law-school buddy."

"You know, I think they may be getting wise to me," Day said. "Rogers threw a few hints today."

Sally took a place in the big upholstered swivel chair behind Gillman's desk and spun around in it slowly like a child playing in her father's office.

"They're just testing you out," she said. "They do that with every newcomer. They're pretty nervous about shoo flies these days."

The swivel chair tilted back to reveal a pink patch of thigh and a sudden flash of printed Pucci bikini. At that close distance Palmer could even make out several golden curls of pubic hair peeping out from under the elastic of the panties.

Sally sat, angled back like that in the chair, her legs spread seemingly for balance, oscillating slowly on the swivel, her crotch swaying like a golden pendulum, until she noticed Palmer's swivelling eyes. She caught his gaze with a calculated look, tilted the chair to a level position, and gave a half-hearted tug at the hem of her short linen skirt.

Her lips parted in a mocking smile.

"You see? There are fringe benefits to working with a woman U.S. attorney." And then she was all business again.

She leaned forward, folded her arms on the desk and looked at him seriously. "What about you? You got any more clues as to what was in that house, or should have been?"

"Hell, I don't even know what I'm *looking* for," Day said.

Sally Friedlander smiled. The expression on her face

was as cold as the inside of a Good Humor wagon. "You don't have to play with us, Day. You must have heard something, because we know something's been going down.

"What's that?"

"We've had a tail for months on Potatoes De Angelo. As soon as he got back to the city and saw what happened to his house, he jumped into his car and drove further out on Long Beach Island to a beach club there. He opened the gate with a key and went inside. We don't know what he did inside there, but when he came out he was sweating even more than ever. He kept wiping those fat jowls of his with a big red handkerchief, and from where our man was watching him, he thought De Angelo was about to break into tears."

"What do you think it means?" Day said. His voice was calm and curious.

"I think that he had the skag they were looking for stashed somewhere in that club and that it's not there any more. Doesn't it look that way to you?"

Day shrugged. "I'm not really up on the case. What do we do now? You still got a tail on him?"

Sally Friedlander moved forward so that her substantial bosom was now resting fully on the desk. Day wondered if she purposefully used those weapons to distract nervous defendants and witnesses, the way detectives waved cigarettes under the nose of a deprived chain smoker.

"That's the problem. We had a tail on him. He parked his car down in Little Italy on Mulberry Street. He went into Luna's restaurant and he must have slipped out the back. The car is still there on Mulberry Street since three o'clock yesterday afternoon."

"Maybe he was on to your tail and he decided to go and pick up the smack some place. Maybe he *knows* where it is," Day said. "That's a possible theory, isn't it?"

Sally looked at him quizzically. "Yes, that's a possible theory. It's also a dumb theory. More than likely, he's terrified and took it on the lam because somebody is going to be very upset when that big pile of junk turns up missing."

"Well, who's got it? It's obvious that Cronin, Shulman and that gang don't know where it is or they wouldn't be so upset."

"That's a very good question," Sally Friedlander said. "I get the definite feeling that Potatoes De Angelo knew that that stuff was still there in the beach club within the past few days. I suspect he checked it fairly regularly. He has a cabana there which is registered in the name of Gennaro. That's his mother-in-law, except she's been dead for two years. We went in here with a warrant this morning. He and his family have two lockers, C-43 and C-45."

"What did you find?" Day said.

"We didn't find anything in C-45. We didn't find anything in C-43 either . . ."

"Oh, that's too bad," Day said.

"Except a gram and a half of white dust. It tested out in the lab test as eight-five-percent pure heroin."

Day whistled appreciatively. "You think that's where he kept the stuff then?"

"It's a definite possibility," Sally Friedlander said. "Meanwhile, keep your eyes open and let us know if there's any action going on involving the Rover Boys over there on your squad. Also, see if there's any place you can drop a bug, hide a microphone, someplace where they talk together privately, maybe a booth in a saloon, in one of their cars or even in the squad room."

"I'll check it out," Day said.

The door opened a crack and Gillman looked in. "Am I interrupting anything?" he giggled maliciously.

"Wish you were," Day Palmer said, "but Miss Friedlander has been strictly business with me, so far."

Gillman came into the room and Sally started to get up from his chair.

"Stay where you are. I'll just sit here." He rested a haunch on the edge of the desk.

"Do you want to see the drums of milk sugar?" Day Palmer asked for the second time. "Like I said, I've got them with me in the car in the garage downstairs."

"Like I said, we've got the reports. I don't need to look at a couple of cardboard containers of lactose."

"Well, I just wasn't sure. They didn't explain to me why you wanted to see me."

"I *didn't* really. The whole thing was Miss Friedlander's idea," Gillman said.

Day Palmer wasn't sure, but he thought he saw a slight flush of color rising in the U.S. attorney's fresh young cheeks. She suddenly became very busy snapping shut the brown pigskin attaché case which lay open on Gillman's desk and slipping into a short linen jacket.

Before she left, Sally Friedlander came close to Day Palmer and took his hand in hers.

"Don't be so distant, Detective Palmer. We'd all *love* to see more of you."

And she was gone.

CHAPTER TWENTY-SIX

Day stuck around for a few minutes, then went down
to the Municipal Garage to reclaim the Nova and the
drums of sugar.

He drove the wagon south through Foley Square,
took a couple of fast zigs and zags through the financial district and finally doubled back up Varick Street
to West Houston, across Houston to Essex and down
Essex to the garage.

It was after five and most of the cars that kept the
garage busy during day hours were gone. Palmer
drove the Nova up the circling ramp to the top floor
and parked it; then he went down, picked up the
Mustang and drove it up to the top floor also, next to
the Nova.

The only employees that tended the garage were
downstairs collecting money at the exit. Day took a
careful look around. Cars approaching would have to
come up the ramp, visible and audible in plenty of
time for him to take any necessary precautions. Besides, it was doubtful if anybody would take notice of

somebody fooling around with the trunk of his own car.

Quickly, Day took out his pocket knife and slit the cords with which he had tied the four gunny sacks full of heroin. He dumped all of the plastic bags loose into the Mustang's trunk and closed and locked it again. Then he opened the tailgate of the Nova and pried open the tin lids of the cardboard containers with a screwdriver. Working as quickly as he could, he emptied more than half of each container into gunny sacks, tieing them up again with the twine he had brought for the occasion. He took the four gunny sacks and put them on the back seat of the Mustang.

There was still no sound of cars from down below and since there was plenty of parking space on the first two floors, Day was sure that no one would come to this top level. He took one of the half empty containers, put it on the ground behind the station wagon, then he took another of the half-empty containers and emptied it into the first one. He now had a completely empty cardboard container. He rolled this over behind the Mustang, opened the trunk and took out one hundred half kilo sacks of heroin. These he placed in the bottom of the empty container. Then he closed the trunk of the Mustang on the remaining bags of smack and rolled the container with the plastic bags in it over to the tailgate of the Nova. Standing on the tailgate to get as much height and leverage as he could, Day lifted the full container of milk sugar and poured its contents into the container with the plastic bags in it that was standing on the ground, until the bags of heroin were covered to a depth of eighteen inches with pure milk sugar. He then replaced the tin top on the cardboard container and lifted it into the Nova. He repeated the procedure until all the bags of heroin were now resting on the bottom of the four containers checked out of the property clerk's office under a thick blanket of milk sugar.

The displaced milk sugar was now packed neatly into the gunny sacks that Palmer had taken with him,

143

and was replaced in the trunk of the Mustang. Palmer carefully locked the battered lid of the Mustang trunk, put the key in his pocket, dusted off his jacket and pants as well as he could, got back into the Nova wagon and drove it back to Broome Street and the property clerk's office.

There he signed the drums in again after waiting fifteen minutes in the line for other officers who were checking their evidence in and out. He got a receipt from the busy clerk, drove around to the rear loading platform and unloaded the containers.

The four hundred pounds of smack were now resting in the safest place they could be—right in the police department property clerk's office, clearly labeled sugar. If anybody wanted to open the containers and reach in they would find that they really *did* contain milk sugar just about as far as a person could reach, and after that—Cesare-pure heroin.

When he had checked the evidence in, Day got behind the wheel of the Nova once more, drove down to South Street and checked it back into the motor pool. Then he went upstairs into the squad room to sign out.

The only one of the four Musketeers that 'was present at that hour was Easy Eddie who was dealing out stud poker hands to himself and making mind bets.

"How's it going, kid?" Eddie said as Palmer came in.

The young detective shrugged. "Nothing. A big pain in the ass. A wild goose chase. They had me down there, asked a few questions. They didn't even want to look at the evidence, just the lab reports."

"Looks like you got a little white powder all over you," Eddie said. "You've got some on your cuffs there and right here on your shoulder." He reached over to wipe it off and then wet a finger, pressed it to the seam of Palmer's tweed jacket and tasted it.

"That's milk sugar, all right."

Palmer managed to look surprised. "What did you *think* it would be? Sweet and Low?"

CHAPTER TWENTY-SEVEN

Christina told Palmer that Frazer Arnold would be playing at the Astoria Courts between six and nine. At five, he called the Task Force office from the pay phone in the ferry terminal. Sally Friedlander answered.

"I want you to meet me at the Americana Hotel, room 2319 in a half hour. Can you make it?" Her voice sounded authoritative, but wistful.

"No sweat, but I did have an appointment tonight. Can it wait?"

"I think you'll be interested in this," Sally said. "It won't take long. Be there."

Palmer was at the hotel in twenty minutes. He grabbed an elevator to the fifteenth floor, got off, pushed the up button and got on to the next elevator to the twenty-third floor.

The U.S. attorney looked smashing in a red silk dress with almost no back and very little material at the shoulders. Her hair was loose and flowed in yellow fullness below her neck.

"Wow," Palmer said, "it's the lady in red. You're sure you're not the one who turned in Dillinger? That's a great disguise for a U.S. attorney."

Sally Friedlander offered a tight smile to his remarks, turned and led the way into the room, which was furnished in modern motel with some Dubuffet prints on the wall and limed oak furniture, a big double bed, an easy chair, a desk and a dressing table. The view was southward toward the Chrysler and Empire State buildings. The windows of the skyscrapers were largely still lighted and made a dramatic pattern against the darkening autumn sky.

"Boy, that's something!" Palmer said looking out. "Like a billion dollars worth of diamonds."

The blonde attorney came to the window for a minute, looking, her shoulder touching his. There was definite electricity in the air.

They turned away from the window.

"There's something I want you to hear," she said. There was a small Sony tape recorder on the desk.

"Would you like a drink first? I ordered a bottle from room service."

There was a jug of Johnny Walker Black on the dresser, a bucket of ice and two tall glasses.

"Make me one, too, while you're at it."

Palmer mixed two stiff ones. He wondered if this interview would make him miss the appointment with Frazer Arnold at the courts, but he decided to play the scene by ear.

Sally accepted the drink from him, lifted it in a barely perceptible toast, took a sip and put it down on the glass-topped desk.

"This is a tape we acquired from the FBI. They made it at a place called The Barn, in New Jersey. You ever hear of it?"

Day shrugged indifferently. "It's supposed to be headquarters for Gyp De Carlo, isn't it?"

"That's right. The FBI has had a bug in it for years. This conversation is between a man named Santini—they call him the 'Sheikh' and Angie

146

Benedetto. We've been watching the Sheikh for a long time and know he's dealing in narcotics and other things. His territories are upper Manhattan and the Bronx but he has some connections to the De Carlo family. Angie is a low level hood and strong arm man; as you'll hear, he's just done some work for the Sheikh. This was recorded in a billiard room downstairs while they were waiting to talk to De Carlo."

She pushed the play button on the recorder.

There were some loud knocking sounds, probably pool balls being hit, then a high, light voice with a heavy South Bronx accent was talking.

"Did you take care of it, Angie?" the high voice said.

"Yes and no, Vinnie, yes and no."

The second voice was husky and rasping as though its owner had taken too many punches in the Adams apple. It had the clogged nasal sound of a fighter whose nostrils had been blocked with years of accumulated scar tissue.

BENEDETTO: We pick up Potatoes outside of Luna's. He's trying to make it out the back door. (Laughs) He's so fucking fat, he could hardly get through the door! He's puffing and sweating like a pig, so I grab him and shove him in Gagliano's car. Right away he starts blubbering and crying and screaming and everything. So I don't want no noise, see, so I show him the shiv, you know, I just poke it a little bit into his big, fat belly. (More laughter) You should have seen him! The son-of-a-bitch must have lost twenty pounds right there in the car. I thought he'd shit. So I say to him, "Listen Potatoes, if you say another fucking word, I'll cut your liver out. But if you play ball, maybe everything will be o.k. Now, stop blubbering anyway."

SANTINI: They should've never made him. The books was already closed, but Joe Bananas insisted that he be a made man. The guy hasn't got any balls.

147

He couldn't break an egg. He never made his bones. He never killed nobody in his life.

BENEDETTO: He ain't like his brother. His brother went with Tony Boy, you know. He must'a iced about ten guys and he never even got made.

SANTINI: Well, that's the way it goes. Some of these guys got connections and pull, whatever. It ain't like it used to be. So what happened then?

BENEDETTO: Well, we take him through the Holland Tunnel. We take him out there to Secaucus, you know, where Chooch has the pig farm?

SANTINI: Yeah, right.

BENEDETTO: We figure it could be nice and quiet there and nobody could come around and bother us.

SANTINI: You done right. That's a good place. Chooch is in with us, anyway.

BENEDETTO: Yeah, I know. That's why I took him there. So we're playing the radio all the way out, you know, they got this opera on WOR. It's really good. They were playing Cavelleria Rusticana ...

SANTINI: Come on. Cut the shit! What happened?

BENEDETTO: All the way out, Potatoes is wheezing and breathing real heavy. I thought he was gonna pass out on us from suffocatin'. He claims he got asthma and it makes him breath like that when he gets nervous. I thought he'd croak before we even got him out there. So we get him out on the farm and we take him into that little room. You know, downstairs—like a refrigerator room?

SANTINI: Yeah, I know it.

BENEDETTO: So it takes about three of us to hold him up and get him in a chair. He's falling down and crying and everything so much. So I give him a rap in the teeth to shut him up like, ya know? And he goes quiet and I say "O.K. you scum bag. Where'd you put the junk?" He looks at me and he says, "I swear on my mother's grave I don't know what happened to it. I checked it out the day before. It was all there, o.k. The next day the cops come, they rip up my joint. They don't find nothin' like I figured, except the key is missing out of the drawer. So I got another key in one of those magnetic things under the car hood. I go running over there to the beach club and there ain't no damage or anything but the locker is empty. There isn't a fucking thing in it! I swear on my children's eyes." That's what he says. "I swear on my children's eyes." So I tell him he's a fucking liar and I get out this ice pick, ya know, and I kind of poke it into him a little bit. Not much, maybe an inch or two, just to let him know I mean business. Now he starts to cry again and the snot starts coming out of his nose and out of his eyes like a regular fountain. So I poke him a couple of more times with the ice pick. "Listen, you big sazeech. You were trusted to hang on to that stuff. You know what that stuff is worth?" "I know, I know," he cries.

SANTINI: That fucking chadrool, you couldn't trust him with nothing!

BENEDETTO: So Chooch puts the chain around his neck, you know, and he starts to squeeze it. Fucking Potatoes' eyes are bulging out of his head like a couple of artichokes and his tongue is going in and out of his mouth. I say, "You gonna tell us where that stuff is? If you don't, I'm gonna cut off your prick and stuff it in your mouth and throw you on your front step."

SANTINI: You really shouldn't do that. That don't show no respect for the family.

BENEDETTO: Yeah, well, I was just telling him that to throw a scare into him. So I give him another couple of pokes and Chooch is pulling like crazy on the chain behind him. He's trying to drag him around the room by the chain but Potatoes is too fat. It was really funny. You should have seen it. Then he starts puking and crawling around. It was really a mess. It was messing up the whole room. He was pissing and everything in his pants like a baby. This guy got no balls at all.

SANTINI: So, did he tell you anything?

BENEDETTO: Naw, I poked him once more, maybe twice, like in the back with the pick. Maybe I hit something. I don't know. The next thing I know, he's pissing blood. Then he sort of goes over on his face and he starts breathing real heavy and then he goes out and croaks. So that was that.

SANTINI: The scum bag got what was coming to him. How the fuck could he lose a piece of junk like that? Now what are we suppose to do? We're gonna be in plenty of trouble upstairs. You know that.

BENEDETTO: I know, I know.

SANTINI: What'd you do with him?

BENEDETTO: Well, there's no bullets in him or anything, right? So we just put him in a big plastic bag, 'cause there was so much puke and shit and everything coming out. We put it on a piece of canvas. It took four guys to carry that fat slob out. We put him in Chooch's pick-up truck. We take him out to the dumps there and we throw him out on the dumps with the garbage. That's what he deserves. Right out with the garbage.

SANTINI: Ya did right. The body will be found and there'll be a lot of good stuff in the papers and whoever those fuckers are who took the junk are gonna be pissin' their pants, too. It'll let them know what they'll get if we ever catch up to them, and we will.

VOICE: (Sound of door opening—voice) "Hey, what are you doing Sheikh? *Che se Dice?* Hey, Benedetto, *Wallyo*. You got a good game goin' there."

Sally reached over and shut the tape off. Palmer took a long pull at the scotch highball.

"It's interesting, huh?"

"It's scary," Palmer admitted. "Those guys are really *bad*, aren't they?"

"They're not Boy Scouts."

Sally picked up her pigskin attaché case and took out two mug shots. One was of a balding man with straight hair pulled back over his ears, a broad nose spread all over his face, thick lips, and squinting, tiny eyes. "That's Angie Benedetto. He's killed at least eight people—that we know about."

She threw another photo on the table. It was of a thin, pale-faced man with a· wavy pompadour arranged in a careful swoop over his brow, a thin mustache, soft, long-lashed eyes. He looked as though he might have been the third violinist in the Radio City Music Hall orchestra. "That's the Sheikh."

Day studied the photos.

"Keep those faces in mind, in case you run into them. You see the connection with the case, right?"

"Right," Day said. "Is that it?"

"That's it," Sally said in a business-like fashion. And then with a smile, "unless you want to help me finish the scotch. I'm off duty now."

"I'd really like that, Sally," Palmer said, "but I've got an appointment . . ."

The blonde U.S. attorney crossed to the bureau and poured herself a second strong scotch.

"You know," she said, dropping a couple of cubes into the glass, "things are changing. There's a lot of opportunity for women now—take somebody like me. There's only three or four of us women attached to the U.S. attorney's office. But we're gonna move up first because there just aren't that many eligible people."

"Well, that's fine," Palmer said. "I'm all for it . . ."

"Yes," Sally said, "they're still a bunch of male chauvinist pigs, but they're learning to listen. They had to put a woman on the President's cabinet, and who knows, some day there might even be a female attorney general."

"Listen, Sally, I've really got to go if we're finished here . . ."

Her voice took a hard edge.

"Sit down," she said. "I'm not finished talking."

Palmer sighed and dropped into an overstuffed armchair. Sally Friedlander's face was flushed now and her eyes had a brightness that seemed to be augmented by the drinks she had had. She took her glass and came over and sat on the arm of Palmer's chair, one hand resting lightly on his shoulder.

"You know," she said, "we might be working to-gether for a long time and what I say will probably have a great deal to do with the disposition of your case. But I don't feel as though I really *know* you yet. You haven't really loosened up with me."

Now her hand crept up the back of his neck and ran lightly through the curly light-brown hair. The message could not have been clearer. Palmer stood up angrily, pushing the hand from his head and nearly upsetting the blonde attorney's balance on the arm of the chair.

"Look, Miss Friedlander," he said, "I'm gonna get out of this deal or I'm not, but I'm not going to bed with Lieutenant Diendorfer and I'm not going to bed with you just to get things fixed. I'm not saying I couldn't go for you, but I don't like being pushed, and you're really leaning on me now."

Sally's face was really flushed now and the pink glow extended down her throat creeping under the tan to the patch of white skin where her deep-cut neckline edged her bosom.

"When I see what I want," she said, "I go after it. The sexual revolution, you know. What's wrong with that?"

"Nothing," Palmer said, "except I like to do my own pushing—if you know what I mean."

He replaced his empty glass carefully on the bu-reau and strode to the door, still stiff with anger. Sally Friedlander stared after him with a thin smile on her face that Palmer felt held a lot of anger.

"Don't get in any trouble, lover boy," she said, as he opened the door to go.

"I'll try not to," Palmer said.

CHAPTER TWENTY-EIGHT

It was after eight by the time Day got out to the Astoria Tennis Courts which were housed in a big, plastic bubble-like structure.

It wasn't hard to figure out who Frazer Arnold was. He was the only black in the place. Arnold was playing on court number three with an intense, whip-thin, grey-haired man. Arnold played a rushing game—serving and attacking the net immediately. The other man, older, played a tricky game full of junk balls, spins, slices and all sorts of weird English and canny placements, dunking shots just over the net in the corner, and then lobbing them out to the base line. Arnold's forte seemed to be slashing drives, hard and low, generally aimed at the side line.

The locker room attendant told Palmer that Arnold's opponent was Bill Forst, the house pro, who had probably filled in when Palmer didn't show.

Arnold turned as soon as he completed his last service and noticed Palmer sitting on the bench near the court. He gave him a curt nod, apparently recognizing him from Christina's description. He introduced himself when the game was over.

"You had some nice shots there," Palmer said approvingly.

"Aw, my game's been off all week. I want to work on those drives, especially my back hand. Do you play?"

Day shrugged. "I was on the college team at Syracuse, but no star."

"I played at Brown," Arnold said. "But I guess I wouldn't have met you. I'm older than you are."

He was a lean, muscular man with dark skin the color of roasted chestnuts. He wore his hair in a modified Afro and had a bushy moustache. The nose was well shaped, but broad with flaring nostrils. The eyes, brown with curling lashes had a nervous darting motion that seemed to be surveying the entire area like a sentry at all times, or perhaps Arnold was just nervous about meeting Day Palmer.

"I'll just grab a fast shower and meet you outside," he said. "I won't be more than ten minutes."

Palmer sucked on a coke from the machine and watched a set of mixed doubles. He had the feeling that the athletes at this court paid more attention to their costumes than to their games. There was hardly a player around that didn't have a little crocodile over his left pocket and most of the women had Louis Vuitton bags for their rackets and tennis clothes.

Frazer Arnold came out almost exactly ten minutes later. He was wearing a blue warm-up suit with gold stripes down the side and a fresh white shirt.

"There's a diner on Steinway Avenue where we can have a cup of coffee and talk. They serve beer, too, if you'd like that."

"It might go good," Palmer agreed.

Outside the courts, Day jumped into his Mustang and followed Frazer Arnold's beige 220SL Mercedes through the streets lined with deserted factories to an old-fashioned railroad-style diner on Steinway Avenue not far from the Queensboro Bridge.

Palmer ordered a cheeseburger and a Rheingold. Arnold had a club steak, no potatoes, a couple of pieces of lettuce and a Tab.

"Trying to stay in shape," he explained. "It's easy to get flabby, working in that office."

There was a moment's silence. Neither man seemed to know exactly where to put the scalpel to open up the conversation. They made some desultory small talk of tennis, staying in shape, and working for the city.

Arnold seemed bitter. He had worked and worked and worked to finally get somewhere in politics.

"I was the big man behind the scenes for Adam Clayton Powell, but when that bubble burst, where was I? Nowhere! Now I'm stuck in a dingy twenty-seven thousand, five hundred dollar job, boring, no connections, no future."

Palmer thought privately that twenty-seven thousand, five hundred dollars was not a bad pay check.

"Sounds like plenty of money, eh?" Arnold said. "How many kids you got?"

"None, I'm not married," Palmer answered.

"Oh, yeah, that's right," Arnold said. And Palmer got the feeling that the black city official knew more than a little about his affairs.

"Well, when a man's got four kids, he can't send them to public schools in this jungle here. So I got to live in Scarsdale. Right? Private schools, clothes, music lessons, dance lessons, golf lessons, tennis lessons, horseback riding, a maid, fur coat for the wife, trips to Bermuda and Haiti. I'm not complaining. It's a long way from the ghetto, but there's no way the money I make can stretch to cover all that, and I got a wife that's really an M.C.—middle-class Negro. She wants it all."

Arnold took a fastidious sip from the Tab. "Well, I guess you're not interested in all that. How can I help you? I understand you're a good friend of my ... Christina's."

155

"We're good friends," Palmer agreed. "You know I'm on the police force."

"Yeah, I know that."

"I'm very interested in what's happening in the narcotics business uptown. I'm not looking to make any busts. It's what you might call background information. I'd like to know who's the big man. Who is capable of making the number one deals. I promise you that this will not lead to trouble."

"I assume that," Arnold said. "And anyway, there's no way you *could* get my man into trouble. The top people in narcotics already know who he is, but they'll never be able to make a bust on him, because he's too well protected, from top to bottom. Time to take a ride?"

"I guess so," Palmer said cautiously.

"You're headed uptown anyway, right?"

"Right."

"O.K., there's a parking lot at Eighty-seventh Street and Third Avenue. Your car will be safe there. I'll pick you up in the Mercedes. Wait for me outside."

Fifteen minutes later, Frazer and Palmer were riding up Third Avenue via the air-conditioned comfort of the Mercedes.

"What's the pitch?" Palmer asked.

"I'm going to show you the biggest drug supermarket in the world," Frazer Arnold said, "and you won't be able to do a thing about it."

CHAPTER TWENTY-NINE

At One Hundred and Tenth Street, Frazer Arnold wheeled the Mercedes west and then north on Eighth Avenue.

"Now, in a few blocks, you'll see what I'm talking about," Arnold said.

As they approached the block, crowded with bars and grills, chicken and rib joints, store-front churches and discount furniture stores, Day Palmer noticed that the sidewalks were crowded on a Hundred and Fourteenth and a Hundred and Sixteenth with groups of people in clusters of twos and threes. The streets were lined on both sides with cars, many of them double parked. Included was a large number of Cadillac Eldorados.

Frazer Arnold pulled the Mercedes up behind one of the Eldorados and double-parked with the motor running. Day Palmer estimated that there were two hundred people on the street in those few blocks.

"You see those dudes?" Arnold said. "They're here for one thing—to buy and sell heroin. If you watch closely, you'll see a lot of stuff changing hands. They don't sell nickel bags here, mainly quarters—an eighth of an ounce. It goes from seventy-five dollars and up according to the market."

"And no busts are made?"

"Oh, yeah! You wouldn't know about it. You're in Group One of the Narcotics Division. This section is handled by Group Two. That covers from Forty-second Street up to the end of Manhattan on the West Side."

"You seem to know a lot about this stuff."

"I may live in Scarsdale," Arnold said, "but to keep up in politics, I got to spend a lot of time in Harlem and you don't spend time in Harlem without learning about things like this. Right now the Narcs from Group Two are pulling a lot of what they call 'buy-busts'. They send in an undercover cop and as soon as he makes a buy, the back-up team of uniformed men from the Twenty-eighth Precinct come in and make the bust. Most of the undercover men have only got a couple of days experience. They're given a special crash course, learn how to talk jive and all that. They try to get as many blacks in the squad as they can, because a white guy, obviously, is under instant suspicion. But ninety percent of the time, these guys are spotted and the dealers burn him by selling him a 'turkey'—some plain white milk sugar with no drug in it at all. So the arrests don't stand up. See those buildings on the other side? The cops got video cameras, binoculars and all sorts of stuff up there. It don't make any difference. These guys just wave at them and smile into the camera. A few weeks ago they tried rounding up everybody on the block and charging them with disorderly conduct, but the court wouldn't let the arrests hold up, because any junk found on the suspects could not be legally used as evidence, as the arrest was based on disorderly conduct. Still, I guess they must bust twenty guys a day, just to keep the action moving."

"Must be a lot of money made here."

"There's a lot of stuff changing hands, but there aren't more than ten guys making the big profits out of it. They got another block like this over on Lennox Avenue and a little further up here, around One Hundred and Twenty-seventh Street. It adds up to a real lot of money. That's why they can't stop it, no matter how many busts they make. There's just too much dough involved. They busted Frank Matthews a little while ago. He was one of the big leaders around here. They laid a three hundred and twenty-five thousand bail on him. He put it up in cash and he was gone the next day. Frank's got his own dealers working in Philadelphia, Baltimore, and all over the South. He could disappear and they'll never find him. But to give you an idea of the size of his operation, when they busted Frank Matthews' place in Brooklyn, they found two and a half *million* glassine bags. There was so much stuff they they left a half pound of heroin behind that they didn't even bother with."

"Sounds familiar," Palmer said.

"Listen, one of the police informants testified that when he went in to pay Frank Matthews, Matthews opened a double door closet and there was money piled up from the floor at Matthews' height—and Matthews is six feet tall. And nobody's gonna rat on him either, because he paid back every bit of that three hundred and twenty-five thousand dollar bail to the people who had put it up."

"What about the new tough Rockefeller laws? The life sentences and all that?"

"Doesn't make any difference, man," Frazer Arnold said. "It's just too big. Did you ever think what would happen if they *legalized* heroin?"

"What do you mean?"

"Well, in the first place, medical research hasn't shown that heroin itself necessarily kills anybody. Just bad dust, hot shots, dirty needles, malnutrition, things like that."

"That's right. But don't people get a worse and worse habit?"

159

"Sure they do, but if the stuff were freely available and cheap, what's the difference? In the first place, you'd get rid of all these big-time grifters and all these crooked cops, if you'll excuse me for saying so. Did you ever think of the money that goes into narcotics enforcement—federal money, city money, Customs department? Would you believe ten *billion* a year? Did you ever think that more than half the street crime is linked to junkies trying to get enough money for their next fix? Even if a few junkies *did* die from O.D.'s, these are people that are already screwed up in their heads. They found that out down in Lexington and Fort Worth Public Health Hospitals, where they try to straighten these guys out. It isn't the *junk* that made them screwy, it's something else, something psychological. You can never cure a junkie till you find out what *that* is, and they haven't found it out yet."

"What do you think they ought to do?"

"As far as I'm concerned, let them have all they want. Give it away. Right away ninety percent of your dealers would go out of business. It's the money that funds crime. And if a few of *them* die from O.D.'s, so what? Better *them* than *us*. Better a junkie sliding into oblivion in some alley than you or me with an ice pick in the back of our neck."

"Why are you showing me all this stuff?" Palmer asked.

Arnold laid a well-manicured hand gently on his knee.

"I just want you to know how much is involved here. This is where the stuff is used. This is where the money comes from. This is the source. The money mine. It's also the poison that's killing Harlem. You notice the Mafia just *sells* the stuff. They don't use it and they don't let *their* people use it.

"But it's different with the blacks. So now a lot of people feel if it's being used to ruin our people, at least the profits should stay with our people. And I'll tell you something," he said, turning earnestly to the narcotics cop, "I'm not saying whether the guy running these junk operations are good guys or bad guys. They're no Robin Hoods, but they put a lot of money back into the community. They help people out like the old Tammany politicians used to do. And they got more friends in this neighborhood than the law has. That's for sure."

Palmer had noticed that the two of them sitting there in the Mercedes were getting suspicious stares from the men busily exchanging packets of money and dope on the street, but their presence didn't seem to actually stop the traffic. Still, he felt that if they stayed there, ultimately there would be trouble.

A tall, heavy-set man in a butter yellow, leather trench coat, almost to his ankles, broke loose from the group he was talking to, and started pushing through the crowd to the Mercedes. Frazer Arnold put the car in gear, backed it up a few feet and started up Eighth Avenue to One Hundred and Twenty-fifth Street, and then left on One Hundred and Twenty-fifth to the West Side Highway.

"Where are we going now?"

"Just before I picked you up, I made a call to a man I think you'd like to meet."

"Where are we getting together?"

"In the bar on the promenade of the Hilton Hotel."

"Not in Harlem?"

Arnold smiled ironically. "Listen, this guy's got *money*. He doesn't *have* to live in Harlem. He just has to go there to pick up his bread. He must have a half a dozen pads. He's got one downtown. He's got a place up on Edgecombe Avenue, just to keep his negritude. He's got a big mansion up in Riverdale where he keeps his white wife so that nobody can see her, except the neighbors. He's got a place in the Bahamas where he used to entertain Adam Clayton Powell and he's got a private island, all to himself, near Cape Cod."

Day whistled appreciatively. "He doesn't do anything small does he?"

"Our man is the biggest," Arnold said.

"Where do you fit in?"

Arnold cast a suspicious glance at him through his warm, brown, long-lashed eyes. "I *don't* fit in as far as you know. I'm nothing but a link, and that's the way it stays. You wired?"

Palmer laughed. "Not on this trip."

"Well, wired or not, you'll never get anything from my mouth that you can use, so keep that in mind."

They pulled up under the huge, modern porte-cochere of the Hilton and Arnold turned the Mercedes over to the doorman for parking. Inside they settled into the large, overupholstered, leather-covered chairs. Palmer ordered a scotch and soda. Frazer Arnold requested Chivas Regal on the rocks—double.

"Always travel first cabin," he said as he slipped the mini-skirted waitress a fin to insure prompt service.

This guy throws around a lot of money for a guy on twenty-seven five with four kids and a big private school bill, Palmer thought.

The fiver must have had a magical effect, because the pert, red-haired waitress was back with their scotch almost before Palmer had a chance to cast an eye around and case the room. Things had been happening so fast that he hadn't really had a chance to check out whether he was being tailed. But he had made quite sure that there was nobody following him to the parking lot on Eighty-seventh Street, and after that, it was unlikely that they would spot him in Frazer Arnold's Mercedes. He'd just have to ride his luck at this point.

A brief shadow fell on the table and Arnold jumped to his feet to shake the hand of the stranger who had just arrived. Palmer followed suit. When he stood up he realized that the newcomer towered at least seven inches above his own six feet two.

"Mr. Palmer," Arnold Frazer said, "I'd like you to meet Doctor Calvin Haynes."

Palmer looked up into a black, broad, smiling face,

fringed by a kinky beard and creased by a huge dazzling white smile. The voice was rich and deep as a church organ and had a timber that made the chandeliers quiver.

"I'm pleased to meet you, sir," Doctor Haynes said enveloping Palmer's hand in a paw as big as a fielder's mitt. His voice was soft and cultured with only the faintest tinge of a ghetto accent.

"Won't you sit down?" Frazer Arnold said with studied formality.

"I don't mind if I do. I've had a busy day with my practice."

The bearded man lowered his huge lanky form into the black bar chair. He was wearing an understated brown English worsted suit with a heavy chalk stripe that only emphasized his height. With it he wore a matching vest, a yellow broadcloth shirt and a paisley tie. His only jewelry was a college ring on his right hand and a small Masonic emblem in his lapel.

Arnold ordered another Chivas for the newcomer. Palmer studied the tall man with care. There was something very familiar about his face and even his manner.

As the "Doctor" wrapped his long spatulate fingers around the highball, Day Palmer could see that the ring he wore was a St. John's college ring, and then everything snapped into place.

"Weren't you "Shooter Haynes" at St. John's a couple of years ago?"

The big, black man smiled, showing his regular piano key teeth in a three octave grin.

"Not *was*," he said. "*Am*. But it's a long time since I made my points playing basketball."

"I must say you were the greatest," Palmer said. "I played myself only a few years later and people were still talking about your college career. But then you quit the pros only after five years. How come? I thought they were going to make you the first black manager."

Haynes smiled his easy, brilliant smile again and

laughed as though in appreciation of a rich joke. "I left that to others. I still think I serve mankind better in my present occupation."

"You're a doctor?" Palmer said.

"I have a vast and appreciative clientele and the work gives me great pleasure."

When Haynes spoke, the words came out formal and straight, but there was always a mocking undertone.

The talk veered to basketball, naturally. They discussed the performances of Bill Russell, Wilt the Stilt, the gyrations of the Harlem Globetrotters and gradually the talk shifted into other subjects, travel—Haynes seemed to have been everywhere, Africa, Asia, South America and most parts of Europe. He spoke appreciatively of the food in the Piemonte area of Northern Italy, a recipe for *rouille* that he picked up in Marseille, of Gao Liang, a potent one hundred and twenty proof liquor served in Taiwan.

Frazer Arnold was able to keep up with him, although obviously from a more limited background.

Palmer wasn't sure exactly when or how to bring up the subject of his four hundred pounds of heroin. It certainly didn't seem like the time or place for an all-out statement. Finally, he decided he had to assume that Frazer Arnold knew what the story was, to some extent, and that the "Doctor"—Shooter Haynes—must have something more to do with drugs than prescribing Darvon to menopausal widows.

"I suppose in your work," Palmer said, choosing his words carefully, "you frequently are involved with very high level deals."

Shooter Haynes' wide grin remained frozen on his face. The only change was in the big friendly brown eyes which now assumed a hooded and watchful aspect.

"I would say that in the realm of finances, my backers and I are prepared to go the limit. We're as big as any of our competitors and more ambitious, because we aim to be number one in our line of work in the near future."

Palmer had not much trouble decoding that. He grabbed a handful of dry-roasted peanuts from the bowl on the table, took a sip of his scotch. "I have a friend," he said, "who may be able to come into the way of a very big piece of business. Something in the five million dollar range. I don't suppose that's out of your class."

Shooter Haynes roared with laughter, as though he'd been told an enormously funny joke. "It's differences like that that make for class warfare, right? But I think we're all in the same ball park or should I say basketball court."

"I wonder if my friend could have a chat with you sometime—in the near future?"

"Well, my man here, Frazer Arnold, he always knows where to get hold of me. Tell you what. You sit tight and ole Frazer will let you know when we can get together. Maybe your 'friend' would like to spend a nice weekend out on my island. It's primitive and a bit chilly at this time of year, but we've got some wonderful lobsters out there. The air is pure. It's my favorite place ..."

"Where is this?"

"It's out in the Elizabeth Islands, not far from Martha's Vineyard. Only two miles long. I picked it up cheap about five years ago. It used to be a big exclusive fishing club—bass fishing. Now the only ones that can go bass fishing there are me and my friends. Why don't you come out?"

Palmer flashed a questioning look at Frazer Arnold, who was listening with interest to the conversation and he thought that Arnold returned a barely perceptible nod of approval.

"Sure, I'd like to come if I can get away. How do I get up there?"

"Why don't you come up Saturday morning? I'll send a car for you and you can come up with Frazer here. You will come, won't you, Fraz?"

Frazer nodded amicably. "Of course. Your tennis courts still in good shape?"

"Always in tip-top condition."

"Then I'm your man."

"You and Mr. Palmer here can drive up in the Jag. George will pick you up and we'll have a chopper take you over from New Bedford, as usual."

"Sounds good," Arnold said. "O.K. with you?"

"If I can get away from work," Palmer said. "I'll sure try my best."

"Bring your tennis racket and shorts and you can even bring a bathing suit. The water's warm up there this time of year. I never even go in till mid August it's so damn cold in the early summer."

"I'll do that," Palmer said. "Maybe we can catch up on that game we missed. Right, Frazer?"

Frazer smiled wordlessly.

Shooter Haynes moved forward, placed a hand the size of a floor mat on Day Palmer's shoulders. "It's quiet there. No outsiders, if you know what I mean. It's a place we can talk without interruption from strangers. You dig?"

Palmer nodded. "It sounds like a fun weekend," he said.

CHAPTER THIRTY

Palmer met the Jaguar at Broadway and 242nd Street where the elevated subway line comes to an abrupt end.

The driver was a dapper, middle-aged Phillipino named Bill. He held the door of the sleek, green Mark IX for Palmer. The inside was upholstered in a coordinated shade of pigskin. The partition separating the rear seat from the driver was upholstered in the same material trimmed with burled walnut.

As the chauffeur put the car smoothly into gear and glided off toward the Sawmill Parkway, Palmer experimented with the equipment in the back of the car. There was a cluster of switches near his right hand which controlled all the windows and the glass panel separating the chauffeur from the passengers' section. One side of the partition dividing the front seat from the rear, pulled out to reveal a small bar, complete with scotch, bourbon and-vodka plus glasses and an ice chest. The other partition pulled out to reveal a Sony television set and a mobile telephone.

Day pushed the button controlling the window that separated him from the chauffeur. "This is quite a car isn't it, Bill?"

"Oh, yes, Mr. Palmer. The boss, he has three like this."

Day whistled appreciatively. "Are you going to pick up Mr. Arnold in Scarsdale?" he asked.

Bill giggled. "Hee, hee! Mr. Arnold, he got out yesterday by chopper."

So it was to be a solo trip.

Palmer pushed the button closing the window, leaned back, fixed himself a Chivas and soda and watched an old Betty Grable Alice Faye movie about World War One on the Sony for most of the way up.

There was a Bell two-seater helicopter waiting for him in the parking lot of a yacht club just outside of New Bedford. The blades were already turning slowly in readiness for his arrival.

The pilot, a rakish young blonde guy, took Palmer's flight bag and stored it behind the aluminum seat of the chopper and helped Palmer into it. Bill stood by the Jag and waved by-by as the chopper rose in the warm autumn sunlight and headed out over Buzzard's Bay. The pilot who was named Charlie Silva pointed out the sights during the short flight which took them over West Island and then on a slight southeasterly course to the Elizabeth Islands.

As the chopper drifted in for a landing, Palmer noticed a small breakwater enclosing a harbor which sheltered what looked like a sixty-foot cabin cruiser, a thirty-five-foot ketch and a number of smaller launches, dingies and skiffs. The chopper put down on a concrete pier paved with asphalt. A Landrover was parked on the pier. Beside it a beefy, unsmiling Oriental waited for Palmer. He took Palmer's bag and the tennis racket from Silva and stored them in the back of the Landrover, then held the door open for Palmer to enter. He drove off down the concrete road and onto a rutted sandy trail sprouted with dune grass.

The drive was a short one. The Landrover simply skirted a low lying rocky outcrop and made a turn. There before Palmer was a cluster of low, modernistic buildings that managed to look like an old fishing village with their white trim and grey barn siding. To the right as they drove up, was a tennis court on which a girl with waist-length red hair and fantastic legs was rallying with a tall, well-stacked brunette who was wearing a head kerchief and a bikini bottom—nothing else. As the Landrover passed the tennis court, the girl in the bikini ventured a friendly wave and a sunny smile and went back to practicing her strokes.

At the end of the court was a stretch of bright green lawn which surrounded a large swimming pool.

A Puerto Rican houseboy in a white coat came out as they pulled up in front of the long grey building. Before the main door was a small, iron jockey with a ring in his hand. His face was painted white. *I guess that puts Mr. Charlie in his place*, Day thought.

The houseboy ran out and took the bags from the unsmiling Oriental and showed Palmer to his room. It was about twenty feet long and one side of it was all glass, looking out over Buzzard's Bay west toward the mainland.

On the floor was a white polar bear rug which must have been ten feet long.

The houseboy, whose name was Feliciano, opened the sliding doors of a row of closets which occupied one entire end of the room and put Palmer's bag and tennis racket into it.

"Shall I unpack for you, sir?" he said.

"No, I'll do that myself," Palmer answered.

There were a number of pieces of small artillery in the bag that he was not anxious to have handled by anyone but himself.

Feliciano pulled back another section of the closet doors and indicated a small refrigerator done in barn-wood tones to match the house. "There is ice and

169

champagne in here," and he slid open another door, "whiskey and other drinks, here."

Hanging in the closet was a thick, white terry cloth robe with the name "Dayton" embroidered across the back.

Palmer found "The Shooter" at the pool, his great sprawling form overhanging a sailcloth banana chair. The dark skin of his well-muscled body was accentuated by a pair of white Adidas tennis shorts.

Haynes reached over his head and tugged a cord which was attached to an antique brass ship bell. A young man with streaky blonde hair and a saddle-leather suntan emerged from behind an outdoor bar, set back about ten feet from the pool. He was wearing bell bottom, white duck trousers, a red sash and a white sleeveless jersey which featured an anchor entwined with the letter H.

"Get Mr. Palmer whatever he wants," Haynes said.

Palmer settled for a gin and tonic. From where he stood now, Palmer could see the pool actually ran under a low glass window into the house itself. It was shaped like a kidney and was bordered with natural fieldstone.

The two girls who had been playing tennis now approached from the direction of the courts, their faces wet and their hair damp with sweat.

"Girls," Haynes said from his reclining position, "this is Day Palmer, a friend of mine. Be nice to him. The red-haired one's named Shirley. Inga is the dark-haired one."

The girls smiled cheerily at Palmer. Inga was still wearing nothing on top. Her body was an even bronze color all over. She seemed totally unselfconscious about her exposure. Shirley mopped her flushed brow with a little red handkerchief.

"Boy, I'm really hot! I've got to take a swim," she said. And without a preamble, unbuttoned the blouse of her white tennis costume. Unselfconsciously, she removed the top and the brief white skirt, revealing a sparse tangle of pubic hair that proved she was really a redhead, and dove neatly into the pool.

After a few minutes two more girls came out of the house. One was tall, slim and elegant with skin the color of caramel and a shock of thick black hair hanging about her shoulders. She wore a floor-length white skirt which was slit to well above the knee and a brown see-through blouse which revealed a pair of firm, neatly molded breasts about as big and hard as a man's fist. Her name was Wendy. Lisa, the second girl, was petite and small-boned, with exquisite lines like a Chinese porcelain figurine.

None of the women seemed to possess last names or any identities of their own. The two tennis players, Shirley and Inga, emerged from the pool, took towels that were handed to them by Richard, dried their nude bodies and then joined the group wearing nothing but the bath towels.

Wendy and Shirley arranged themselves comfortably at Palmer's feet, refilling his gin and tonic when it showed signs of dipping below the halfway mark. At intervals Richard, the pool attendant, passed among them with a tray on which there was a liberal assortment of vari-colored pills, sodium amytal poppers, and an antique silver bowl which must have held five thousand dollars worth of coke.

Palmer resisted the pills and coke, but finally under dulcet persuasion from Wendy accepted a giant King Kong Bomber of pure Panama Red.

By the time Palmer finished the enormous joint, he was on his third gin and tonic. He was feeling so mellow that he almost didn't care if they *never* got down to business. But he fought to bring his rapidly fading consciousness under control. There were bigger things at stake here than the swelling in his jeans.

"Where's Frazer Arnold?" he asked the Shooter, who was at this point enjoying a neck message administered by Shirley, the red-haired one.

The ex-basketball star waved a long arm back toward the main house.

"Resting, man! He's *been* up here since yesterday. Got to get himself in shape for the night program. Feliciano'll show you the room." (Palmer noticed that Shooter was serviced by every kind of minority except black.)

If Arnold wasn't coming down to the party, Palmer felt, he'd better go to see the city official himself. In fact, a private conversation was called for before Palmer got too stoned to navigate.

Arnold's room was a few doors down from Palmer's own quarters. His voice sounded relaxed and lazy as he answered Palmer's knock.

"Come in, anybody!"

CHAPTER THIRTY-ONE

The trim, athletic-looking black man was lying sprawled out on the king-sized bed, puffing lazily at the mouthpiece of the Nargilah bubbling on the night table beside his bed. He was nude except for a bath towel covering his loins. He looked up lazily as Palmer entered the room.

"Oh, it's you, man," he said dreamily. "I figured you were about due."

The room was so filled with the spicy smell of hash, that Palmer thought he could've gotten a contact high with a couple of deep breaths. His head was already buzzing from the bomber he'd puffed downstairs.

"Beautiful set-up, Frazer," he said. "Really beautiful." The wallpaper in Arnold's room was a tangled pattern of rosebuds on an eggshell background. And now Palmer's senses were so heightened by Mary Jane, that he could swear that the room itself smelled from the flowers on the wall. It was like walking into a greenhouse.

"You been out here a while, right?" Palmer said, settling into a fur-covered reclining chair at the end of Arnold's bed.

"Yeah, man," Arnold said. "Had some business with the big Shooter—choppered in here yesterday."

"Big night?" Palmer asked politely.

"Out of sight."

"Which one did you stay with?"

A puzzled frown crossed Arnold's brow.

"Who remembers? *All* of them, man," he said after a pause.

"Listen," Palmer said, "are we just gonna fly around the moon up here, or are we gonna take care of business?"

Arnold blew a perfect hash smoke ring.

"Easy, baby, there's no rush. We gotta feel each other out. I mean, you're out here, you get stripped down, jump in the pool. You see the Shooter knows there's no way you could be wired and there's no transmitter or bug that'll reach the land. There is also no way you could call down any sudden raid out here. So it's all fun and games, but he knows what he's doing."

"What's your part in this?" Palmer said. "I figure you got to get a little taste, right?"

"I'm getting my taste right now, man," Arnold said. "Some people might consider me a boojie nigger these days, but there's no way I can forget what it was like down home. All them cotton-picken suckers working chump jobs for fat back, collards, grits and gravy. They call that *soul* food now. Shit, man, that was just the garbage that the white folks threw out. I get a kick from these dudes that go slumming in the soul food joints eating fat back and black-eye peas. Shit man, I'm scoffin' Smithfield ham and artichoke hearts. My daddy was a Georgia field nigger and I had a long way to come, but I made it now and there ain't nobody gonna rush me."

Relaxed now and away from the city, Palmer noticed that Arnold affected soul brother's jive rather

174

than the Ivy League accents he had favored in the vicinity of the tennis courts. But hadn't Christina said that her father was a New Jersey pullman porter? Probably one of them was just lying for affect, but which one? Or did it matter?

Arnold finally got up on one elbow and tried to bring the tall white man, lounging on his recliner chair into focus.

"Look, baby, just listen to me. Stay cool. Go down, talk some trash, blow some grass, do your thing. But when the time comes, the Shooter will run the game down to you. Right now, I'm bottomed out, so it's no use to talk to me anyway." With this, he lay back on a pillow and composed his face in a beatific smile, closed his eyes, and drifted off into another world.

"Frazer," Palmer said. "Hey, Frazer?"

No answer.

"Shit."

Palmer closed the door softly behind him and wandered back to the swimming pool. The booze and pot were beginning to have a strong effect, and Palmer realized that no matter how hard he concentrated there would be little more business transacted that night. Drowsily he accepted another joint from Feliciano, the industrious little houseboy, and a top-to-toe back rub from Inga, the tall dark-haired job. At his head, easy to reach Feliciano placed a refill of his gin and tonic that tasted as though it had about a pint of gin in it. Palmer drew a blank on the rest of the night, but it must have been a beauty.

In the morning when he awoke on gingham-checked sheets, he was aware that there were two figures in bed with him. One, Liza, had a tawny leg thrown across his, the other, Shirley, crouched half-way down the bed, the red hair splayed across his pelvis, her breath making hot dancing rhythms on his hips.

"You're up I see."

It was the rich, black, unmistakable voice of Shooter Haynes. He was sitting at a coffee table on

175

the terrace outside of Day's room. On it was a cheery pitcher of orange juice, a steaming silver coffee service and a basket of hot bagels. Haynes, sprawling in a captain's canvas chair in a white warm-up suit, had a light sheen of sweat on his brow. "Just doing a little jogging to keep in shape," he said indicating the suit. "Have a bagel with a little lox? I'm a freak on bagels. I have them flown in every morning from Zabar's."

Palmer roused himself, somewhat reluctantly, from those warm recumbent forms. The girls stirred and purred like contented cats and went back to sleep in each other's arms.

Day reached into the closet for the terry cloth robe and joined Shooter Haynes on the terrace. The juice was fresh-squeezed and tangy. Day accepted a bagel, which looked no bigger than a subway token in Haynes' giant fingers.

"Now that we got all that other shit out of the way," Haynes said, "what's on your mind?"

Day swallowed his mouthful of bagel, washed it down with black coffee and said, "Would you believe 200 keys of Cesare——pure skag?"

Haynes whistled appreciatively. "That's a nice piece of junk all right. What kind of money did your people have in mind?"

"To get rid of it in one piece, they'll take five million untraceable small bills," Palmer said. "That's less than $25,000 a key."

He put his coffee down carefully to avoid letting Haynes see how his hands were shaking now.

Shooter Haynes bit a bagel in half with his huge alligatorlike choppers and said nothing. Palmer let the subject lay.

"That was some party you threw last night, Shooter," he said.

"If you thought the *party* was good, you ought to see the *video-tape*," Haynes said, laughing and slapping his thigh. And Palmer realized that Haynes was kidding on the square.

"They'd never get a crack at network prime time," he said.

"No," Haynes admitted, "but you could collect an awful lot of money at private showings."

"That isn't your game, is it?" Palmer said sure of his ground here.

Haynes roared with laughter. "No, that's just my insurance."

"What about the five million?"

Haynes dropped the jocular tone and segued into a strictly business tone as though a switch had been turned on.

"Palmer, I may be the big nigger up in Harlem, but five million dollars in small bills is a large piece of action for anybody. It takes time to put that together and I'm not even sure I could lay my hands on it. Suppose we meet in the Oak Room at the Plaza on Tuesday? You'll have my answer."

"No sooner?" Palmer said.

"Hell, I ain't going *back* till Monday. But I tell you what I'll do. I'll have the chopper put you right down at the Twenty-third Street pad so you won't have to take the long ride in the Jag."

"I didn't mind that too much," Palmer said laughing.

Now the crisp morning air, whose silence had been broken up to this point only by the sound of the sea and the distant call of sea birds, was polluted with the harsh grinding roar of machinery.

"What the fuck is that?" Day said.

"That's the cement mixer. They're pouring a few more concrete blocks for my breakwater out there," Haynes said pointing to the small harbor below them. "We had a couple of bad storms recently and I think the boats could use more shelter."

Day looked out and could see that the breakwater was composed of huge blocks of concrete, each about six feet long and four feet square.

"Wouldn't it be easier to make that out of natural rock—and more attractive?" Palmer said. The large grey blocks looked incongruous against the otherwise natural setting.

"The blocks serve my purpose better," Haynes said.

Day Palmer wondered if it was his imagination, or had he heard an undertone of implied menace in the Shooter's last seemingly aimless remark?

CHAPTER THIRTY-TWO

There was a surprise waiting for Day Palmer when he got back to the family homestead in the Bronx on Sunday afternoon. The first thing he noticed was the garage. He had had the cement floor of the old building patched only a month before. Now it was ripped up as though by jack hammers and the remaining sacks of patching cement and sand had been slashed, their contents scattered wildly around the floor.

Insulation batts had been ripped from the side of the old wooden building and emptied sacks of rock salt and garden fertilizer added to the obscene mess. Quickly Day proceeded to the house itself, entering through the kitchen door, his police thirty-eight ready in his hand in case the vandals had not yet departed. Here the scene was, if anything, worse. Every bit of the upholstered furniture had been slashed and mutilated. Every kitchen container of salt, sugar, and flour had been dumped at random on the floor. The floors themselves and the walls had been ripped to the bare shell.

179

Upstairs, too, mattresses and cushions had been slashed and torn. Feathers swirled ankle deep in the faint fall breeze coming through the window.

The closed room formerly occupied by Day's parents, had also been invaded. The mattresses slashed, the bureaus emptied haphazardly on the floor. The ceilings ripped to the beams. In the middle of the floor of his parent's room, someone had left two gross and enormous human turds, as though in a final gesture of anger and defiance. The only time Day had seen such thorough destruction had been at Potatoes De Angelo's house on Long Island.

It seemed obvious that if the U.S. attorney's office knew that the residue of heroin was found in the Gennaro locker rented by De Angelo, others, by now, were also informed.

Palmer's first reaction was a suffocating sense of rage. Then forcing himself to be calm, he rose from the torn carcass of the daybed he'd been sitting on, made his way to the kitchen, found an undamaged bottle of Grant's, and poured himself two fingers in a jelly glass. He'd taken one hard pull of the warm straight liquor, and was about to finish the rest when there was a startling sound of a ringing doorbell.

Somehow to him, the house was now dead and the jangling sound was a gross intrusion.

Day made his way through the debris to the front door; through the small window he could see a blue hat and a silver shield. At this point the uniform meant anything but certain protection to Day. He took the thirty-eight from the holster again and held it in the side pocket of his jacket, opening the door. Outside was a NYPD station wagon, the sort used by the Forensic Department. At the door was a cop in a police hat and coveralls. He was carrying a large plastic bag over his arm.

When Day opened the door, the man looked at him and said, "We're from Forensic. Where's the stiff?"

Day looked at him uncomprehendingly. The cop looked contrite.

"I'm sorry. Are you with the family?" he said, removing his hat.

"What are you talking about?" Palmer asked.

"We got a squeal that there was a body to be picked up here for Forensic. This is the Palmer residence, isn't it?"

Day shot the man a cold hard stare but then saw that the cop was playing it straight. The squeal could have been phoned in from anywhere.

"Sorry, someone must have been playing a joke on you," he said, closing the door.

The cop went off down the steps scratching his head. Day recognized the gambit as a logical follow-up in a campaign of terrorism. Somebody had him marked for sure; whether it was the guys on his own squad or maybe the Mafia.

For that matter, when a piece of dope the size of the one involved here was a bone of contention, was *anybody* clear of suspicion who knew about it? This now included the U.S. attorney's office and the IAD shoo flies. One thing was clear. His value was shot as rollover cop. He was burned but good. It was also apparent that if he was going to take any action it would have to be fast.

At this point he could only think of two people to whom he might turn for help—Christina and Sally Friedlander and he wasn't *positive* about either of *them.*

CHAPTER THIRTY-THREE

One thing was certain, even one more night in the family house would probably be dangerous. Day Palmer jumped back into his Mustang. He picked up the Henry Hudson south at 233rd Street, not even bothering to watch for tails. Whoever was after him was good and professional and would probably be able to switch cars back and forth. A tail would be difficult to spot.

Day drove down along the Hudson, over the Harlem River and down toward the George Washington Bridge. This was a route he knew by heart. Every half mile or so there was a lay-by where the highway widened a bit for cars with emergency breakdowns.

At the last lay-by before the turn-off to the Cross Bronx Expressway, Day swerved across a line of traffic without signaling and pulled in. Any cars following him now would have to keep going in the line of traffic, or at the very best, stop at the next available parking space and wait for him to appear again. After waiting for five minutes, Day pulled out again cautiously and turned left to the Cross Bronx Expressway.

He followed it east across the Triborough and finally exited the city highways at La Guardia Airport. He left the Mustang in the airport's long-term parking garage. In the arrivals terminal he signed up for a Budget rent-a-car. For his purposes he would have preferred a Porsche or a Lotus, but this was not the sort of thing you rented at a budget center.

He settled for a green Nova coupe. It felt sluggish under the pedal after the hopped-up responsiveness of the Mustang, but it would have to do.

From the airport, he called the special night number that Sally Friedlander had given him. Her at-home voice was sultry and open. An entirely different quality from the slick, probing, aware timber he had been conscious of in her business encounters.

Palmer's experience was such that he had not much confidence in the privacy in *any* telephone, particularly that of a U.S. attorney. But what he had to say would not be of much use to the enemy in any event.

"Sally, this is your friend, Rolly. I don't know if you remember me. We had a date one time at Charlie Brown's and another one at the Americana? I told you I'd call again as soon as I could."

There was a pause as Sally Friedlander absorbed the information and tried to readjust her sights.

"Why, yes," she said icily. "I thought we were going to see each other more regularly."

"Well, I intended that," Palmer said. "But something came up. A pretty big deal in my line of work and I think you'll really be interested in it when I have a chance to tell you. It's such a big thing that I don't think I'll even go into my office tomorrow because I have to attend to the details."

"I really hate for you to get into business deals that you might not know anything about," Sally said cautiously. "It can be very risky. Are you sure you want to do this without calling in some of our people for advice?"

"I'm afraid it isn't that kind of deal," Palmer said, "but I'd like to get your opinion and some of your friend's ideas on the subject, a little later. I'll call you back when I have more details. 'Bye."

As soon as he hung up, Day dropped another dime into the phone and started to dial Christina's number but then he realized that this was a stupid gesture. He wasn't positive that anybody had yet linked him to Christina; not as closely as they might have. But even if he called from a pay phone, he realized that his voice might be recognized, and a dangerous connection established. Yet he felt that it was essential that he see her before the action got more heated and set up some sort of code system for communication in the future.

It was only a ten-minute drive from La Guardia to Forest Hills. Once in the area, Palmer decided not to circle the block. There was always the possibility that someone could recognize him behind the wheel. Instead he drove to Sixty-fourth Road, the street immediately parallel and behind Christina's. It was now after ten o'clock at night, and most of the houses were already dark or had lights on only in the upper stories. Palmer counted down five houses from the Bay end of the street. The house was a sprawling mock-English Tudor one. There was a big yellow LTD parked in the driveway indicating that the master was home.

Palmer parked the Nova on the far side of the street and sat for a moment watching the house. A flickering light in the upper window indicated that the only inhabitants awake were probably catching the late news on television. That was good, since it would mean they would not be especially alert to any noises in the yard.

Palmer was still wearing sneakers from his holiday with Shooter Haynes and his steps hardly made a sound on the asphalt driveway. He only hoped that Mr. LTD didn't have a dog. In the rear of the house was a small goldfish pond about five feet across and a rock garden backed by a wooden, picket fence about five feet high. Using the stones as a climbing aid and staying close to the cinderblock garage wall, Day was able to surmount it without getting impaled on the sharp wooden spikes, but on the other side he had a close call. His left foot landed in a red kiddy express wagon that Jennifer had no doubt left there for his benefit, but he managed to grab a piece of garage wall and maintain his balance.

Once over the fence, Palmer didn't bother much with precautions. He doubted that they were watching the rear entrance, even if they might have had a stake-out on the front.

Taking his wallet from his pocket, he selected a Master Charge card and slid it behind the latch of the kitchen door. There was a slight resistance to the pressure of the card, but ultimately the latch gave fairly smoothly and he opened the door as soundlessly as possible.

He made a mental note to remind Chris to get dead-lock bolts for all the doors. He was tiptoeing across the linoleum floor of the kitchen when his eyes were suddenly seared with what must have been the beam of a six-cell flashlight. A calm voice behind the blinding light said, "Freeze, Mister, or I'll blow your head off!"

CHAPTER THIRTY-FOUR

Chris Navarro breathed a sigh of relief when she recognized the face temporarily frozen in the beam of her light. She lowered the twenty-gauge shotgun that she had been cradling, awkwardly, in her free arm.

"Advance friend and be recognized."

"Christ!" Palmer said. "How can you recognize me? Didn't my hair turn white in the last few minutes?"

Christina turned on the kitchen light, put the safety on the shotgun and leaned it against the copper-toned refrigerator.

"No, your hair didn't turn white but judging from your face, you're the *palest* white man I've ever seen. Don't you know that's a dangerous way to visit a lady? After all, I'm not married anymore. It's perfectly legitimate for you to call on me through the front door."

"It may be perfectly legitimate, but it's dangerous," Palmer said.

"Well, it's kind of chilly out here," Christina said hugging her bare shoulders. And now for the first time Day Palmer realized that the light from the hall was streaming through her thin nightgown, backlighting her figure in such a way that every line and hair underneath the sheer fabric was clearly visible.

"I guess we can talk just as well in bed," Palmer whispered. "Besides we'll wake Jennifer talking here."

"I thought you'd never ask," Christina said, lighting their way up the stairs with the big flashlight.

In the bedroom, Christina leaped for the rumpled covers and pulled them up over her goose-pimpled shoulders.

"Brrr," she said, "I'm freezing!"

"I'm not surprised," Palmer said. "That's a hell of an outfit to greet strangers in. After all you didn't *know* it was me."

Christina favored him with a tight smile. "Anybody else wouldn't have lived to enjoy what he saw."

Palmer took off his shoes and lay down, fully clothed, on the bed beside her.

"Aren't you going to get in here with me?" Christina said, wistfully.

"I can't get my mind all steamed up now. I have a lot of things to think about and we have plenty to talk about."

"What happened out on Pascag Island? Was it good?"

Day looked at her suspiciously. "What do you mean 'good'?"

"I mean did you accomplish what you set out to do?"

"Oh, yeah, it was a quiet weekend, but I think that we can do business with Mr. Haynes."

Christina looked at him suspiciously out of the corner of her eyes.

"From what I've heard about the Big Nigger, his weekends are anything *but* quiet."

"Well, it certainly wasn't *noisy*," Palmer said, ducking the issue. "The problem is, he's not sure he can raise the money very quickly and I think we got to get something in motion pretty soon."

187

"Why is that?"

Palmer explained what had happened to his house in the Bronx and about the visit from the Forensic truck.

"What are you going to do?"

"Well, I figure as far as the Narcotics Squad is concerned, I'm already out of the picture. If I show up back there, I may not even make it through the day. I kind of reported to Sally Friedlander. I'm hoping to stay on the good side of the Feds in case I need them. I'd like to leave as many options open as possible. Meanwhile, I'm sure that they're watching my place full time and that my phone is as public as Shea Stadium. That's why I came in through the back door tonight. I think your phone must be covered, also. And probably they've got surveillance on the house. I'll call Frazer tomorrow and give him some numbers where you can reach me. You call Frazer from a booth, and he'll give you the numbers and then you call me from a different booth."

"What about Jennifer? Do you think she's in danger?"

"I think we're *all* in danger but she's in less of a position to cope with it than we are. I don't want to scare you, but I guess I'd better tell you what happened to Potatoes De Angelo; or maybe I won't tell you *exactly* what happened. I can just say that he's not around any more, and the way they took him off would make Torquemada look like a pussy cat.

"Look, I don't think there's any way you can stay here any longer either. Is there someplace you can take Jennifer, or better yet, can you *send* her some place? If everything works out, it might be only a matter of days—a week at the most."

"I still have an aunt living down in Atlanta. It might be interesting for Jennifer to see how other black folks live."

"Well, look, take your car tomorrow to the Independent Subway on Queens Boulevard. Take her down in the subway at Seventy-fourth Street, wait until the doors are just about closed, then jam the door and jump out. If you're certain that nobody jumped out after you, then go upstairs and take a taxi to Frazer's place, turn over the kid, and see if you can set up some place to live through him."

Palmer got up and started lacing his shoes.

"Aren't you going to stay?" Her hand roamed insinuatingly over his crotch.

Palmer shook his head ruefully. "Honey, believe me, my head is someplace else. I don't think I could perform if my life depended on it, and right now, I think my life *does* depend on keeping a clear head. I don't want to take a chance going through that backyard again tomorrow and I sure don't want to be seen leaving here."

"O.K., I'll give you a pass this time, but are you sure it wasn't that 'quiet' weekend at Shooter Haynes' island that got you so worn out?"

Day walked around to her side of the bed, got on his knees and took her warm, honey-colored body in his arms. His lips touched hers once or twice tenderly, then they were avidly entwined with open mouths and penetrating tongues. After a few minutes, Christina's caressing hands found their way down to the tube of flesh nestling in Day Palmer's jockey shorts ...

CHAPTER THIRTY-FIVE

The sharp, metallic noise cut through even the sound
of their heavy breathing. Palmer put his hand over
Christina's lips, held his breath, and listened carefully. There was no other sound. Signalling to her for
silence, he sat up carefully in the bed trying to avoid
the sound of creaking springs.

Still in his stocking feet, he walked carefully across
the room, pulling the thirty-eight from its harness
hanging from a chair back. At the head of the stairs
he waited, taking very shallow breaths, listening for
any other sounds. There was nothing he could iden-
tify, but there was a definite aura. It was as though
you could smell the presence of another human being
in the house below. Keeping as much as possible to
the edge of the risers, Palmer began to work his way
down the carpeted stairs and he wished like hell now
that he had grabbed Christina's flashlight before he
started out. But he had the advantage of knowing the
territory very well. If it was a prowler, he would at
least be handicapped by not knowing the layout.

At the foot of the stairs, Palmer paused again, trying to keep his breath shallow and soundless. Now there was definitely another sound from the direction of the kitchen; just a slight squeak of a floorboard under pressure. It might have been caused by expansion of a wooden beam in the damp night air——or the pressure of someone's foot waiting there in the darkness.

Palmer dropped to his belly and crawled across ten feet of rug separating the base of the stairs from the door to the kitchen—very slowly. As he neared the kitchen door, he was almost certain that he could hear the sound of quiet, muffled breathing. When he reached the frame of the kitchen door, he slowly eased himself erect keeping his body behind the door frame. The switch, he knew, was just to the right, outside the kitchen on the living room wall. Holding the gun in his left hand, he edged it out beyond the frame and moved his head so one eye could peer into the kitchen. Then quickly he switched on the bright overhead light and said in police fashion, "Freeze, you son-of-a-bitch, or I'll blow your head off."

The answer was a shattering sound of a heavy caliber pistol echoing off the cheerful yellow walls of the Navarro kitchen. Palmer saw the flash of a black wooly head and some tanned skin ducking behind the shelf of the breakfast nook alcove at the end of the room. The bullet hit the door frame about six inches over his head and sprayed the doorway with a shower of splinters, as it ricocheted off somewhere into the darkness.

There was another entrance to the kitchen a few feet to his left which gave onto Jennifer's room. Peripherally, Palmer was now aware of a white figure crouched low there, reaching slowly towards the area of the ice box. It was Christina who must have slipped down the back stairs which led directly to the corridor feeding into the child's room.

At first he was irritated by her intrusion into the affair. It was dangerous and it might get both of them hurt. Then he realized that she was crouching and reaching slowly and carefully for the shotgun he had left leaning against the refrigerator when she had surprised him coming in the outside kitchen door.

Now a voice came from the direction of the breakfast alcove.

"Take it easy man. Let's talk this over."

Palmer risked a quick peek from behind the door frame. All he could see was the faint nimbus of kinky hair.

"O.K.," he said from behind the sheltering wall. "Throw your piece out, and come out with your hands in the air and then we'll talk."

"You ain't gonna shoot me, man?"

The voice had a metallic timber and its tone was distressingly familiar.

"Look, if I was gonna kill you, I could have nailed you through that skinny piece of wood you're hiding behind. Just throw the piece out, and come out hands up and we'll talk."

There was a cluttering sound of heavy metal on the vinyl floor. Palmer risked a quick peek and saw a shiny automatic pistol lying in the center of the kitchen floor.

"O.K., now come out slow with your hands in the air."

He knew damn well that the son-of-a-bitch might have a hold-out piece on him somewhere. A lithe, tawny figure with a bushy Afro rose now from the breakfast alcove hands in air, and moved into the light of the kitchen. The face looked very familiar. In fact, Palmer knew who it was ...

BLAM! His eardrums were nearly shattered by a deafening explosion to his immediate left and then BLAM! another one. There were two flashes of red and one of flying black. One of the blasts tore off the side of the intruder's head and sent the Afro wig he had been wearing flying against the window. The other left a gash like a giant slice of beefsteak tomato in the man's black turtleneck just above and to the left of the naval. The figure reeled backward, slumped against the kitchen counter, knocking over the Waring blender perched there, and fell to the floor with a gurgling sound.

To his left, Christina stood incongruously clad in her sheer nightgown, holding her ex-husband's smoking shotgun in her hand. Her eyes were glittering, bright with excitement. There were reddish spots, like fever blushes in her cheeks, but otherwise no sign of fear.

"Jesus Christ, Christina!" Palmer said. "The man was coming out with his hands up."

He looked down at the figure slumped at the base of the kitchen cabinet. The head was thrown back and the eyeballs showed only white and the blind stare of death. What was left of the head was shiny brown and bald.

"It's fuckin' Easy Eddie Evans!" Palmer said. Didn't you recognize him?"

Christina put down the shotgun, walked over and stared curiously at the huddled figure.

"You know, I think you're right," she said. "I guess I just couldn't make out his face under all that bush."

Palmer took a fast look around the kitchen and then out the door keeping himself carefully out of the line of fire from any possible accomplices.

"Somebody must have heard those three shots," Palmer said. "This place is gonna be crawling with cops in a few minutes."

Now he saw that a light had gone on in the brick house next door. He turned apologetically to the woman who was still standing over the crumbled corpse of her victim.

"Chris, I got to cut out or we're gonna blow this whole deal. When the cops come, all you got to say is you heard a burglar and you blasted him. A widow living alone has the right to keep a loaded shotgun handy, and besides, there's evidence that he took a shot at you. I'm splitting. You know how we'll get in touch. I'll call you as soon as I can."

Already in the night, he could hear the sounds of sirens approaching from Queens Boulevard.

CHAPTER THIRTY-SIX

Day had no trouble slipping over the fence, through the rock garden and onto Sixty-fourth Road to the waiting Nova in the pre-dawn darkness. There was a scream of straining tires and an intermittent flashing light as a squad car came barreling down the street from the direction of the bay and made a squealing turn at the corner, obviously heading towards Christina's house.

Before the whole area could become a beehive for police activity, Palmer slipped into the Nova, made a fast right and took off in the direction of Queens Boulevard. The traffic-free streets at that hour made it almost impossible for anybody to tail him without being spotted—even if they had somehow tied him to the new rental car.

Thinking hard now about the many steps to be taken, Day drove down Queens Boulevard, through the Midtown tunnel, north on Third Avenue, and then turned west on Forty-second Street, following it all the way across the river where there was a big flashy motel called the Manhattan Motor Lodge—as good a place as any to hole up temporarily. He stowed the car in the motel's basement garage, went upstairs to the desk, and registered for a single with bath. An elderly queen with plucked eyebrows took a key from the row of pigeonholes behind him and led Palmer to a room on the nineteenth floor decorated in *kitsch*. From the windows of the room Palmer's eye could range the Hudson from Hoboken to the Statue of Liberty.

In a brochure on the modern limed-oak dressing table listing the motel's services, he found to his satisfaction that there was a car rental bureau on the premises. This would mean the he could change every day to further confuse anybody who was maintaining surveillance on him. Also, there was a choice of three exits leading from the motel, to further complicate the problem for any unwanted watchers.

Palmer thought of calling Christina's place to see what had happened. He knew it was risky, but he couldn't go to sleep not knowing. Feeling a little foolish resorting to such an old gag, he covered the mouthpiece on the house phone with a handkerchief and dialed Christina's number. There was a direct dialing system for outside calls. A man's voice answered, startling him for a moment. "Sgt. Pacelli, this is Navarro's residence. Who's calling?"

"This is a neighbor. I heard noises. Is Mrs. Navarro all right?"

"She's all right," the voice said. "It's the other guy that's in trouble. She just shot a burglar."

"Oh, oh, I see," Palmer said and hung up before the call could be traced.

Just to be sure, he dialed one more call to the 110 Precinct in Forest Hills.

"Precinct," the tired voice answered.

"May I speak to Sgt. Pacelli," Palmer said.

"He's out on a call. Can I take a message?"

Palmer said nothing but hung up. He was now at

least reasonably sure that Christina was safe until morning.

Palmer climbed into the queen-sized, firm motel bed and tried to get some sleep, but his mind was still whirling with the excitement of the evening. What had Eddie Evans been doing at the Navarro house? Did he figure that there was some information about the French Connection dope stash hidden in the house? Or was he trying to grab the kid or Christina and use them as leverage against Palmer? He wondered too about Christina's shots. Evans was out in the plain light of the kitchen with his hands in the air. Even in the wig, it should have been easy for her to recognize him. She must have known him well. Then why had she blown him away like that?—almost cold-bloodedly. Was Eddie some kind of a threat? Or was she just afraid that he would queer the deal for two hundred keys of dope?

Then the tension of the evening began to tell and his eyes grew sandy.

He fell asleep while still trying to puzzle out in his mind what he would do if Haynes came up with the five million. Would he proceed directly to Mexico or Canada having Christina and Jennifer follow? Or should he and Chris leave Jennifer in Atlanta until they were sure they were settled and bring her down at a later date? And did he *really* want to be tied to Christina for the rest of his life? He hadn't really known her that long; but so far, he had never felt such a unity with any woman. There was a feeling of direct communication with her that left out any subterfuge—usually. But she was so smart it made him nervous. Why had she been so insistent that he get the money rather than take the dope south for sale?

The whole situation reminded him of the stories of treasure hunters whose partners remained straight and loyal until the treasure was actually surfaced and then they split up in murderous bickering. But on the other hand, Day argued with himself, a woman like Christina needs a man to complement and reflect all that sexy brilliance. What good would the money be without someone you loved to share it with?

For a man it was different. He could go anywhere in the world—Europe, the Middle East, Argentina and *hire* feminine companionship. Sure, it wouldn't be love, but it could be pretty satisfying. It didn't seem to him that Shooter Haynes was having any conflicts on the subject.

For a woman, it would be more difficult to hire herself a bevy of mindless weight lifters and body guards. Somehow, he couldn't see that as being Christina's style. There was the kid, too. Jennifer needed a father. He didn't think Christina would sacrifice the child's well-being even for the millions involved.

On the other hand, how did he know she didn't *already* have a man of her own set up. And Palmer, in his semi-coma of fatigue, felt an unreasonable searing blast of jealousy.

He fell into a deep sleep punctuated by confusing nightmares in which he was fleeing through an endless labyrinth of strange city streets that seemed to change locale from block to block. One moment the street seemed to be Paseo de la Reforma in Mexico City. But then he saw a long unprotected vista of huge glass-walled buildings, maybe in Brasilia someplace. Later he seemed to be trudging across the rocky beaches of an Atlantic Island with crabs scuttling at his feet, nibbling at his heels, impeding his way. He was dragging a giant Syracuse Athletic Department duffle bag which was packed with money. And always he was being chased. The identity of the chasers changed from scene to scene, like those quick-cut summaries at the beginning of a television series that run through the protaganist's life in thirty seconds before the opening commercial.

One minute it was a bunch of Keystone cops waving straight razors instead of clubs. Then it seemed to be a gang of female musical-comedy pirates with torn shirts, bandanas, cutlasses and bare breasts bobbling in hasty pursuit. In one part of the dream he escaped into a porno movie house which turned out to be Radio City Music Hall. On the stage was the cast of the Metropolitan Opera Company singing the drinking song from Traviata. But as Palmer ran down the aisle the house orchestra rose from the pit on a moving platform. Instead of musical instruments, the band was equipped with an assortment of sub-machine guns, Browning automatics and M-sixteens, all of them pointed at him.

Palmer ran through the back of the theatre over a thick carpet that kept yielding underfoot like quicksand and slowed his movement to a frantic sluggish broken-field run. Now he saw that the lobby was completely lined with solid gold doors, carved three dimensionally in the shape of women's breasts.

Behind one of the doors he knew was Christina—safety. But the problem was to find the door. His progress through the quicksand rug of the lobby was further impeded by the presence of the Harlem Globetrotters who seemed to be playing an exhibition at one end; except as he got closer he saw that the man doing the fancy dribbling and shooting was Doctor Calvin Haynes and the rest of the team was six foot six inch versions of Shirley, Wendy, Liza and Inga.

He awoke after four hours sleep with gritty eyes and a burning throat. He downed an iced coke from the refrigerator in the room, took a scalding hot and then an ice cold shower, toweled himself vigorously and opened the suitcase which he had hurriedly packed on leaving the house in the Bronx. It contained a denim leisure suit, a couple of sweaters, his Paul Stuart blazer and grey Daks slacks, a shoulder holster (the Daks had no belt), an ankle holster—just in case—his regulation police snubnose thirty-eight and a small Browning thirty-two automatic for the ankle.

He shaved and dressed carefully, selected a navy blue Turnbull and Asser shirt his father had brought him from London in the good days, and a yellow-and-blue British Regimental tie sold to him with haughty reluctance by a Jermyn Street haberdasher during a summer holiday in London. ("Are you, sir, in fact, a member of the Queen's own guards?" the clerk had asked.)

He was stalling for time. He doubted that Frazer Arnold could have arranged shelter for Christina that soon. But he was burning with curiosity to know whether she had gotten away safely and was settled somewhere so that he could talk to her.

Things were happening so fast it was hard for Day Palmer to grasp the fact that in a matter of days or hours, he might be a free-swinging, playboy millionaire with a beautiful tawny wife and a ready-made, three-year-old daughter—or a corpse with an icepick in the brain floating in the Harlem River off Mc-Comb's Dam Bridge—or maybe the filler for an elaborate concrete breakwater on an island off Cape Cod.

One thing he had learned in college—worry was a nonadjustive response. If there was nothing you could do about a situation, there was no sense brooding over it. He reached for the pink touch phone by the bed and dialed Frazer Arnold's number.

CHAPTER THIRTY-SEVEN

Palmer reached Frazer Arnold's secretary at the City Controller's Office. He was reluctant to give her his name. A phone running through a switchboard was not only wide open to taps, but accessible to simple eavesdropping. Palmer knew from his police experience that one of the easiest ways to get information was to take the switchboard operator out for lunch, a few drinks, or whatever.

"Who's calling, please?" the tinny voice said at the other end of the line.

"Tell him it's a friend of Mr. Haynes," Palmer said and in a few minutes Frazer Arnold's smooth modulated voice was on the line.

"Who is this?" he asked, cautiously.

Without answering the question, Palmer said, "I called to thank you for arranging that nice week'end out on the Island with Mr. Haynes. Do you know who this is speaking? There's no need to mention my name."

There was a pause and a dry voice answered. "Yes, I know."

"I asked this girl friend of mine to come over and speak to you this morning about a job. I wondered if you were able to arrange anything for her?"

"Yes, as a matter of fact, I was," Arnold said. "I had just the opening in an office and secretarial service in which I am ... associated."

"Oh, that's a relief," Palmer said. "She needed help so much and I felt it was the least I could do. Tell me, I haven't seen her in some time. How is her child? My friend's child, that is."

"Oh, she's fine," Arnold said. "She's planning to go down on a holiday and visit with her aunt in the near future. It's for her health, you see."

Down deep, Palmer wondered how effective all this obfuscatory bullshit was. He remembered listening to tapes where the caller would reach a connection and ask for "one shirt" or "two shirts" for a customer. It was when they asked especially for "one sleeve" or "one half of a shirt," the phone tappers had no difficulty in deciphering the "shirt" code into keys of heroin.

But there was no sense in making it easy for any eavesdroppers on the line.

"I'm in the Manhattan Motorlodge," Palmer said. "I'll be in the coffee shop in about five minutes. I wonder if you could take the time to call me from another phone and give me a number where I might reach my friend?"

Arnold's voice was calm. "I think that can be arranged."

Day Palmer went down to the coffee shop on the main floor and ordered a cheese danish and coffee, selected a seat near the phone booth in the corner. The coffee was just turning from lukewarm to tepid when the phone rang. Day answered without giving anyone a chance to intercept. It was Arnold's voice. There was no conversation, only a number with a Murray Hill exchange repeated twice. "And your friend's name is Tina Johnson," the voice said. "Have you got that?"

"Right," Palmer said.

He called the number given from the booth. A voice answered. "Zebra Office Services."

Palmer asked for Tina Johnson.

"I'll connect you," the voice said. And then Christina was on the line.

"Is everything o.k.?"

"It's o.k., so far," Christina said.

"What happened?"

"They took me down to the precinct and the detectives took my statement and then the homicide guys came and questioned me. I don't think they know Eddie's connection yet to Pancho, but they'll find that out soon enough. However, I'm not sure what they can do with that. They want me down at homicide again tomorrow."

"O.K., we'll just play it cool for the minute," Palmer said, "and see what happens tomorrow. What about the kid? Is she all right?"

"Yes," Christina said. "Jennifer is on her way to Atlanta. Frazer's wife is taking her down, along with a couple of her own kids. I'm working here at the secretarial service. I can make a few dollars and it'll keep me busy. Can we get together?"

"God, I really want to, sweetheart. But I think that with the heat that's on now, and for your own safety, I'd better take care of business, if you know what I mean. I don't think it should be more than a week at the most. Can't be. But right now everything is very much up in the air—except my feelings about you. We really don't need all this. I wish we could go back a few squares in the game and start all over with the funeral."

"If I hadn't asked you to check out what happened to Pancho ..."

Day interrupted. "I would have done it myself."

"Yes, but now it's been just like picking at a piece of loose thread, and pulling and pulling until everything unravels. Anyway, the way it's working out, we may wind up happy and rich yet. Maybe it's a blessing in disguise."

"Well, baby, the chance to play it straight is long since gone. So you might as well get used to the idea of being a millionairess and see if you can learn to live with it. Where can I reach you later?"

"There's a twenty-four hour service on this line. They'll let you know where to call me."

"All right. Love you." And then he hung up.

Day Palmer showed up at the Plaza promptly at noon on Tuesday and was pleased to see that Shooter Haynes was already occupying a table in the Oak Bar. With him was Inga, the tall, dark-haired, topless tennis player. Palmer was surprised. He expected Haynes to be alone. The Shooter stood up and engulfed Palmer's hand with his giant paw in a firm handshake but one that he had obviously learned to control to keep from crushing punier digits on contact. Inga stood up, also, and greeted him with a warm, friendly open-mouthed kiss. "It's good to see you again," she murmured.

Palmer noticed for the first time that Inga had a slight accent, indefinable but definite—as though she had learned English as a second language at a very early age.

"Inga here is my main squeeze, this week. She was keeping me company and taking a few notes till you came. You can run along now, honey," he said, slapping her firmly on her trim buttocks. Inga winced appreciatively, brushed Palmer again with her soft lips and trotted off through the gathering lunch crowd like a winning thoroughbred.

"I like your life style," Palmer said appreciatively watching the girl's disappearing rump.

"*Style* is what it's all *about*, man," Shooter said.

They ordered bloody bulls from the trim waitress. Haynes slipped her a five in advance. It certainly made for good service.

"There's a lot of people," Shooter lectured, "who

203

have the money, but don't know how to live in style. Take some plumber, he's making forty thousand a year, double time and overtime every way he turns around. He's got a tacky house in a development in Valley Stream, fifteen hundred dollars worth of inlaid vinyl tiles, a slate pool table and a wall to wall color television in the basement. More color television in all the rooms of his house. He owns a couple of big flashy Cadillac 'Rados, vacations in Miami and Vegas, and pisses away his money on the gambling tables.

"Now *another* guy with the same amount of money might have a neat little boat house in the Thimble Islands, a small ketch, a Fiat 124, one TV and take his vacation in the ruins of Chichen Itza or cruising down the Inland Waterway. That's the kind of thing I used to do before I had *real* money. Now, except for a few details, like the women and the cars, it doesn't seem that much better—just more secure."

Shooter was friendlier and more expansive than he had been on the island and Palmer felt that the big man genuinely liked him; but so far there was no talk of the business at hand.

After they finished the drink, Haynes suggested that they go to the Nippon Restaurant on Fifty-second Street for a Japanese lunch. The chauffeur was waiting outside with the Jaguar Mark IX.

They feasted on raw salmon, and bonita with little balls of rice, small, warm, ceramic flasks of Saki and shrimp tempura, followed by green tea.

"Healthiest stuff in the world," Shooter Haynes said deftly manipulating his chopsticks. "Keeps you in shape. Doesn't put any weight on. Good for the old sex life too."

"Listen, you got any word on that *deal?*" Palmer said impatiently, finally unable to control his curiosity.

"Easy, man," Haynes said. "Everything in its place. Why don't we make this a whole Oriental afternoon? I got a place I want to show you."

Haynes stood up and waved at a mod-looking, young

Japanese who was tending the cash register and said, "Put it on my bill." He left without signing the tab or even waiting to see what it was.

Outside, Bill was waiting, reading the Daily News leaning against the Jaguar.

"*Ichiban* Club, Bill."

The Jaguar proceeded a few blocks, turned up Third, took a right in the East Fifties to a tall brown-stone with a modest brass plaque at the head of the stairs. Opening the door, they might have been in a *Ryo-Kan* in Kyoto. They were greeted by a pretty but discreet, black-eyed Japanese girl in a formal kimono who sat them down on a *tatami* platform, kneeled at their feet and removed their shoes.

Smiling, she led the two men down a long hall to a small room with cushions, sliding screens and a long low table on which a bottle of champagne rested in a cooler. Two frosted glasses were waiting on a table.

"Which girls did you like best out of the island?" Haynes asked him in an apparent non sequitur.

"God, I liked them all," Palmer said.

"Well, for this kind of work, I think you might try Liza. She didn't spend that much time with you, anyway. She's got a light touch."

He turned to the Mamma-san who had brought them in and said, "Bring us Dawn and Liza."

Mamma-san said nothing; simply bobbed her head and covered her toothy mouth to suppress a giggle.

Shooter Haynes had barely finished pouring them each a glass of champagne when the two girls appeared, each dressed in a short see-through happi-coat with Oriental characters along the border reaching just a few inches below the crotch line.

As Haynes and Palmer sipped the champagne (it was a Charles Heidsieck sixty-one) the girls began with deft gentle fingers to remove their clothes. Palmer's shoulder and ankle holsters caused a slight shock and Palmer felt embarrassed.

"Just professional habit, wearing those, I guess," he said apologetically.

Haynes laughed richly. "That's o.k., man, but that's one of the reasons I do business here. It sort of puts everything on a one-on-one level, if you know what I mean."

When they were stripped, the girls took each of the men by one hand and led them to the far end of the room where a pair of decorated, rice-paper panels slid open to reveal a red painted steel door with a wire-reinforced glass window in it.

Behind the door was a room tastefully decorated in Japanese tiles. There were two unpainted scrubbed wood benches. Between them was a ceramic table fitted with gold spigots and control valves for various devices in the room.

Haynes indicated that Palmer should take a seat on one of the benches and sat down opposite him. The girls removed their flimsy happi coats, hung them on a pair of hooks on the wall, poured two more champagnes and busied themselves with the valves. After a couple of turns on the gold handles, there was a hissing noise and the room began to fill with steam from hidden nozzles near the floor.

"Now, we can really talk," Haynes said expansively, topping off Palmer's glass of Heidsieck.

As the men chatted, the girls gently massaged them from the roots of their scalps down to the base of their spines. Palmer wasn't sure how anyone could concentrate under these circumstances. Haynes seemed to give himself over completely to the sensual ministrations of the tall blonde behind him for a few minutes and then leaned forward—all business, while the blonde continued to work on his back.

"Look, we got a problem," he said. "We're not gonna be able to come up with the kind of cash you're talking about, all in small unmarked bills. That would take at least a month; but I've got a proposition that you can make *double* the money, and a nice safe easy deal. Know anything about hot securities?"

Palmer shrugged. "Not in my line. That's usually handled by the FBI."

"Well, you know there's a ready market going on all the time in that stuff. All sorts of hot paper. It's one of the Mafia's big business operations."

"Yeah, I heard that," Palmer said diffidently, not certain what the Shooter was getting at.

"Now I'll be the first to admit that you could probably live a pretty good life, even as an ex-patriate, on five million dollars in small bills, but on *double* that amount you could live *twice* as good, right? Suppose I deliver to you, not five million, but ten million dollars in untraceable city bonds; bearer bonds with no names, and no registration. You can check them through. They're not recorded stolen."

"What would I do with them?"

"Man, you've got Mafia connections. Those guys handle that stuff every day as though it were a push cart of bananas. You can check it out with them before you give me your answer."

"City bonds, you say? Anything to do with Frazer Arnold?"

"Listen, man. Do I ask you where you got your skag? You just check out my idea and get back to me with an answer and we'll do some business. Meanwhile, relax and enjoy yourself. Looks like all that health treatment is beginning to get to you," Shooter said noticing a growing protuberance between Palmer's clean hairy legs.

Liza peered over his shoulder sympathetically and then walked on her bare feet around the bench and kneeled before him.

"Shall I finish you off before you go in for a rub down?" she asked politely.

CHAPTER THIRTY-EIGHT

Alfredo "Home Run" Pugliese was an informer. Day Palmer had used him for policy and loan-shark collars in his TPF days. Pugliese won his nickname by hitting "home runs" off the knee caps of several of his debtors in the loan shark business who had not come up with their vigorish on time. He was a soldier in the family of Sheikh Santini.

Palmer had not seen him for some time. The loan shark was not very well connected in the narcotics business; but Palmer now remembered that Pugliese had become sophisticated since his early days of building a batting average on the patellas of slow payers. In recent years he had taken to accepting gold, jewelry, TV's and the like as security against his loans, selling them within a month, if not paid. The advantage of this was that the value of the security was always at least five or six times the amount of the loan. Pugliese had become kind of a delayed fence.

Pugliese was a freak for Jewish delicatessans. So Day Palmer arranged to meet him at the Carnegie on

Sixth Avenue in the Fifties for a short course in estate planning.

Over a *knubblewurst* on rye and a Miller Highlife, Palmer exchanged financial notes with the pudgy-faced loan enforcer.

"Suppose," Palmer said, playing with a side order of coleslaw, "that someone could get some bearer bonds, unregistered city bonds; guaranteed not listed as stolen. Would such a person have any trouble moving the stuff?"

Home Run Pugliese favored him with a smile studded with caraway seeds. *"Nada problema!* The family moves that stuff every day just like it was cash. Even with names, it's possible. It just makes it that you gotta be a little more careful, if you know what I mean. If you got names, you just have to sign it. What we usually do, see, is: say I got a guy owes me a G or two and he's got a family and all. So I lean a little on him. I explain that I don't have to play baseball with his kneecaps if he gives us a little help. So maybe this guy works in the stock room at a brokerage house. Now in the main offices, everybody is very Wasp, you know, straight shirts, ties, the whole *schtick*. But in the stock room, it's different. They pay them *bubkes*, and they're all sweating in their shirt sleeves in some ratty loft sending these stocks back and forth: half the time without receipts or anything, by messenger. It's very easy to get mixed up. So, anyway, the guy goes into some portfolios and pulls out, say, two hundred G of Xerox.

"Now, we take that stuff, but we don't *sell* it, see, because it's got *names* on it and it could be hot. What we do, is we get some *other chadrool* in a *different* brokerage house who's into me for a few thousand simoleons. Now the *second* guy rips off *another* couple of hundred thousand in Xerox, but he puts the *first* two hundred thousand in its place, in the portfolio. You got it so far?"

"Let's see," Palmer reasoned, "the *first chadrool's* two hundred thousand is given to the second

209

chadrool, who puts it in the portfolio to replace the stuff that he has stolen. Right?"

"Right," Pugliese said biting off half a garlic pickle. "Now we take the *second* two hundred G and we sell *that*, see? Now that stuff is *never* gonna be marked stolen because when they look in the portfolio it came out of, there's something *in* it. Meanwhile, the *first* stuff, if they look in the portfolio and find it missing, they list *that* as stolen. But *that* isn't ever gonna turn up in the market. It just stays lost. So like I say, it's *nada problema*."

Among Mafia clansmen, Home Run was known as something of an internationalist. He was one of the few who didn't mind dealing with Puerto Ricans, Blacks or Jews—even Wasps—as long as they had money. Of course, he passed out enforcement without regard to race, creed or color either.

Palmer wondered if his father had known Pugliese, or someone like him.

"Well, what about these unlisted Municipal Bearer Bonds?" he asked.

"Those are great because you don't have to pull any switches at all. Those are just like cash. Only thing is, if there's a big lump, you can't dump it all at once. It makes too big a splash."

"Suppose somebody came in with a really heavy score, do you think the family could handle it?"

Home Run's pride was hurt. "Are you kidding? My family can handle *anything*. Christ! We even own a couple of *banks* out there in the Midwest and a couple down in the Cayman Islands and a casino in Freeport. What's the problem? You got some stuff to get rid of?"

Home Run found it not surprising at all that a cop might be dealing in hot stocks. He already had a number of excellent connections with members of the Safe and Loft squad. They were good solid men who had been feeding him loot for years.

"Let's just say I'm checking for information at this point."

"O.K., O.K.," Home Run said wiping yellow mustard from his chin with a paper napkin.

"Listen, you finish up," Palmer said. "I got things to do." He picked up the tab from the table.

"Now, I know *something's* going down," Home Run said. "Since when did you ever grab a tab?"

From a phone booth in the Hilton, Palmer called Shooter Haynes' uptown office. A recorded voice answered. In the background a group was chanting Burt Bacharach's "You Are the Sunshine of My Life."

"Good afternoon," the recorded voice said. "Doctor Calvin Haynes is out on hospital call. He will be back shortly and will be pleased to attend to your problems. If you would care to leave your number, please, do so when the music has stopped and at the sound of the beep." Palmer waited patiently through the end of "Sunshine" and said, "Haynes, this is your stockbroker friend out on the Island. About those . . ."

Now the call was broken into by the rich, chocolatey voice of Shooter. Apparently the answering device was one of those where the telephone could monitor the call and decide whether to accept the taped message or break in personally.

"How you going, my man?" Haynes said. "You got any information for me?"

"Bearer bonds, Municipal Bearer Bonds, unregistered, unreported are okay. Try to get the amount you mentioned because I may have to take a loss when I sell them."

"Cool," Haynes said. "Check me tomorrow morning. I'll let you know details about delivery. What about those 'shirts' I ordered from you. The two hundred 'shirts' you were gonna sell me?"

"Don't worry about them. My shipping department is working on it, and as soon as we know we have the securities, we can make the deal."

"Right on," Shooter said. "Later, man," and hung up.

Day left the phone booth, took the down escalator to the basement of the Hilton, shuffled through a cluster of registering conventioneers from the Metal Trades Industry and exited by the escalator at the far end.

All this cloak-and-dagger with the coded words and the constant tail-shaking was becoming a habit to him. Day realized that the more involved he had become with this deal, the more his actions had become those of a criminal—his whole way of life. Rather than being someone on the other side of the fence, now he was on the *same* side *with* the "fence."

From a sidewalk phone booth, he called Christina at the Zebra office. He explained that he would not be able to see her that night, but would keep in touch.

"How did things go down at homicide?" he asked.

"They questioned me for an hour or so. I think they figure there was something funny going on between Pancho and Eddie, but they don't connect me to it. They figure Eddie was breaking in to get at something that Pancho had. I have a feeling they're not too anxious to interfere in a problem between cops."

"Well," Palmer said, "let's hope that IAD doesn't get wind of it. They'll sure be interested."

"Don't worry your darling head," Christina said. "Let's just take care of business. Is everything going down all right with the soul brothers?"

"Things are moving, sweetie. But we'll just have to suffer a little deprivation and stay apart till we get it set up. This hurts me more than it hurts you."

"Lover," Christina said softly. "I'm expecting you to pay me back for all those times you're missing at bat."

"If I *got* it, baby, you'll *get* it," Palmer said. "The kid o.k.?"

"Yeah, she's getting a kick out of being the only *ofay* in the Atlanta ghetto."

"O.K., talk to you tomorrow. Love ya," Palmer said and hung up.

He gave some thought to calling the Narcotics Squad to explain his absence those last few days. But then he realized the die was cast. According to regulations, if he was out and didn't call in sick within the next three days, he would be automatically suspended. But he was hoping everything would be taken care of by then.

In any event, there was no sense in giving any enemies he might have on the squad even a clue as to how to chase him. The best deal was just to drop off the face of the earth.

He stopped in to an Elpine hot dog stand on Times Square and had a coconut champagne while he sorted out the threads of his problem and how he was going to handle them. As he sipped the sweet tropical drink, he watched the tacky parade of sightseers, homosexual cruisers, transvestites and pimps lending their color to the Great White Way.

Narcotics isn't such a bad bag, Palmer thought. *They could have put me on the pussy patrol.*

A gypsy cab rolled by cruising for fares. The sign on its side said, "We're not yellow, we'll go anywhere." A tall, slick pimp was talking to a mini-skirted, pimply-faced whore while waiting for the light to change on Broadway. He was wearing a green, crushed velvet jump suit with a purple velvet scarf and a wide brim, fuzzy felt hat to match the suit. Around the hat was the stiff wiry billow of a modified Afro. On his arm the pimp was carrying a tiny black Chihuahua in a jeweled collar. Idly, Day wondered where they got those rigs. Certainly, they weren't on sale at any haberdashery he'd ever been in.

There was something about the movements of the pimp as he spoke and gesticulated with his jeweled fingers that looked vaguely familiar, as did the black fuzzy hair creeping out from under the broad-brimmed hat. Dark glasses concealed a large part of the pimp's face.

Take off all of that flash, Palmer thought, add a grey flannel suit and a school tie and the dude could have been Frazer Arnold.

CHAPTER THIRTY-NINE

Palmer knocked back the cool sweet drink, threw down thirty-five cents and blended into the crowd moving south on Forty-second Street. En route, he lost four dimes trying to make phone calls from jiggered phone booths. Finally, in a booth near the Allied Tower he was able to get a dial tone. He called Sally Friedlander.

"Hi, Sally. Miss me?" he said.

"Where in Hell have you been? Everybody's looking all over for you! If you don't call in by tomorrow, they're going to suspend you from the department. Lieutenant Diendorfer at IAD is not exactly happy either."

"Look, Sally, I can't give you details, but I'm working on something very big now. So big, I don't think I can afford to let anyone in on it until it's all set up. And as far as the squad is concerned, I'm really burned there. If I show up, you'll have to open a charge account for me at Campbell's funeral home and I don't think they'll give me an inspector's funeral."

Sally's voice sounded genuinely worried. "Listen, Day, don't get in over your head. That was Pancho's problem, and you know what happened to him. Pancho had a terrific future. He would have . . ."

And now Palmer was surprised to hear that the U.S. attorney was crying over a dead Narc. Or was it over a Narc that was soon to *be* dead? Her voice faded away and then came back.

"Excuse me," she said. "I just choked on a piece of . . . chewing gum."

But Palmer knew she didn't chew gum.

Now she had control again and her voice was harder. "You know, you've still got those indictments hanging over you, Palmer. So this deal you're working on better come out *good,* otherwise I'll see to it that they give you one of the nicest rooms up in Danbury."

"The Federal Pen Hilton?"

"You get the picture."

"I'll do my best. Bye."

Now Palmer pushed past the porno movies and gay crowds (and they were "really gay" on West Forty-second Street) to his new home at the Manhattan Motorlodge.

In the lobby, he bought an Ed McBain 87th Precinct mystery and copies of *Time, Newsweek,* the *Post,* the *Times* and the *News.* He had a long, lonely night ahead of him.

He took the reading matter upstairs along with a bottle of Grants he'd acquired during his walk home. There was nothing to do now but sweat out Shooter Haynes' report. He would really have loved to have had Christina up in that plastic room with the view of the Hudson but there was no sense in exposing her to any more risk than necessary.

He sat on the big hotel bed and turned the radio on to CBS twenty-four hour news. He poured himself a Grant's over ice from the machine in the hall and added a little water from the bathroom sink. He would have preferred soda but the machine was out of that and he drew the line at Scotch and Coke.

He enjoyed reading these realistic McBain police yarns. The best thing he liked about them was that everything always turned out very clear and everybody got what was coming to them in the end. Only in real police work, it didn't turn out that way. Half the time you didn't know who was on your side and who was against you. And the biggest crooks got away by making deals with lawyers, copping a plea, bribing judges, or threatening jurors. Usually the guy who had to do time in the end was simply some lesser fry that was taking a fall for his boss.

When you added to the pot of confusion caused by political loyalties and payoffs and side-switching stool pigeons, you got a mix-up where you couldn't tell the good guys from the bad guys without a score card and even then ... But in paperback novels everything turned out nice and clear and wrapped up in the end.

That night he couldn't concentrate on the 87th Precinct mystery. He folded his hands behind his head, breaking the pose for an occasional sip of Scotch, letting his unconscious play scrabble with all the puzzle pieces in his head.

He wondered what had been going on with Sally Friedlander and Pancho Navarro. It sounded like it was something more than a heavy collar. On a hunch, he went to the closet and pulled out Pancho's blue telephone address book. On the back pages he found a notation that had puzzled him earlier—S.F. Americana Hotel, flowers.

S.F. ... Sally Friedlander? And there were plenty of other S.F. dates—all at hotels.

By eleven o'clock he had finished all of *Time*, *Newsweek*, the *Post*, the *Times*, the *News* and half of the bottle of Grants. But still sleep came hard. And it was probably three o'clock before he dozed off with WCBS still blaring its endless repetitive news bulletins, "And in the Bronx a three alarm fire took four lives ..." At least there were no bulletins about run-

216

away roll-over cops—yet. Nor was there anything about the shooting of a burglar in Queens who turned out to be a cop.

In the morning at ten, Palmer called Shooter Haynes from the coffee shop downstairs. "Have you got my order ready, yet, Doctor?" he asked.

"I told you to stay cool, man. We got the whole batch in five thousand dollar denominations. Easy to move."

"How about delivery?"

"Well, in those small denominations, it takes up quite a lot of room. Our connection in City Hall had it sent over to the Zebra Secretarial Service. Your friend Tina Johnson over there has already accepted delivery."

Palmer was surprised. "You trust her with all that?"

He gave a rich chocolate laugh. "I wouldn't say *trust*, man. Let's just say we're holding your main squeeze for security. If you don't deliver the shirts, then you can forget about playing mod squad with your sweet meat and that goes for the little picaninny down in Atlanta, too. Are you runnin' with me, Herbie?"

"I gotcha," Day Palmer said. "But how do you know I just won't jump off and leave the dame and the kid?"

Another rich chuckle from the Shooter. "Let's just say I have faith, baby. And besides you ain't going no where in a hurry with all that paper. It takes up a box about the size of a case of oranges. And then you still got to convert it. That'd give us plenty of time to catch up with you. Now what about delivery on your end?"

Day Palmer had given a lot of thought during the night to the question of removing the skag from the property clerk's office. There was no reason for it, but there was always a possibility that they might have the office staked out. Maybe somebody had figured that he had the junk and where he'd put it. But even

217

if it weren't staked out there would be some chance that he'd be spotted when he signed it out.

"You got a panel truck you can make available to me?" Palmer asked Haynes.

"Sure," the Shooter said. "Got lots of wheels. What kind you want?"

"A small panel truck or even a van. Nothing that will attract attention."

"Sure, I got the Countee Cullen Soul Food Supply Company. I can pull a truck out of that warehouse whenever I want. Our motto is, 'Grits and gravy will make you groovy.'"

But Palmer was in no mood to play the dozens with a soul brother now. "Have the truck parked in the Manhattan Motorlodge garage by noon. Can you handle that?"

"Right on."

"Leave the parking ticket and the key at the motel garage in an envelope with my name on it."

"Gotcha."

"Now where do you want the stuff delivered?"

"You just drive up to the Down Home Chick'n Ribs. That's on the West side of Lennox between 127th and 128th. Go inside and tell the man you got a delivery for him. He'll come out, jump in the van and check out the shipment. If everything's o.k., I'll give the word to spring the paper over at Zebra."

"What makes you think you can trust those people?"

"Man, these aren't 'those people.' These are 'my people'.

"Dynamite!" Day Palmer said. "I'll keep in touch." And he hung up.

They were really getting down to the short strokes now. All he had to do was dump off the dope, pick up the paper, and trade it off through Home Run Pugliese for enough cash to live forever with Christina and little Jennifer in some distant paradise. On second thought, who wants to live forever?

CHAPTER FORTY

His night of insomnia had not been a total loss. Day Palmer had a thorough plan worked out in his mind for picking up the skag from the clerk's office and delivering it uptown. As soon as he had finished the call, he walked a couple of blocks east on Forty-second Street to the big army and navy store where he picked up white workers coveralls. In a cut-rate theatrical drug store on Eighth Avenue, he bought the darkest pancake makeup he could get and a jar of cold cream.

He pushed his way through a group of booted, hot-pants, ten-dollar hookers to the "Belle Hair Wig Shop" across the street where he bought a big black bushy Afro job in nylon for nine ninety eight—just like the ones Easy Eddie used to wear.

Returning to the hotel he tossed his purchases onto the seat of the Mustang in the motel garage. Then he went downstairs to the Avis desk and asked for the Chevy delivery van that he had ordered just after his conversation with Shooter Haynes.

"It'll be ready in a few minutes," the girl at the check-out counter told him apologetically. "They're just cleaning it up."

"Look, never mind cleaning it up. Just get it out here. I *like* it dirty," Palmer said. "No kidding, I'm in a hurry."

The girl shrugged, picked up a telephone, called down to the garage and told them to send the van up. It was a boxy job and didn't have much pick-up, but it would have to do. There was no way he could fit those four big cardboard containers into the Mustang.

Palmer drove the van out of the motel over to the West Side Drive, down to Canal Street where he got off and drove across, up Lafayette Street to the property clerk's office. There he waited impatiently in line for six detectives ahead of him to sign out their stuff. At the desk he filled out the sheet with the case docket number, signed the name Detective Edward Evans and put in a badge number out of his head. He wasn't sure who would be after him, if anybody, but there was no harm in leaving false clues behind.

He went outside and picked up the van and backed it up to the loading platform and rolled the four drums in. They were heavy but not too much for one strong man. He was almost certain there was nobody on his tail, but on the way back, to be certain, he headed east instead of west to First Avenue, across Forty-ninth Street, then down Second Avenue. He was almost sure as he made the second turn that there was a black Plymouth Coupe behind him, hanging back about a block's distance, but showing up in his rear view mirror with disturbing regularity. This was just why he had chosen this route. He kept hitting the staggered lights just as they changed, pushing and pushing so that his shadow was forced to stay at least a block or two behind by the lights. At Forty-third Street, the Plymouth was still a block-and-a-half behind. Palmer knew that there was no way that he could outrace anybody in the bulky tub he was driving with six hundred pounds of mixed powders in the back.

He took a fast right turn on Forty-third Street. There were three or four parking garages on the block plus a National car-leasing office. Day Palmer knew the area well since his days as a rookie pulling guard duty details around the U.N. As soon as he was positive that the Plymouth had not made the turn, he took a sharp right into the Meyers Parking Garage, kept going past the rows of cars waiting to be driven to the parking ramps upstairs and emerged on Forty-fourth Street eastbound. Now, he drove very slowly, to give the Plymouth time to turn into Forty-third and wonder where he had disappeared to. He was back on Second Avenue, retracing his steps. As he passed Forty-third he had a reassuring glimpse of the Plymouth parked by the curb, probably trying to figure which ramp he had turned into. He continued to Forty-second, took a right and drove clear across town back to the motel, into the garage and up the ramp to the third level where he parked the van next to the Mustang.

Leaving the van, he picked up the package with the coveralls, makeup and the wig from the seat of the Mustang and returned to his room. In the bathroom he applied the brown makeup all over his face and hands and half way up his arms to his elbows, careful to darken the areas inside his ears, behind the ears and around the neck. The color was not black but rather the shade of a well done Toll House cookie. When he was sure his face was well covered, he took the Afro wig from the paper bag and slipped its elastic bands over his head. Cool man! He could have passed for an older member of the Jackson Five.

He removed the police thirty-eight from his belt holster, put it on the dressing table and slipped into the white coveralls. Then he replaced the thirty-eight in the side pocket of the work garment. The coveralls were of one piece and it would have been impossible to get at the holster once he had them on. Of course, if his plan went well, there would be no need to get at the piece; but there was no sense taking chances.

Now, he opened the door of his room a crack to make sure there was no one in the corridor, left it quickly and proceeded down the hall to the elevator where he pressed the button for the exit giving direct access to the garage. In the garage he approached the attendant and asked if there was an envelope in the name of Palmer. He was startled to see that the young garage attendant had a complexion and hair style not unlike his own new head; but the light in the cellar was gloomy and the attendant wasn't too concerned. He pulled an envelope off the bulletin board where it was hanging from a spring clip and tossed it to Palmer.

"Here y'are, my man!"

Palmer felt that he had been accepted as one of the brothers.

In the envelope were a claim ticket for the parking garage, a car key, a card for the Down Home Chick'n'Rib on Lennox Avenue "where the elite meet to eat" and a Win button—a real Shooter Haynes touch. Palmer stuck the Win button on his breast and gave the claim ticket to the attendant who pointed to a Volkswagon delivery van parked in the rear of the garage.

"The motor must still be warm," the bushy-haired kid said. "It only come in here about an hour ago."

"What do I owe you?"

"Nothing, man, the cat laid five skins on me. You must have a good boss."

"The most!" Palmer said.

The van which had a sign on the outside announcing that it was the property of the "County Cullen Soul Food Supply House." As Palmer drove past the little office where his look-alike garage attendant was listening to Ray Charles on his eight track stereo and leafing through a copy of Penthouse, he honked his horn. Reluctantly, the kid put the magazine down and came to the small check-out window of the garage.

"Listen," Palmer said, "I don't have to be uptown for another half hour. I'm gonna pull this heap upstairs and take a nap, o.k.?"

"O.K.," the kid said and slammed the window down.

Palmer doubled back in the van to the third floor, where he parked it next to the Chevy van, which in turn was next to the Mustang. He was acquiring quite a fleet.

He opened the rear doors of the Chevy, rolled the four heavy drums out and eased them slowly to the floor. He closed the Chevy doors, rolled the drums behind the County Cullen van, braced each drum against the tail board and lifted it up until he could roll it in.

When all four drums were in, he got inside the van and put them upright again to keep them from sliding around the back. The whole operation took just fifteen minutes. Now he backed out the Soul Food Delivery van, circled down the three tiers of the parking garage and rolled out the Forty-third Street side of the motel to West Street, then up to the West Side Drive to 125th, across to Lennox and up Lennox to the Down Home Chick'n'Rib, which incongruously enough was decorated with a bamboo and palm, mock-tropical exterior. (In its previous incarnation it had been the Hawaiian Luau.)

It was now about three o'clock in the afternoon and the Down Home was empty. A fat smiling man the color of bittersweet chocolate in a white cook's hat and apron was sprinking sawdust and sweeping the place out. He looked like the man in the ad for Uncle Ben's Rice.

"I got a delivery here for Mr. Haynes," Palmer said. "You know anything about it?"

The man flashed a brilliant smile and put down the broom. "Right on," he said, "just let me take a little look."

"Do you mind if I make a phone call first?"

"Help yourself," the man said with another brilliant grin. There was a pay phone on the wall. Palmer slipped in a dime and called Shooter Haynes' private number. He waited patiently through the recorded announcement until the beep came for the message.

"Are you there, Haynes?" he said. "This is your delivery man from County Cullen."

There was hardly a pause before the Shooter's voice came on calm and natural. "Everything cool, baby?"

"Solid," Palmer said. "The grits have been delivered and they're mellow."

"My man check them out?"

"He will, as soon as I call Zebra and find out that everything is cool down there."

"No problem," Shooter said. "You just grab a snack, while my man is checking, and call Zebra in about twenty minutes. Everything will be straight."

Palmer hung up and went over and talked to "Uncle Ben."

"How about fixing me up some collard greens, ribs and black-eyed peas? Then you can go out and check the load, right?"

"You talk funny for a nigger," the man said and passed through the swinging doors to the kitchen.

In a minute he was out with a big ironstone plate. The ribs were tasty and crisp but the greens were soggy; and the black-eyed peas on the lukewarm side.

"This is the off hours," Uncle Ben said apologetically. "Can I go out and unload the grits now?"

"Sure," Palmer said.

He reached into the side pocket of his coveralls, pulled out the thirty-eight, and flashed it discreetly to "Uncle Ben."

"No monkey business, eh, brother?"

"No, man, I ain't in the monkey business."

"O.K., just roll those drums inside the kitchen door and I'll show you how to check out the inventory."

Palmer finished the plate of soul food in a leisurely

224

fashion. He hadn't had anything since breakfast and then only an English and coffee. As he ate, he sat and watched the chef, sweating heavily, roll the four drums in through the swinging doors of the kitchen. When the fourth drum had been rolled in, Palmer mopped up his plate with a piece of cornbread, finished off the last of his coffee and passed through the doors into the kitchen to join the chubby cook who was still panting with the effort.

"Man, those things are heavy!"

"In this case," Palmer said, "the heavier the better."

He drew a couple of heavy plastic garbage pails from the corner of the kitchen and had "Uncle Ben" pour off the top layer of milk sugar into them until the layers of white powder in plastic bags were visible. "Uncle Ben's" eyes were as white and round as marshmallows.

"Man, I never saw so much shit in one place in my life!"

Palmer smiled. "There's the same amount in every one of these drums."

The black man reached his arm into the drum and pulled out one of the plastic bags, slit the end with a chef's knife and tasted its contents carefully.

"Whoo-boy, that stuff is really down! You got a deal, brother."

"You want to check the rest of the drums?"

"No, the Shooter say you his man. I take you on faith, brother."

There was another wall phone in the kitchen. This one not a pay phone. The cook got on and dialed Haynes' number.

"Looks good to me, Shooter," he said. Then he listened for a moment and hung up. "He say you can call Zebra anytime."

Palmer got on the phone and dialed the number of the secretarial service.

"Zebra Secretarial Service," the voice said. "Black or white, we got it right."

Palmer asked to be connected to Christina. In a

225

few moments that honey-sweet voice was cooing on the line.

"You got the paper, doll?" Palmer asked.

"Ready and waiting," she said. "But are *you* o.k., sweetie?"

"I'm great!" Palmer said, "but you should see me now. I really got 'soul'."

"What do you mean?"

"I'll explain later," Day said. "Go out and buy a suitcase big enough to hold the paper. Put the bonds in it. Go down to the Port Authority Bus Terminal and check it in a locker. Then come over and meet me, say, at five o'clock in the coffee shop of the Manhattan Motor Lodge. Can you handle that?"

"Right."

"Won't be too heavy?"

"No sweat."

"The kid o.k.?"

"Aces."

"O.K., then. I'll see you. I love you."

"Love you too." And they both hung up.

As Palmer replaced the receiver on the hook, the black cook reappeared from the main dining room with a bottle of Wild Turkey under his arm and two glasses in his hands.

"Here man, you deserve a taste, after all that. Boss say to give you a drink."

He poured a couple of inches of neat Bourbon into the tumblers.

"You want ice or water or something?"

"No, that's o.k.," Palmer said. The glasses were resting on the stainless steel top of the big kitchen table. At one end of the table was a finely calibrated apothecary scale, a lot too delicate for the ordinary requirements of soul-food cookery. Next to it was a deck of playing cards. The sight of it jogged Palmer's memory. There was a coating—a very fine coating—of white powder on the table. It logically could have been flour. Day took a deep swallow of the Bourbon, then wet his finger, and passed it lightly over the smooth steel surface of the table. Thoughtfully he licked the white residue from the tip of his index finger. The taste was bitter—and familiar.

"You cutting the stuff right here? Right in this room?" Palmer asked thoughtfully.

Now the brilliant Uncle Ben smile vanished from the black cook's face.

"You just worry about your end of things, man. We'll take care of business here. Now you better drink up and go."

"Thanks a lot," Palmer said to the fat cook. "I'm splittin' now."

"Cool," the cook said, "but just let me give you two pieces of advice 'brother.' One is: don't ever cross the Shooter; and the other is—don't let any *other* 'brothers' get a look at you in that outfit, you'll never pass."

CHAPTER FORTY-ONE

Day Palmer stepped on to Lennox Avenue, hailed a gypsy cab and had it drop him off at the Port Authority Terminal.

In the bus station he went into a pay toilet. From a side pocket he took the small jar of cold cream and the makeup wipe-off pads that he had brought with him. Sitting on the toilet behind the locked door, he rubbed off as much of the coloring as he could from his face, hands and neck. He took off the wig and the white coverall and wrapped the wig in the coverall, first taking the thirty-eight from the pocket and replacing it in his clip-on belt holster. At the wash basin, he gave himself a good scrubbing and wipe-down with paper towels. There were still a few streaks of brown in the nostrils and the corner of the eyes which he managed to wipe clean. After all, nobody said he had to be *spotless*, only *white*.

Now with the coveralls and wig under his arm, he left by the Ninth Avenue side of the terminal for the short walk back to the motel. There he stashed the disguise in his suitcase. It was just ten to five. He inspected his face in the mirror and saw that some of the brown dye was still in his ears. He removed it with the corner of a washcloth and went downstairs to wait for Christina.

He supposed he could have her meet him in the Port Authority Terminal. It was only a few blocks away; but in the back of his mind was the fact that he hadn't seen her in a long time.

Palmer dawdled over a cup of coffee in the coffee shop, went to the phone and called Zebra and ascertained that Christina had already left some time ago. He sat down again and stirred the coffee aimlessly. By five after five, he was beginning to sweat. At six minutes after the hour, her fine, tan, athletic frame, the white-streaked hair swinging loosely around her shoulders, came through the swinging doors of the street entrance.

She ran to him, put her arms around his neck and kissed him on the cheeks, the ears, and the lips about a hundred times. Day held her back for a minute at arms length.

"God, it's good to see you," he said. "Can you just hold off for about four minutes?"

"What for?" Christina said looking puzzled.

"That's how long it will take us to get in the elevator and go upstairs."

On the way up they stopped at the machine in the hallway and picked up some ice and club soda. Palmer was pleased to see the machine had finally been restocked. From another machine he was able to get several bags of potato chips.

"Say this is gonna be a regular party, isn't it?" Christina said. Her smile was broad and brilliant and Day had never noticed before how deep the little dimple on the left side of her cheek was.

In the room he threw the bag of supplies on to a chair, and they fell on the bed in each other's arms. There was an urgency to their lovemaking that had never been there before. Day took off only his shoes and socks and his pants and undershorts.

"I hate pantyhose," he said stripping off the feminine garment, "especially with someone who has such smooth brown legs as you."

And then they were twined together and he was penetrating her and they were doing it in short, hot, heavy, urgent strokes. It was all over in minutes and Palmer lay back laughing. "I'm sorry, sweetheart. I just couldn't wait. I've missed you so much."

"Are you kidding?" Christina said. She was still breathing heavily from their exertions. "I was running with you the whole way. Now, maybe we can get our minds on other things for a little while, talk, straighten things out, make some plans and get back to some *serious* lovemaking."

"Right," Palmer said, bringing glasses from the bathroom and pouring them a pair of drinks.

Briefly he sketched in the events of the day.

"Boy," Christina laughed. "I'd give a nickel to see you in black face."

"It gave me an idea of how the other side lives," Palmer laughed. But then he was grimly serious.

"Listen, sweetheart, did they give you a hard time up there?"

"What do you mean?"

"Shooter Haynes and those people. They said they were holding you as hostage till the delivery of the goods and they'd get the kid too, if I didn't come across."

Christina frowned, puzzled. "I didn't know anything about it. It's true that I never left the place. I slept in the back room and ate there, but I thought that was what *you* wanted me to do. Of course, they know where Jennifer is . . ."

"Well," Palmer mused, "as long as they had you under control, there was no need for them to tell you. I wonder what would happen if you tried to walk out on them . . ."

"I guess we'll never know now, baby," Christina said.

"Do you think that Frazer is gonna get half of that deal?"

Christina laughed. "Nothing like that, honey. He'll get a small cut for helping provide the paper."

"It came out of his office?"

"In a way; you see he's in charge of ordering the bonds from the printing company. On a three hundred million dollar bond, it's not going to be noticed if he orders up an extra ten million. The printing company down in Philly doesn't know anything about it. The certificates are all numbered consecutively, of course, but when they get to the city vault, Frazer just slips out a stack of certificates from the middle. That way, even if they check the top or the bottom numbers, they won't notice that there's anything missing. The certificates haven't even been sold yet, so they're not recorded anywhere. When he sells them, it's just paper. In a sense, he's not taking anything from anybody, is he?"

Palmer thought that over. "I suppose not. Nobody's bought this batch yet."

"Right."

"The whole thing's fantastic. It's like play money."

"Except," Christina pointed out, "that it's authentic, noncounterfeited, and not reported on any stolen list. Like your Mafia friend says, 'It's practically as good as cash.'"

Palmer rolled over now, took the glass from her hand, put it on the floor and kissed her tenderly and gently.

"You are some terrific woman," he said.

She slowly unbuttoned his shirt and slipped it off over his shoulders, caressing him with her mouth as different areas of skin were unveiled.

"Oh, my!" she said. "You still got a touch of the tar brush around your neck. I think we better wash that off. Come on. Momma will give you a real good scrub down and shower—from head to toe.

231

She took his hands in both of hers and pulled him off to the bathroom.

"You know," Palmer said, "if we pull this deal off, we're going to have a beautiful life together."

"Yeah," Christina said, "if ..."

CHAPTER FORTY-TWO

They decided she might as well spend the night. To avoid hang ups they went downstairs and registered her as his wife. The clerk shrugged. He didn't care what kind of broads a guy had in his room if he paid the price for a double.

As Day Palmer suggested, Christina had taken all of her important papers with her; her birth certificate, passport, driver's license and so forth. And when she left Zebra, she took the small weekend case, out of which she had been living for the past few days.

"I'm positive we're safe here, honey. And I don't think you should go back to Forest Hills on any account. If things go right, everything should be cleared up in a few days and then we can take off."

Before they went to bed that night, he put in a call to Home Run Pugliese.

"Listen, the treat's on me, this time," Home Run said. "Meet me at Katz's on Houston Street at Essex."

"Don't you ever eat in anything but Jewish delicatessens?" Palmer said laughing.

"Listen, I have to eat with these *goombahs* all the time. I get tired of pasta and olive oil."

They arranged a meet for eleven-thirty, before the lunch hour crowd set in.

In the morning, Chris and Day went down to the Port Authority Terminal together. En route they stopped for breakfast at the coffee shop. The waitress by now was beginning to recognize him. Watching them, she smiled and said, "Newlyweds, huh? I can tell every time."

"That's right," Palmer said. "You've got a good eye on you."

In the Port Authority Terminal they took out the heavy, cheap suitcase that Christina had brought the bonds down in and took it back to the motel. There, Palmer threw the suitcase on the bed and unlocked it with a key that Christina supplied him.

Inside were four bundles wrapped like reams of typing paper in brown manila. Day slit one of the packages open with his switchblade throw-away knife. There it was—crisp, gleaming and beautiful, engraved with pictures of old New York mayors, City Hall and the Seal of the State of New York—two thousand five thousand dollar bonds for the construction of the Battery Park Housing Projects, payable to the bearer on demand.

Palmer slipped one of the bonds off the top, folded it and put it in his inside pocket. "A sample," he explained. He took his wallet from his pocket and peeled fifty dollars from his dwindling supply of cash.

"Here, while I go downtown, why don't you get yourself some more clothes in case we have to pull out in a hurry?"

She pushed the money back at him. "Don't be dumb, sweetheart. I still have all my credit cards."

"O.K., I'll see you later. By this time tomorrow you may be able to buy out the whole store."

"If nothing goes wrong," Christina said.

Palmer kissed her goodbye, decided not to take the

Mustang, in case somebody recognized it. He returned the Volkswagen van to Avis and hailed a cab outside the motel for the trip to the Lower East Side and his meeting with Pugliese.

CHAPTER FORTY-THREE

Home Run Pugliese had selected a table that could accommodate only two persons. He sat at it boxed into a corner with his back to the wall. Nobody was going to pull a Joey Gallo on Home Run!

Day ordered a mixed cold-cut plate: salami, pastrami, corned beef, liverwurst, chicken salami, tongue and turkey, served with a side order of potato salad and a plate of half sour pickles, with a Dr. Brown celery tonic to wash it down. Home Run was having matzohball soup, followed by knockwurst "specials" and sauerkraut with a side order of fries, and a diet cream.

Courtesy required that the first few minutes went to small talk; sports, sex, and food. Finally Day Palmer brought up the subject of primary concern.

"About that hot paper, this friend of mine was able to get. I understand there's quite a lot of it available, maybe ten million. You think your bunch can handle it?"

Home Run grunted, his mouth full and held out his

hand. Palmer assumed he was asking for the sample and pulled the folded, engraved piece of paper from his inside pocket.

Home Run carefully wiped the grease from his fingers and spread the paper before him. He nodded with approval as he masticated the garlicky morsels. "Looks good," he said, "but I'd have to have six or seven to make sure it's not counterfeit."

"What do you mean?" Palmer said.

"Well, they float these pieces of material in the paper when they're making it. If you hold a couple up to the light, you'll see the pieces all come in different places. If they don't do that, it's phony. A lot of buyers are getting really savvy these days."

"Assuming it's good—I can guarantee that—what do you think you can get me for it?"

Home Run shrugged. His mouth was full and a couple of strands of sauerkraut were dangling from the corner of his greasy lips.

"Maybe two or three points."

Day Palmer wasn't sure that he heard right. "Two or three *points?* You mean two or three cents on the *dollar?*"

Home Run nodded, seemingly unconcerned. "The usual," he said.

"You are trying to tell me that for ten million dollars worth of City Bonds, you were gonna give me about two hundred thousand dollars?"

"Give or take," Pugliese said unconcerned.

"No way!" Palmer said tensely, almost shouting. "No way! You think that I'm gonna give up everything I got for a lousy couple of hundred grand?"

And do you, Palmer, think that that tall, tawny and terrific Christina is gonna take off with a guy who could deliver an income of maybe twenty grand a year? Not that million-dollar baby from the five and ten cents store. Three dead men, and one maybe on the way. For what? For a lifetime career as a lammister?

"This whole deal sounds like a rip-off to me," Palmer said, his voice anguished.

"So sell them in the stock market," Home Run said. "That's the price; in fact with City Bonds, it would be more like two points because they ain't listed AAA anymore. People don't have confidence in the city."

Palmer had never been good at doing fast math in his head. He patted the side pockets of his jacket, looking for the stub of a pencil he usually carried there—nothing. From his right pocket he pulled an assortment of junk: a pocket handkerchief, the pearl-handled, throw-away switchblade, a handful of keys and change, and a pocket comb, but no pencil. The other pants pocket yielded only the keys to the Mustang and a crumpled Kleenex. Finally, feeling in the breast pocket of his jacket, he found what he was looking for: a little stub of a pencil nestled in the bottom.

With difficulty he extricated it, and made some rapid computations on a paper place mat before him. But the scribbling only confirmed his mental calculations. At that rate he would get two hundred, two hundred fifty thousand in cash—ten years of living at twenty-five thousand each, living off the principal. Or maybe he could live indefinitely on fifteen or twenty thousand if he invested it in some safe securities and just lived on the interest. That sort of money didn't go far these days in any country. Especially if you had to be on the lam—involved with pay-offs to local officials, all sorts of bribes, cover-ups and so on. Besides, he'd be supporting three people—maybe more.

What Day had envisioned of his life in exile was something like the sort of establishment Shooter Haynes had, only maybe without the fancy women—except for Christina. The kind of money they were talking about was less than he'd be earning on the force or at a straight job; certainly less than he and Christina could make combined. And there'd be no pension, plus the constant fear of someone looking over your shoulder; never knowing who would rat on you. He felt so deflated and drained that he could hardly hold himself erect on his chair. The spicy meat before him suddenly tasted like slices of rubber floor mat.

"What's the matter? Don't you like the cold cuts?" Home Run said. "I'll give you a hand there." He reached over and stabbed about a quarter of a pound of goodies from Day Palmer's plate and transferred them to his own, which was empty.

"I think my 'friend' would like to look some place else," Palmer said. "That deal don't sound so good to me."

"It's a top price for that kind of stuff. If it wasn't such good paper, you wouldn't get *that* much," Home Run said reasonably.

"Well, just the same, I'm gonna look around."

Home Run leaned over and laid a pudgy paw on Palmer's hand. "Look, kid, you can look until your face turns green as them notes. Without you got a connection through a bank or a broker or something, there's no *way* you can convert that stuff. The way we do it, see, is we got banks in the sticks, we got banks down in the Bahamas, the Cayman Islands, all those places, Panama. You can't just walk in with that kind of stuff and pass it. Sure, you got maybe five or six pieces maybe twenty-five grand you might unload it for five or ten points. But you're dealing wholesale and every time you try to spread it around, you're exposing yourself to being nailed. Believe me, kid, I know this business. You think ten million's a lot? In my family alone, we handle maybe ten times as much as that in a year, maybe more. And what do you think *we* get for it? *Peanuts!*"

Day felt completely deflated. He pushed himself hurriedly away from the table. The restaurant now was beginning to fill up with soul brothers and Puerto Ricans from the neighborhood and even a few black hookers who had begun to infiltrate the formerly all-Jewish quarter.

Looking around him, Palmer saw no face with which he could communicate. It all added to his sudden feeling of isolation. He was in it now—way over his head. He had burned himself out of the Narcotics Squad; all sorts of people were after him for the junk. If he wanted to stay alive in New York, he'd have to stay undercover forever. And there was Christina to think about. She'd committed everything to him now.

He had to have time to think.

"Look, Home Run, I'll be in touch with you if my 'friend' thinks this deal should go down. It doesn't sound too good to me."

"Take it or leave it. That's the price. I know my business."

Palmer reached for his wallet; but the loan shark-fence waved his hand. "Never mind, kid, this one's on me."

CHAPTER FORTY-FOUR

Day Palmer changed a couple of dollars into dimes. There was a phone booth at the corner of Essex and Orchard, one block down. He kept feeding dimes into the phone calling all the connections and contacts he could think of: FBI men he had dealt with in the past, known criminal informers, people in the stock market he'd gone to school with. It all added up to the same thing. It was almost impossible single handed to market hot stocks.

All of the countries that were famous for dealing in funny money, Switzerland, Luxembourg, Liechtenstein, the Bahamas, Mexico, the Cayman Islands, they either checked the stock back to its source or paid for it only on collection. Of course, in asking the questions, he always indicated it was a case he was working on and wasn't too specific about the kind of securities, but the answers were the same.

One of the best ways to convert stolen stock into liquid cash was to use it as collateral on a bank loan; but to do that you needed bank connections and at that you'd have to give a big piece of action to the bank. By the time all that was finished, you wouldn't get much more than the two or three points Home Run had offered, and working that way there was the added disadvantage of dealing with strangers.

Herman Woodfield, an IRS investigator, refused to give any information on the phone. Day had known him at Syracuse and saw him once in a while at basketball games. He arranged to meet Herman for drinks in the bar of the Schrafft's on East Forty-third Street. Herman preferred that bar because, as an IRS man, he was subject to slurs on his reputation for sobriety. By personal experience, Herman had discovered that Schrafft's gave enormous drinks, but who would think anything wrong with an IRS man staggering slightly as he left a place traditionally more known for its tunafish sandwiches and ice cream sundaes.

Herman himself was somewhat of a stiff but a few Wild Turkeys mellowed him enough to give Palmer the lowdown on unloading phony stock. Palmer explained it all as part of a secret investigation for the police department. One of his suspects, Palmer explained, had a load of phony stocks but no heavy connections. Palmer was wondering whether the man could unload the stuff in some fashion.

"It's not as easy as people think, old pal. There's a lot of problems and also there's problems getting the money into someplace where it won't be noticed after he's got it. You know we've had a law for about a couple of years now that any money taken out of the country in excess of five thousand dollars, has to be declared and also the bank has to declare withdrawals that are sent overseas in excess of that amount. Of course, there's a million loopholes in that one, but like any other business, it takes experience to know them. You say your man is not experienced in this kind of manipulation?"

"No, he's always been in another business," Palmer said.

"Well, he probably wouldn't have the facilities then to transfer amounts in quantities that you're speaking of. Say a million or so."

"Well, what about the stocks? Can he unload them either here or in another country?"

"Easy enough if you're in the mob. I remember I worked on an investigation of Phil Dio Guardi. You know, he was Johnny Dio's nephew. He had so many connections through his own family and the Genovese's with stockbrokers and banks, that he could sell anything, until we nailed him.

"Then I remember a case I worked on myself, you may have heard of it, Edward H. Wuensche. They used to call him the paper hanger. He dumped hot stocks in banks all over the country. Counterfeits, too. He worked with all sorts of big outfits like The Long Island Trust Company, First National Bank of Miami, and the Cook County Federal Savings and Loan Association. They all lent him dough on hot stocks and bonds and on phonies. He even somehow managed to take a Zurich bank for seven and a half million in stolen securities. And those gnomes are sharp.

"He borrowed ninety-five thousand dollars from that Long Island bank on a couple of hundred thousand worth of Federal National Mortgage Association Bonds——Fanny Mays. In Chicago, he managed to dump more than five million in fake Tennessee bonds, but the bank explained that they were relying on the credit and reputation of the guy that acted as Wuensche's go-between. According to Wuensche, he unloaded at least forty million dollars of fake or hot securities in his career, almost always by using the paper as collateral for a bank loan."

"How much could he get on that?"

Herman shrugged. "If the stocks looked good, he may get up to two-thirds of the face value. The thing is he had to kick back about five percent to the banker. Banks weren't as innocent as all that in this deal, but they had a good cover."

"Is that the going rate for the banks?"

"No, some of them held him up for even ten percent or more. But he was investigated finally by Congress. He said that if we knew how much hot stocks went through those banks, it would shake us to our boots."

"But that kind of deal is limited to a man who has ins, right?" Palmer said.

"No other way. Stranger walks in with that stuff, the banker would reach for his phone in a minute to check him out and there's a lot of ways he could check him out. That's why the Rebozo deal looked so fishy."

"What was that?"

"You know. I'm talking about Bebe Rebozo, right? The President's buddy—ex-President, I should say. In 1970, he loaned a hundred and ninety-five thousand on nine hundred thousand shares of IBM stock which was then valued at about two hundred and eighty-five grand. According to Rebozo, he didn't know they were stolen. But all the assurance he had on that came from some guy named Walter something who had been involved in the Bobby Baker scandals and Donald Nixon, the President's brother. Also a guy named Jim Crosby, who was Chairman of the Board of Resorts International which was formerly the Mary Carter Paint Company. That's the outfit that was involved in Freeport and Paradise Island.

"It always goes around in circles. But if you're not *moving* in those circles, forget it. Even guys with connections get nailed once in a while. As a matter of fact, Tony Salerno was indicted for trying to pass stolen IBM stocks through that same bank."

"So what you're saying is that it's not easy to get rid of a big chunk of hot stocks unless you're connected and maybe not even then."

"That's about the picture," Herman said floating another Wild Turkey. Herman had been known in college as the world's champion freeloader and never passed up a chance for a free drink.

"I could tell you this, old buddy, that suspect of

yours hasn't got a chance in hell to unload the stuff. He'll just have to dump it for whatever he can get and that won't be much."

An Irish waitress with a brogue as thick as country ham came to collect the bill. Sadly, Palmer paid it and left.

"See you around, Herman. Don't check any wooden tax returns."

Feeling discouraged, Palmer walked back across Forty-third Street and by habit ducked through Grand Central just in case there were any tails coming out on the Vanberbilt Avenue side. He walked the nine blocks back to the hotel. At that point, he didn't even feel he could afford a taxi.

Christina was dressed and waiting when he came back. She was wearing a bleached denim patchwork jacket, skirt to match and a yellow cotton turtleneck shirt. Her hair was pulled back and tied with a yellow ribbon. Standing there in the sunlight sifting across the Hudson through the motel window, she could have been eighteen years old. The back lighting from the afternoon sun ran a golden line around the rim of her forehead and cheeks, accenting the dusky olive tones of her complexion.

She was arranging a big bunch of gladioli on the dressing table when he came in.

"I got these from one of those corner florists near the subway. I thought they'd brighten up the room," she said.

He picked her up and kissed her thoughtfully.

"My, my, you have got something on your mind. Don't you? That kiss didn't show much spirit."

"I do have, honey. I don't know what we're gonna do with these bonds. It looks as though your 'brother' Frazer and Shooter Haynes really ripped us off. Those stocks aren't worth beans. You know what we could get on the whole ten million? Maybe a couple of hundred grand. Not exactly a fortune for a family on the lam."

"Maybe they didn't realize what they were doing."

"Are you kidding?" Palmer said disgustedly. "Those guys ripped us off for five million bucks worth of dope and it cost them nothing. Frazer just snatched those bonds out of the vault with no investment whatsoever. Talk about profit markups. There's only one way to take care of a son-of-a-bitch like that and I'm gonna do it."

Palmer reached behind him and patted the thirty-eight in the clip holster.

"Don't be dumb, sweetheart. That isn't gonna get you the dough and it'll just get you deeper in trouble."

"No, but it will give me a lot of satisfaction," Palmer said. "Him and his friend the trick-shot artist."

Christina walked to the window and gazed at the sun now setting behind the Hoboken slums.

"Two hundred grand isn't much, is it, for what we planned?"

"You said it," Palmer said. "Considering that I have to give up my job, my pension, and everything else and become a fugitive for the rest of my life. I'd be better off on the job and so would you be if we stayed together. We *are* staying together on this, aren't we?"

"Sure, sure, honey," Christina said impatiently. "I'm just trying to figure some way out of this. I didn't plan on getting in to this deal for peanuts, either."

"Is that why you scrubbed Evans? You were afraid he'd show up for a cut or blow the whistle on us?"

Christina looked at him with what almost seemed contempt. "You're supposed to be the big hard-boiled New York dick. How many guys do you want in on this deal anyway? Pancho always figured that Evans would cross him some day. He told me himself that Evans knew too much."

"I thought he didn't discuss those things with you?"

"He didn't," Christina said, "not in detail. But sometimes his attitudes were very revealing."

Palmer looked at her with a mixture of respect and awe.

"I got to hand it to you . . . I think. Not many women could be sharp enough at a time like that to wax a guy because he might cut into her share of the loot or handle it so coolly."

He had only *talked* about offing Frazer and Shooter Haynes, but Christina had actually taken Evans off. Palmer poured himself about half a finger of Scotch and tossed it off neat, then mixed a pair of drinks for the two of them while Christina went out to the machine in the hall for ice.

He sat at the dressing table sipping the warm drink and doodling on the room service menu with the motel ballpoint pen. Briefly he considered whether he might be able to take the two hundred and fifty thousand dollars to a don't-give-a-damn country like Brazil where they had no extradition and put it into some kind of business, become a local tycoon. Shit! That wasn't what it was all about. If he'd wanted to live that sort of life he could have taken up business administration in the *first* place.

He tried to retrace his steps and see how he'd gotten so deeply and inextricably involved. All he had been trying to do was find out what happened to Pancho. And now, here he was with Pancho's widow and kid facing phone tapping, fraud, grand larceny, maybe murder and God knows what other raps, with an alternative of a life on the lam.

It didn't seem right to take Christina and Jennifer off into some weird banana republic and stick them with a fugitive life on the fringes of civilization. He didn't think Christina wanted that either.

His grim thoughts were interrupted by the unfamiliar jangling of the telephone. Day was startled. Who would be calling him here? Maybe it was Christina. Maybe she had done down to the lobby and wanted to ask him something. Maybe it was the desk about the bill.

Day picked up the pink princess phone and held it to his ear.

"Hey, there, Palmer." The voice was high-pitched,

husky and familiar. "How you doin'? It's Home Run Pugliese."

Palmer was startled.

"How did you find me here?"

"No sweat. You pulled your room key out of your pocket when you were looking for the pencil. I happened to notice it."

Palmer pounded his head with the palm of his hand. Dumb! Dumb! Well he wasn't too crazy about the motel anyway. Time to move.

"Listen, I was talking to one of the wise guys about that material you were showing me. You know, that *green* material?"

"I know," Palmer said.

"Well, my guy says it's very good material. There's a good market for it. A lot of demand for them kind of things now. Whadda 'ya say to *ten* points?"

Even in his head Palmer could figure that out. Just move the decimal point—a million bucks. That was a long way from two hundred thousand bucks. On a million bucks he could probably be pulling down seventy-five thousand a year on interest alone, even with bribes, payoffs and the rest. The three of them could live pretty well on that.

"What made you change your mind?" Palmer asked cautiously.

"Well, you know, I handle a lot of things," Pugliese said. "I'm not always so up to date on some of these materials that we deal with; so I went to some experts."

"We talking about payment in the same form we discussed before, small bills, nothing over hundreds, no consecutive serial numbers?"

"Sure, sure, any way you want it," Pugliese said.

"No Las Vegas skim money that the FBI's got bulletins on?"

"No, no, this is strictly kosher, like Katz's delicatessen."

"Sounds good," Palmer said. "When can we set it up?"

"I'll give you a ring tomorrow. You gonna be in?"

"I guess so," Palmer said cautiously, "but just in case, can I still reach *you* at the same number?"

"Oh, yeah, you can get me there," Pugliese said.

"O.K., see ya."

There was a rattling of a key in the lock, and Palmer reached for his thirty-eight. But it was only Christina with the ice and a couple of egg salad sandwiches.

"I thought you might want a snack," she said. Then noticing the gun, "What's up? What were you afraid of?"

"I did something stupid, Chris. The wise guys know where we are. I flashed the motel key by accident when I was talking to Home Run Pugliese. He just called me."

"But why are you so jumpy?"

"Look, I've been dealing with those guys for a long time. They don't let a chance go by to make a buck. If they figure I got ten million worth of negotiable hot stocks here, they're gonna try to rip it off, right? Who am I gonna complain to, the police? Get everything together. We're splitting right now. I figure that call from Pugliese was just to make sure I was *here*."

"Go!" she said and started to gather the few odds and ends she had distributed around the room.

Palmer took the suitcase full of bonds from the closet, and his own suitcase.

"We'd better hang on to all the cash we can, Chris. Why don't you go down and pay this on your American Express card? I'll move the stuff down. I'll meet you in the Mustang outside and then we'll figure out where to go."

He was not parked on 42nd Street for more than a minute when Christina came through the revolving door eating up the sidewalk in fast swinging strides. Palmer had the car in gear, rolling, almost before she had the door of the Mustang closed.

"You know, Day, I think you might be right."

"About what?"

"Wise guys. As I was checking out, there was a call from somebody asking for our room. The clerk let me pick up the phone at the desk. I got on the line—it was just open air."

CHAPTER FORTY-FIVE

Palmer drove the Mustang erratically around the city streets in a general southerly course. He kept a constant eye in the rear view mirror, made a lot of fast no-signal turns and a couple of times, pulled into a bus stop and waited in heavy traffic, watching to see if any other cars also pulled over.

Unless it was a major stakeout complete with mobile units and walkie-talkies, he didn't think that anybody had him covered at the moment.

"That's some brother you got, Christina," he said, pulling into traffic again. "With friends like him, you don't need enemies. Is he really your brother?

"What do you mean?" Christina asked.

"I don't know. It was something he said."

"Well, he's only my half brother."

"Where were you on Friday anyway when I was driving up to the island?"

"What is this, jealousy? I didn't think you were like that. I was talking with the cops and getting myself under cover, right?"

"Yeah, right," Palmer said, his eyes on the rear view mirror and the traffic. "Well, when I get a hold of those guys, it's gonna make what happened to Potatoes De Angelo look like a communion breakfast."

"Don't waste energy, honey. You might as well go right ahead and see what you could do with this stuff. After all, Frazer was only acting in the American tradition, wasn't he? That's how the Rockefellers, the Mellons and the Fords made it."

He glanced at her sharply out of the corner of his eye. It wasn't possible that she could have been in on this. If so, what was she doing here? He dismissed the thought from his mind.

"Well, I'm learning a lesson from all this, but I don't know if it'll do me any good."

"What's that?"

"It's one thing to be a good professional *cop* and it's a different thing to be a good professional *crook*. When it comes to thieving, I'm just a bush leaguer trying to make it with the pros."

She put a warm hand over his, which was resting on the Hurst shifter.

"Grifting is a profession and I guess you just don't learn any profession over night. But what are we going to do now?"

"I got a plan I've been working over and thank God I left a few doors open on my side of the fence."

"You want to tell me about it?"

"Later. I haven't got things worked out yet. Meanwhile, let's pick up a copy of the *Times* and take a little ride."

Palmer wheeled sharply to Times Square where they were able to pick up an early edition of the paper, then over to the Drive, up the Henry Hudson and the Sawmill toward Westchester County.

"Where are we going?" Chris said.

"On a pre-honeymoon. o.k. with you?"

"Anywhere, as long as it's with you," Chris said. "What's the deal?"

"The deal is, I think it's better for us to get out of

Manhattan entirely, for the moment. Between the cops and wise guys, there's too many people looking for my ass and they might recognize both of us. Don't forget, whatever it's worth—a quarter of a million, two million or ten million, there's a lot of very fancy paper in the trunk of this car. And if word reaches former friends of Pancho's as to whatever happened to all that skag—it's probably all cut up into quarters and being peddled all over One Hundred and Seventeenth Street by now—they may get mean with me just on general principles; not to mention you and the kid."

"No place to hide?" Christina said.

He put a comforting hand on her denim knee. "We'll work it out, honey, but it takes time and we haven't got much of that."

Day finally pulled into a place called Gita's Motel, just north of Brewster on Route Twenty-two. The roads had been empty enough on the way up, so it was a sure thing they had not been followed——unless somebody had planted a beeper in the car itself.

At the motel, to be on the safe side they registered as Mr. and Mrs. Charles.

Better pay cash, Palmer, figured, and forget about the credit card. That would leave a record behind them.

The cabins were all done in Swiss Chalet style. There was a large deserted empty swimming pool in front of the attractive cluster of white and brown cabins. Day selected one where the car could be parked behind a tree, out of sight from the road.

He moved their suitcases and the bag full of bonds into the room, and then went out with a flashlight to check over the Mustang. As far as he could see, there was no sign that a beeper had been attached.

A beeper was a small transmitter, no bigger than a pack of cigarettes that could sometimes be attached to a car, so that it would emit a radio signal that could be picked up by a receiver in a following vehicle.

It was doubtful that the wise guys had this kind of equipment. But cops had it and Palmer was not in the mood to trust anyone.

The room was cheerful and clean; although not as big as the one in the Manhattan Motorlodge. Through the front window, which was framed in an attractive yellow print curtain, they had a clear view of Route Twenty-two, the swimming pool and the wooded hills beyond.

"There's a restaurant just up the road I think you'll like," Day said. "Le Beau Sejour. Terrific French food. Three stars from Craig Claibourne."

"Sounds good. You seem to know an awful lot about this neighborhood."

"Well, I was raised in the North Bronx, as you know, and this territory isn't so far from there. Everybody in the gang knew about this place. Even back in those days they didn't ask questions when you registered here; but I could never afford Le Beau Sejour then."

"And now, it's go for broke?"

"Right."

"Can we go dressed like this?" Christina said, indicating her denim outfit.

Palmer looked over her trim figure, the firm triangular thrusting breasts, the smooth unlined neck, the dark almost Oriental eyes. "Honey, you'd be an ornament anywhere."

While Christina freshened up in the small but complete john, Day found a fresh shirt and tie to put on under his sport jacket and slacks, picked up the room phone and made a reservation for two for Mr. and Mrs. Charles at the restaurant.

As they pulled out of the motel parking lot, he stopped the car just short of the entrance and ran over to the roadside phone booth, set back about ten yards from the highway. From his pocket, he put a selection of change on the steel counter of the booth and dialed a New York number.

A high-pitched, husky voice answered. It sounded

muffled as though the speaker had a mouth full of something.

"Pugliese?" Palmer asked.

"Yeah, what?"

"Palmer here."

The voice exploded in laughter. "You son-of-a-bitch! You pulled a run-out powder on us."

"Oh, then you checked?"

"Sure, what else? Where are you now?"

"I'm staying with some relatives out on the Island."

"Oh, yeah, yeah, right," Pugliese said.

It was a funny conversation, since neither of them believed anything the other was saying.

"That deal you were talking about. Is it still on?"

"Sure, sure," Pugliese said. His voice was thick.

"Eating again?"

"Yeah, fuckin' lasagna. I wish I was down in Katz's."

"Well, what about that deal?"

"Sure, when do ya want to meet?"

"I'll call you back tomorrow."

"Sure, sure," Pugliese said laughing, "and next time don't leave no motel keys around, right?"

CHAPTER FORTY-SIX

At the restaurant they had a simple, but expensive dinner. Smoked trout for starters, a rack of lamb *persillé*, a bottle of *Givry*, a sorbet and afterwards *Poire William*.

From the table they could look through the trees and see the still waters of Croton reservoir. It was a scene out of a Japanese print.

Christina had combed her hair loose on her shoulders. Around her slim neck she wore a chain composed of tiny golden ducks—a Mayan design. She was wearing a clinging, scooped-out cashmere sweater that night, and a long pleated skirt. A wide belt with a golden buckle repeated the Mayan motif. She was radiant and looked happier than he'd ever seen her.

"What's up with you, honey?" Palmer asked. "Here we are up to our ass in trouble, the base falling out of our plan with possibly no future—cut off from damn near everybody in the world and you're smiling like a row of Mah-jong tiles."

"It's being away like this; in this setting, away from

256

the house and all its associations with Pancho, away from the city with all the creepy people waiting to snipe at us one way or another. I suddenly realized that whatever happens, this one thing we'll always have—this night."

There was a certain fatalism to her point of view but Palmer could understand it. There had been nothing but strain since Pancho's death. And for her, judging by what had been coming out in the course of this caper, the strain might have gone on a long way before. They returned to the motel after dinner, taking the unfinished bottle of Givry with them. They both were feeling beautiful, warm and relaxed.

When they got back they sat on the bed and drank the mellow red wine slowly. Christina put her glass down and lay back on the bed, her arms stretched over her head. Her hair and it's odd white streak splayed out on the counterpane. Palmer leaned over and kissed her right where the hairline joined her forehead. She put her arms up and pulled him to her. And then they began to make love very slowly and beautifully, taking their time over each step, undressing one another, caressing each patch of bare skin as it became uncovered. When they were completely nude, Day held Christina in his arms a long time, just feeling her warm breath on his collar bone and the occasional gentle thrust from her pelvis pressing against his leg, and smelling that flowery fragrance that was her trademark.

He entered her very slowly and lay again for a long time, without moving, just feeling the warmth of her around him. He remembered in college of hearing of something called *karezza*, an Indian yoga sex exercise in which neither partner in the act of love moved and eventually after an hour, or even *hours*, an orgasm took place by sort of spontaneous combustion. He'd never tried it, because according to the book he read you have to give up drinking and smoking for months, and eat only vegetables before this would work.

257

But now he was holding himself inside her as still as he could to prolong this magic time of being together in relative peace. And, in fact, it was an hour before the two of them slowly began to twist and turn from the pelvis in uniform rhythm, finally reaching the longest, deepest and most achingly beautiful orgasm Palmer had ever known.

In the morning they showered together, rubbed one another down with the skimpy motel towels and went back to bed for a brief happy session in the dappled sunlight coming through the Swiss curtains.

They drove into Brewster for breakfast at a diner, and Palmer sighed over his coffee realizing that the night's activities were only a tiny recess in the program of their life. He turned to the real estate section. Under "One room apartments, furnished," were several listings. All were either short term sub-leases or residential hotels that rented by the week or by the month. All were on the Upper East Side.

"Here's the deal," Palmer said. "I think we have to stay away from almost every hotel or motel. They're too risky. I also want to stay out of Group One Narcotics area which is below Forty-second Street. We're likely to run into Pancho's buddies there. The West Side is too involved with narcotics and again we're liable to run into some familiar faces. So I'm picking the Upper East Side. When we get to town, you check these places out and see if you can find one you like. I'll give you a blank check and you can fill it out for a deposit.

"Just take the place for a week or a month, the shortest time you can get it. There's a public telephone at the south end of the Brooklyn Bridge station. Get the number from information and call me there at four o'clock this afternoon. You can tell me where we're living then."

"O.K., now we got living quarters settled. What's the rest of your plan?"

"They made me roll over once. I'm gonna try to roll

back. How'd you like to be the wife of a straight, legitimate federal agent, honey, in say, El Paso, Texas?"

"Well, it's not exactly the French Riviera, is it?" she said. And there was an edge to her voice that Palmer never noticed before. Who could blame her, considering the strain they'd been under?

"I know," he said softly. "It's not exactly the big plan we had for being the millionaire play couple of the western world. But in some ways it appeals to me. I'm not really crazy about being hunted for the rest of my life."

"What's the difference?" Christina said. "You'll still be a slave. Chained to your job for twenty years and then paid off in peanuts."

"You don't want to back out, do you?" Palmer said. It was a thought he couldn't face at this point. She ignored the question. There was a long pause, and finally she said, "What's your plan?"

"Well, I haven't worked out all the details, but when I have it worked out, I'm going to need your help. Can you drive?"

"They don't call me 'Junior Johnson Navarro' for nothing."

"O.K., we're going to give the roulette wheel one more spin and put all our money on double zero."

CHAPTER FORTY-SEVEN

Day Palmer arranged to meet Sally Friedlander at the Oyster Bar in Grand Central. She seemed tense, nervous and very worried about him on the phone.

"Just get your beautiful ambitious ass up here," Palmer said. "It shouldn't take more than forty minutes from now, allowing you time to go to the powder room. If you're not here in fifty minutes, I'm splitting; but I can tell you this. We're going to talk about the biggest bust you ever made ... make your rep overnight. But come alone. Don't bring anybody with you."

Finally, reluctantly, she agreed.

As Palmer proceeded through the great hall of the station, he passed a flower cart tended by a cheery girl in a red and white striped apron. On an impulse, he stopped.

"Give me five dollar's worth of those yellow ones," he said. "The chrysanthemums."

The girl smiled and wrapped up a sizeable bouquet in white paper; and Palmer took it with him down to the lower level where he ordered an oyster stew to pass the time while waiting for Sally.

Exactly forty-five minutes after he'd called, she arrived looking flustered and concerned.

Palmer had selected a seat where he could watch both entrances. When she came in, he took the flowers and went to greet her.

"Surprise! Surprise!" he said. "It's the autumn equinox and these are to cheer you up."

The blonde U.S. attorney took the bouquet with gratitude, threw her arms around Day Palmer and kissed him impulsively on the cheek.

"No, you deserve better than that!" She took his face between her hands and kissed him full on the mouth.

Palmer was sure he could detect the penetration of her pink tongue between his lips. The girl wasn't easily discouraged.

"How did you know I loved flowers?" she said, smiling happily. And Palmer noticed that her eyes were actually wet.

"I just guessed," he said. "Maybe I read it some place."

Sally sighed and looked at him in an amused fashion. "You are an A number one weird-o. What we call a hoople downtown."

Palmer shrugged. "It keeps me alive."

He threw a quarter on the counter, left the exact change for the oyster stew on the cashier's desk and hustled Sally Friedlander out of the bar.

"Hey, don't I get an oyster stew? I got to feed my hormones also."

"Later maybe," Palmer said. "What I have to say to you, I'd rather say in a moving subway train."

He went downstairs to the platform marked "Trains to Flushing and Queens." It was early afternoon and the cars were nearly empty as was the platform. Palmer stood on the westbound side of the platform. From there the trains went one stop further to Times

Square, waited briefly, then reversed and proceeded eastward out to the Island.

He took Sally Friedlander by the arm and led her into the middle car. It was empty as he had hoped. Just to be safe, he sat in silence till the train got to Times Square.

"What on earth is this all about?" Sally said impatiently.

Day waited till the Queens passengers got on. There were only three or four of them and they sat in the far corner of the car away from the other riders.

"What I have to say, I don't want on record and I don't want any more witnesses than necessary."

"Why did you bring me down here?"

"I figured if anybody was tailing you or you were carrying a wire, we'd be able to shake them this way; on the train we'd be out of the range of any receivers you might be transmitting to."

Sally pouted. It was a girly, feminine thing, not in keeping with her usual business-like demeanor.

"You think I'm carrying a wire?" She held her arms up over her head. She was wearing a tweedy, wool jersey dress with a monk's hooded collar. The dress looked as though it was just about one size too small.

"You want to search me?" she said. Her tone was provocative.

"No, it doesn't look as though you could hide anything under that," Palmer said eyeing her well-curved figure appreciatively, "but I'd like to take a look in this." He took the brown-saddle leather shoulder bag from her, unsnapped it and peered briefly inside. The only thing he could see other than the usual woman's junk was a shining, chrome-plated Walther PPK automatic.

"Satisfied?" Sally said.

He took her hand. "Look, Sally, I know I'm acting weird, but there is a lot at stake.

"All right, clue me in."

"How would you like to make a raid where you can pick up Angie Benedetto, Home Run Pugliese,

Vincent "The Sheikh" Santini and ten million dollars worth of hot Battery Park Municipal Bonds—stolen directly from the city vault?"

Sally whistled appreciatively.

"That sounds like a very heavy collar, but it's a little out of line for a Drug Task Force, isn't it?"

"You can work that out with the U.S. Attorney."

Sally's eyes narrowed speculatively. "How did you get involved in all this? You were supposed to be after the French Connection dope."

Palmer smiled. "Well, one things leads to another and that's where I am now."

"O.K., so I say yes, then what?"

"I want a deal. I want immunity on the phone tapping indictments and any other irregularities that come out of this deal."

Sally nodded noncommittally.

"And I want a transfer out of the New York Police Department, out of IAD into the Drug Enforcement Administration. And I want to be stationed very, very far from New York, preferably along the Mexican border."

"Why there?" Sally asked.

"If I'm going to be working in the drug business, I might as well be where the action is and besides I like speaking Spanish and lots of sunshine."

The train was pulling into Queensboro Plaza. Day helped Sally out across the platform to the Manhattanbound side and they got into a train headed for Times Square. Sally said nothing until they were settled on the Manhattan train.

"What if I say o.k. What's involved?"

"I haven't worked out the details yet," Palmer said, "but I think I may need a big strike team; plenty of cars, maybe even helicopters."

Sally sat in thoughtful silence for several minutes and then finally turned to Palmer, "I can't do this on my own. What do you want me to say?"

"Nothing," Palmer said. "I'll call you and that'll give you time to check, right up to the Attorney Gen-

263

eral if you want. But remember, there's going to be a lot of headlines when somebody finds ten million dollars worth of hot stocks that disappeared right from the mayor's own vault."

CHAPTER FORTY-EIGHT

The apartment Christina had found was nondescript but serviceable. It was a sublet on Third Avenue in the seventies which she had acquired through the Pat Palmer agency. The rent was four hundred and fifty dollars in advance. Day looked over the worn-out, overstuffed furniture, the dark alcove that served as a kitchen and the windowless bathroom with worn spotty tiles and a noisy ventilator.

"Well, what can you expect for four hundred and fifty these days?"

"The kitchen isn't much, but at least I can make us a decent home-cooked meal," Christina said.

"Let's hope we won't be there that long."

"When is everything coming to a head?"

"Tomorrow, if things go right," Day said. "Listen, I can't stand this place. Let's go to Allen's or some place for a hamburger over on Third Avenue."

"I don't think that's so smart, honey," Christina said. "We've only got a couple of days. If we're hiding out, we might as well stay under cover as much as possible. In the end, this is a small town and you never know who's going to spot you by accident."

"I suppose you're right," Palmer muttered disconsolately. "I'll run across to Foo Chow's, the Chinese place up the block and get some food to go. I've got to go out to make a phone call anyway, in a while."

When he got to the corner of Third Avenue, Palmer dialed Home Run Pugliese's. As usual, the loan shark was eating. Palmer could hear loud, smacking noises as he got on the phone.

"What are you eating now, Home Run?"

"Scungilli! I hate the stuff. I got to make believe I like it for the wife. She's very sensitive."

"You got the money?"

"Sure, sure, like I told you."

"How much space does it take up?"

"Well, it's small bills you know, like you said, fits in a big suitcase."

"O.K., load it in a suitcase and then get me a nice small foreign car. It doesn't have to be a Ferrari or a Porsche just something small and fast, maybe a Volvo eighteen hundred or an Audi, something like that. And don't fuck me over on this. I'm going to take the car and give it a complete going over and try it out on the highway."

"All right, all right, I think I know where we can borrow one."

"O.K.," Palmer said, "but make sure it's got a clean pair of plates on it. I'll check those out with motor vehicle identification. I don't want to be picked up for driving a hot car."

"Sure, sure," Pugliese said. "What about them bonds?"

"O.K., when I get the car and try it out, I'll get in touch with you again and we'll set up the meet, and listen, when I hand over the stuff, I don't want to be dealing with any two-bit messenger boys, right? I want to make sure this stuff goes to the head man. After all, if I cross up the family, my life won't be worth a nickel, right?"

"Yeah, right, right. I'll see what I can do."

"Don't *see* what you can do. *Do* it. This is the cleanest stuff you ever saw. You guys can make a fortune on this. Two or three million, maybe more.

"All right, all right," Pugliese said. "Don't sell me already. Where do you want we should leave the car?"

"Leave it in the Coliseum Garage. Leave the key and the parking ticket at the office with my name on it."

"O.K., your fucking majesty. Is that it?"

"I'll be in touch tomorrow about the meet."

The food from Foo Chow's was good even though they had to eat it off garish Melmac plates—the only dishes furnished with the apartment. Christina had bought a bottle of Scotch and some club soda and a bottle of Korbel champagne to drink afterwards.

"Might as well celebrate," she said, "tomorrow's the big day. Are you ready to clue me in?"

"O.K., sweetheart, here's the scene. I want you to get it right, because I'm going to need your help. Basically the idea is to cover ourselves in all contingencies. I figure the Santini mob is out to rip us off any way they can, as long as they can get their hands on those bonds. If they get a chance, they'll snatch them. If they find out where they are, or they'll grab one of us and try to get the information out of us. So we got to make that very difficult for them. Now, from my checkouts, they weren't really lying when they said the run-of-the-mill price for that kind of paper was two or three points and at the most five. If they say they'll pay *ten* percent, the chances are that they're lying. They're never going to come up with the money. But a million dollars is a very nice nest egg for a couple that's just getting started. I'd hate to blow it if they actually came up with the dough."

"Keep talking," Christina said, "I'll just rinse off these dishes."

"Now I had to have the Mafia supply us a car. I

267

don't care if it's their own car or stolen, because when I'm ready, I'm getting in touch with the Task Force."

"I don't understand," Christina said. "Why do you need the car?"

"Because I'm telling the Task Force that I'm *buying* the hot stocks, not *selling* them, so the stocks can't very well turn up in *my* car."

"R-i-g-h-t! But how will the Task Force *know* what's going down?"

"That's another part of the plan. I'll explain it to you on the way down to Lafayette Electronics. They're open late tonight. We have some equipment to pick up."

CHAPTER FORTY-NINE

At the electronics shop he bought a pair of cheap
practical two-way CB battery-powered transmitters
made by Sony. "We'll keep in touch with these," he
explained on the way out. "There's nothing to it, we'll
set the frequency, check it out and then all you got to
do is talk.

"Gotcha," Christina's eyes were sparkling. "You
know, Pancho was into a lot of stuff. I kind of knew
about it and I overheard a lot, but I never got to actually take *part* in anything myself. This is kind of
fun."

"You won't think it's fun if anything goes wrong."

"Still, I'd rather be part of the action and know
what's going on, then just be set aside and told what
they think it's good for me to know."

"By the way," Palmer said. "Do you know who
Sally Friedlander is?"

"Sure, she's that blonde lawyer in the U.S. attorney's office. She's the one who got Pancho to roll over. If that hadn't happened . . ."

"Yeah, I guess a lot of things would be different," Palmer said.

They were in a taxi riding up Third Avenue to their hide-out apartment. Christina was watching the store windows as they passed by, thoughtfully.

"You know," she said, "Pancho and Sally spent a lot of time together on that Task Force. I always wondered . . ."

"What?" Palmer said.

"Nothing, just the sort of thing a woman wonders."

They were both restless and uncomfortable that night and even their lovemaking had a hasty, nervous quality.

"Jesus," Palmer said, shifting to avoid a broken spring in the mattress. "I'm glad the balloon is going up tomorrow. I couldn't take too much of this place."

In the morning Christina and Palmer ate breakfast in a local coffee shop. Palmer called Pugliese from the pay phone and ascertained that the car, a Datsun 24OZ, bright red in color was waiting at the Coliseum.

"Now, here's the deal," Palmer told Chris as they drank their coffee. "I figure there's a good chance they're going to have somebody watching the garage, that's why I picked the Coliseum. There's about five ways you can go out. I don't think they'll try to snatch me right there. It's too hard to make a get away. I want you to take the Mustang and wait at the Sixty-second Street exit. On second thought, let's rent a car. They may recognize the Mustang. Now you wait there and I'll drive around inside the building for a while to see if anybody's on my tail. You keep the motor going and as soon as I pass you, I want you to take the rental car behind me and stall it long enough to block anybody that's chasing me. Get out and lift up the hood or something. You only have to stall them for a minute or two. I hate to expose you to this but I can't see letting anybody else in on the deal at this point."

"You ask me if I can drive and now you ask me to stall the car like a helpless female."

"That's just a *role* you're playing, honey, *later* you'll get a chance to drive. Now, when I get out with the car, I'm going to take it over the Queensboro Bridge to a diner on Steinway Avenue. It's a place where I first met your 'brother.' Here's a matchbook with the address. It's easy to find. It's right near the exit from the bridge. Turn in the rental car, pick up the Mustang from our garage and meet me there. Meanwhile, I'll have set up the meet with the money boys or whatever."

Day took a deep breath and exhaled slowly. "O.K., we'd better get going. It's almost nine and I want to meet you there no later than eleven o'clock, right?"

"Right."

"Take the CB receiver with you when you go to rent the car. That way we can check the reception to make sure nothing goes wrong."

Christina took his hand impulsively. "Day, what if something goes wrong? What if they grab you and hijack the stocks, and maybe kill you?"

"Gee," Palmer said, "I never thought of that."

On their way back from the coffee shop, Palmer stopped by a sporting goods shop and picked up a twenty-gauge Browning double barrel shot gun and a box of shells. It set him back two hundred and twenty-five dollars, but Palmer felt the money was well spent on his life insurance.

In the apartment they had collected their separate suitcases, plus the third suitcase with the bonds in it. Fortunately, there was room in each of their personal suitcases for one of the CB transmitters. "Go through the place," Palmer said, "and see if we left anything. There's a good chance we won't be coming back here."

Christina searched the apartment, checking closet, drawers and anyplace else where they might have left

271

some of their belongings; but they had really never unpacked so there was no problem there.

Downstairs they took a taxi the short few blocks to the garage where Palmer had left his car, transferred all three suitcases to the trunk of the Mustang and put the shotgun in as well.

"Put the Mustang into the Hilton garage. There's a car rental place right there and then rent a car and go up and wait for me where I said. Keep the CB receiver on in case I have any last-minute messages. We'll time it so I'm leaving at the Sixty-second Street exit at just eleven, right?"

"Right."

They grabbed a cab on Third Avenue for the Hilton, where Palmer went downstairs to make a phone call and Christina went to the National Car Rental desk.

Sally Friedlander was waiting for Palmer's call.

"Everything clear on your end?" he asked.

"Yeah, there was plenty trouble, but I managed it. But this better be a good one. What are you going to need for your caper?"

"Plenty of unmarked cars, some riot guns, tear gas maybe, and if you could have a chopper alerted, it might help. I'm going to try to pick a big open area for the meet, where there's plenty of visibility. I haven't decided exactly where yet. But I'll let you know in time. Meanwhile, where do I go to get wired?"

They set up a meet in one of the discount men's clothing stores near Sixteenth Street and Fifth.

"That's a funny corner to pick," Day Palmer said. "Every Italian in America knows that corner."

"Why is that?"

"It's where Mussolini's thugs executed the socialist leader Carlo Tresca, just before the Fascists took over."

"I'm sure Rothberg's Men's Clearance House is not too into that. I'll meet you there at noon, right?"

"Right!"

When Palmer had finished, he checked at the National desk.

"Did a pretty girl with dark hair and a white streak just check out a car?"

"She left a few minutes ago."

"Good!" Palmer said.

He grabbed a cab for the Coliseum Garage, stood in line for a few minutes at the glassed-in booth before he could ask for the envelope with the key in it. It cost him a dollar and a half to take the car out. This meant it had been there more than an hour. The Datsun was a beauty, all right. A late model fire engine red, equipped with Alabama plates, which Day realized could be gotten by the dozen without proof of ownership. He got in and turned the key. The car started with a soft mellow roar. He depressed the clutch and ran the gear shift through the four forward speeds to get the feel of it, and wasting no time warming up, eased out of the parking space.

As he passed, he saw that the attendant in the glass booth was on the phone to somebody. Palmer wondered who.

He began to wind his way through the confusion of signs and arrows, twisting and turning to the exit several floors above.

As he did so, he noticed a Buick Electra taking the curves behind him. Of course, every car in there was there for the purpose of ultimately getting out. But Palmer didn't like anybody riding his tail.

The Datsun was very responsive to steering, and quick on the uptake. He had no trouble putting a couple of turns between himself and the Buick. But behind him, he heard screeching tires that indicated that the Buick was really trying to catch up with him, or making more speed than was decorous in those confined quarters.

Now, Palmer really accelerated the Datsun, swinging around cursing drivers in cars that were backing out or pulling in. Behind him he heard more shrieking tires and the mellow blast of the dual Buick horns.

They're either after me or they're in one big hurry to get out of here, Palmer thought, as he finally spotted the sign on the Sixty-second Street exit.

As he rolled onto the out ramp, which was up a steep slope, Palmer had a quick glimpse of a black-haired girl in a yellow Impala sitting with the motor running near the entrance. He lifted his hand in a half salute and shot out the entrance on Sixty-second Street as the Impala began to move slowly onto the ramp.

Behind him, as he started across Sixty-second Street he was sure he heard the clunk of smashing fenders and the tinkle of falling glass. But this was nearly drowned out by the sound of shrieking brakes.

I hope Chris took full insurance on that Impala, Palmer thought as he headed downtown for his rendezvous on Fifth Avenue with the Task Force.

CHAPTER FIFTY

Day Palmer took the elevator to the ninth floor of the old office building at Sixteenth and Fifth. There were signs in the elevator indicating fantastic bargains in men's clothing; and a big painted sign over the door, *Rothberg, Men's Clothes, Giant Discounts!*

Inside a chubby, balding man with a tape measure around his neck greeted him.

"Something in a suit or sport jacket, maybe, a pair of slacks?"

"Is Mr. Diendorfer here?"

The chubby man's face fell. "Yes, in back; the third dressing room. Please don't take forever, we have business to do here. The others are with him."

The big, hawk-faced IAD lieutenant was waiting for him along with De Groot, the cherubic Fed and Sally Friedlander. Diendorfer looked angry.

"Strip," he said, "so we can get this thing on you."

The white harness and book-size transmitter were hanging from his hands trailing grey wires. Palmer looked significantly toward Sally.

"Come on," Diendorfer said. "Don't be a shmuck. She's seen a guy without a shirt on before."

Palmer shed his jacket and sport shirt and the two men set to work taping the wires to his body. Sally Friedlander, perhaps, had seen a man without his shirt before, but you couldn't tell from the way she was looking over Day Palmer's muscular torso with its pale chest hairs.

"I don't like any of this," Diendorfer grumbled. "If it was up to me, you'd be behind bars by now. This is all out of our hands. It has nothing to do with Internal Affairs anyway. From now on, you're strictly a federal informant as far as I'm concerned."

"I'm sorry, lieutenant," Palmer said. "Those crooked cops just aren't very trusting; somehow they never believed I was one of them."

Diendorfer turned away in disgust.

"Look, lieutenant," Palmer argued, "I don't mind being a cop. I *like* being a cop. That's why I picked the work. But I didn't join up to turn other cops in. And you know damn well, nobody else would do it, if you didn't twist their arm to make them roll over."

"What are you? An idiot?" Diendorfer exploded. "These men we're after are *worse* than criminals. They're thieves and murderers and they use their badges to profit from the public."

At least Diendorfer believed in what he was doing.

"You coming along for the collar, lieutenant?"

"Shit!" Diendorfer said. It was the first dirty word Palmer had ever heard from him. "We'll leave that up to the Feds, with the precinct to back them up."

He gave the wires the last tug to make sure they were secure. Palmer slipped his sport shirt back over his head.

"All right," Sally Friedlander said. "Let's hear the plan—and it better be good."

"O.K.," Palmer said, talking carefully. "I've arranged a meet. They've promised that Santini and a couple of other big shots will be there, along with the hot stocks. Did I tell you they were Municipal Bonds?"

"Yeah, yeah," Sally said patiently.

"We haven't hit upon the exact spot of the meet. I'll have to arrange that later. You can pick it up on the transmitter. I'll stall so you'll have time to get your units in place. I'm going to make the meeting at three P.M. this afternoon. When I say *Anybody got the time? Exact time?* move in as quick as you can. If possible try to have your units deployed somewhere out of sight nearby so you can move fast, because if you don't move fast enough, I'm a dead man."

Sally moved forward and placed a hand compassionately on the side of his face.

"Are you sure you want to do this, Day? I . . . I mean, we already lost *one* good man trying to play a double game like this."

"Sally, you know damn well what I want. I want to be one of the good guys. The way I've been going is leading to nothing but trouble. You hold up your end of the bargain, and I can start again, straight and fresh. I don't want to be looking over my shoulder for the rest of my life."

De Groot looked irritated. "Come on, Sally," he said. His usually cherubic face twisted into a frown of concentration. "We've got a lot of stuff to get coordinated before three o'clock this afternoon. Let's get the show on the road."

"Knock it off, De Groot," Sally said. "I told you I'm handling this job."

De Groot looked crestfallen.

CHAPTER FIFTY-ONE

The man with the tape measure was still standing near the door looking worried as Palmer departed. It was obvious that business was lousy.

"Listen," he said as Palmer pushed his way through the frosted glass door. "We got a terrific selection of extra talls. Maybe you'll come back some day."

"I hope so," Palmer said.

Riding down on the elevator, he was conscious of the unexpected bulk of the transmitter on the small of his back. This, added to the presence of the thirty-eight on his hip and the small caliber automatic in the ankle holster and the switchblade in his side pocket, made him feel like a one-man-war going somewhere to happen.

It was one-fifteen when he pulled the Datsun up in front of the diner on Steinway. He was a bit concerned to note that the Mustang was nowhere in sight. Anxiously, Palmer bolted up the few steps to the long railroad-style diner, and breathed a sigh of relief when he saw Christina waiting for him in a booth in a corner.

Before entering the diner, Palmer reached under his shirt, grabbed the spaghetti-thin antenna-wire and gave it a sharp tug, pulling the plug-in jack completely loose from its socket.

Chris was wearing a blue, floppy-brimmed denim work hat, her familiar patchwork blue jacket, and a pair of bell bottom jeans. Her hair was tied back and braided like a Sioux warrior. If Palmer didn't know who she was, he would have mistaken her for a hippy road bum.

"I see you got your battle fatigues on," Palmer said, slipping into the booth.

"Might as well be ready for anything," Christina answered. Her face was serious as she leaned across the narrow table and kissed him warmly on the lips.

"Where's the Mustang?" Palmer asked, worried.

"I parked it around the corner. No sense in leaving it where somebody might recognize it, like, for instance, Frazer Arnold."

"You're right," Palmer said. "I didn't think of it, but there is a possibility he could show up here. Don't *you* trust him either?"

Christina shrugged. "At this point why trust *anybody*, except you?"

A harried blonde waitress in platform shoes and a foot-high beehive trudged over to take his order. Palmer asked for a black coffee and a toasted English. Chris had already ordered coffee and a Bialy.

"What happened back in the Coliseum?" Palmer asked.

"That Buick started after you, and it was coming out fast. I pulled my car onto the ramp and stalled it the way you told me. But the Buick couldn't stop in time and hit my left fender. Two guys jumped out of the car and left it right there. Then they went running out into the street looking for a cab. I just got myself out of the Impala and walked out of there. Later, I called National Car Rental and told them

279

that somebody had hit my car—that they should come and pick it up. It's fully insured and I used the Third Avenue apartment for an address. I don't think we'll hear from them for a while."

"Did you get a good look at the two guys in the car?"

"No, I was pretty busy ducking broken glass and so on. Just a couple of regular guys. In their thirties maybe. They both wore suits."

"What color?"

"Blue."

"No, I mean what color were the guys?"

"Oh," Christina said. "They were grey."

"Well, I guess that's logical," Palmer said. "The Harlem contingent is off and running. They've got nothing to go after my ass for anymore. In fact, when this is over, *they're* the ones who are going to come out of this better than anyone else."

Christina shrugged. "Let's just worry about *us* for the moment."

"O.K.," Palmer said, "here's the plan. I'll set up the meeting place with the wise guys before we leave here. There's a phone booth in the corner. You and I will keep in touch on the CB transmitters. You follow behind me but stay at least a block away at all times. I'll keep sending you coordinates so you'll know where I am. When we finally get located for the meet, you find a phone booth somewhere in the vicinity. Park right next to it. If anybody starts to use it, jump in there and start dialing like crazy. Just make sure that the phone booth is free when you need it."

He took out his pencil and wrote a number on a piece of paper torn from the placemat. "This is the U.S. Attorney's private number. Remember, I've told the Feds that I'm *buying* the hot paper, not *selling* it. If the wise guys *really* deliver the small bills, which I doubt, we'll get together via the CB transmitters and grab a shuttle from La Guardia to Montreal. After that, we'll play it by ear, but I'll leave a confusing enough trail that it will take the Feds a couple of days to figure out what's going down."

"What about Jennifer?"

"Don't worry, sweetheart, we'll send for her the minute we're settled. But it would definitely make it a bit conspicuous to travel with her if we really have to move. In fact, we may have to move separately if the heat is on. Meanwhile, in Canada we can deposit the money in a couple of bank accounts and draw it out down in Panama or the Bahamas or one of those banana countries."

"Day, do we have to do this?" Christina said.

"We're in a box, aren't we? In the beginning, I thought all I was going to do was even things up for Pancho and maybe get your widow's pension, but now I'm caught in the same trap that Pancho was in, and you and I know that when the story comes out, Pancho isn't getting any pension anyway."

Christina dropped her head, the denim brim of her hat hiding the expression on her face.

Palmer lifted her chin with his forefinger and was surprised to see that her eyes were bright with tears.

"Sweetheart," he said, "I wish more than anything else that those hoods play true to form and come up with a couple of suitcases full of cut-up paper. I can't see a life made up of fishing, lying in the sun, hooking a golfball around the green or swishing a tennis racket through the air all afternoon. That's not a life. That's a hobby. And I can't see making a profession out of being a full-time fugitive.

"Sure we'd have money," he continued pursuasively, "but if a man can't look forward to what he does every day when he gets up, what the hell good is the money? Other than that—a career of squealing on my pals, or on other cops even if they are bastards—that's not for me. That's not what I joined the force for. I'm no gung-ho little boy blue—I actually *like* my work, or I did, until now. If we're lucky we'll wind up watching the cactus sprout down there in Texas some place . . ."

"Or pushing up daisies," Christina said.

"O.K.," Palmer said decisively. "That's enough philosophy. I got just one hour to make my calls to the wise guys, set up a rendezvous and tip off the Feds so they'll be ready to have the Task Force in place. When I give you the signal, you call Sally's number and tell them the shit is hitting the fan and they better move those units out pronto. You're the key communications link in this whole operation."

Christina didn't look happy. Palmer took her hand.

"Listen, sweetheart, in just about two hours, the balloon goes up and it will all be over one way or the other. Are you with me?"

"I'm *with* you," Christina said, with a brave, but forced smile.

Palmer wondered why he had at the last minute held out the information that he was carrying a Federal wire. Maybe he just had gotten the feeling that it was better for *nobody* to know more than they had to.

CHAPTER FIFTY-TWO

Home Run Pugliese was waiting for Day Palmer's call.

"O.K., I've got your shipment ready," Palmer said. "What do you say we meet in the parking lot of Shea Stadium? There's no game today and it will be empty."

Day had chosen the big parking field and the time in order to get plenty of space around him where he could avoid an ambush. There were enough ways to get into the parking field, but the wise guys wouldn't be able to block them all. And besides, Palmer with his badge, could get in through one of the 'service only' entrances.

"I want to see you, Santini and Benedetto on the scene—no one else. We'll just meet there quietly, make the switch and we can each go our way. You got the cash, don't you?"

"A suitcase full of it," Pugliese said.

There was talk in the background.

Then Pugliese's voice: "O.K., you kids, here's a

quarter a piece. Now, go out and play in traffic. You kids are nickel-and-dimeing me to death here. And bring me back two Sabrett hot dogs with everything."

Palmer interrupted the parental lecture.

"I want you guys to park your car outside of the gates. I'll be there in the Datsun. I want all three of you to come on foot and bring the money with you."

"So you could bump us off and take off with the mill', right?" Pugliese said laughing.

"Don't be dumb," Palmer said. "If I wanted to do that, I wouldn't have you bring two guys with you, would I? And I wouldn't risk having the whole combination after me the rest of my life for knocking off a *capo*."

"Yeah, I guess that's right," Pugliese said reluctantly. Then after a moment of silence, he said, "Listen, you're calling all the plays," another pause, "except one. *We'll* pick the meeting place."

"Where did you have in mind?"

"Guccione's junk yard, Hunts Point. It's in a big open field just like you want. No way for anybody to sneak up on you. You can park near the fence there and you'll be protected from that side. There's no traffic out that way this time of day. Nothing but swamps and empty lots. You can find it easy. It's on Clason Avenue, right off Hunt's Point Road. It's just standing out there in the lots."

"How come you're so fussy about where we meet, all of a sudden?"

"Listen, it's *pride*. *We* got to have something to say too, don't we? It's a million bucks."

Day calculated the distance to Hunts Point. He could duck back across the Triborough Bridge and be there almost as fast as he could be out at Shea Stadium. But time was getting close.

"O.K.," he said, "I'll see you there at three o'clock."

"Right and bring your shipment."

"Right," Palmer said and hung up.

Immediately he dialed Sally Friedlander's number.

"O.K.," he said. "The meet is set for around three o'clock. It's in the South Bronx, Hunts Point Section. Get your troops over there in the general area of Hunt's Point Road. There's no tall buildings or anything so you ought to be able to pick up the transmissions nice and clear. I purposely picked this spot for that reason," Palmer said embroidering it a little.

Sally's voice sounded taut. "O.K., we'll be there, and . . . be careful."

Palmer replaced the receiver. His face was set in a tight grin as he reached into his pocket for one last dime, and dialed the number of Group One Narcotics. He stripped the cellophane from the pack of cigarettes in his pocket and put it over the telephone mouthpiece. After three rings a hard voice answered: "Group One, Detective Rogers speaking."

Palmer cupped his hand around the mouthpiece, and dropped his voice to a low guttural drawl.

The conversation was short and purposeful, and at the end, Palmer was almost certain his voice had not been recognized.

Now they had to move out fast. Day picked Chris up from the booth where she was dawdling over the last of the coffee, dropped a buck and a half on the table and led her out the door. Together they drove in the Datsun around the corner and parked near the Mustang.

Quickly, Day transferred the suitcase full of bonds and the shotgun to the small trunk of the Datsun. He went back to the car, taking one CB transmitter with him and turned the switch to talk.

"Testing, one, two, three, testing, one, two, three. I love you, Christina. Do you read me?"

The voice came crackling back. "I read you and I love you."

He dropped the CB transmitter on the seat, and came back to say goodbye to Christina who was standing by the Mustang. They kissed once, very seriously, and then separated.

"O.K., it's the big one," Palmer said quietly. "You can follow as close as you want until we get over the Triborough Bridge, and then hang back at least a block, maybe more. I'll keep talking to you."

He went back to the Datsun, put it into gear and started smoothly off down Steinway Avenue, heading for the Triborough. When he was over the bridge, he tested the CB again.

"This is Day. Do you read me, Christina?"

The voice crackled back. "I read you."

"O.K.," Palmer said, "I'm going to pull into a lay-by and move the shotgun from the trunk into the front seat. I didn't want to carry it over the bridge. There might have been questions."

"O.K., honey," Christina warned. "But be careful what you say. Don't forget this might be picked up on another CB unit."

"You're right, although I doubt if there's any around in our small range. Take it easy now. Lay back for a while and pick me up later. The meeting place is Clason Avenue and Hunt's Point. Find the nearest phone booth to there and stick with it. Kay?"

"Ten four!" Christina responded. She'd been watching too many cops and robbers movies.

Palmer laid the shotgun down so its muzzle was between the bucket seats, where he could reach it easily. He loosened the thirty-eight in his holster.

Over the bridge it was mostly open land—big vacant lots, building sites, abandoned demolished buildings and an occasional auto wrecking or scrap iron yard.

Clason Avenue was a right off Hunts Point Road in the direction of Manhattan whose towers could be seen dimly through the dirty air in the distance. To his left was Baretto Point and across the East River the grim pile of the Riker's Island Penitentiary. Straight ahead, the Triborough Towers loomed in the sky. There was the constant whine and swoop of jets settling into La Guardia Airport. Other than abandoned junkers on almost every other block, there seemed to be no cars in the area.

He passed one junk yard where a crane operator was busy piling auto wrecks on top of one another. Guccione's Junk Yard and Automotive Recycling Center stood like the Chateau Mont St. Michel alone in its beach of flattened debris. He noticed that one corner of the sign said 'Cast Iron, Steel and Scrap, Plants Dismantled, Acetylene Burning. But there was no sign of movement or life at the Guccione's citadel and the streets around it—only the weeling of sea gull scavengers above and haunting boat sounds from the river. The fence on the Clason Avenue side ran for what must have been half a city block. It was of corrugated tin and seemed to have no door or gate in it on that side, which was all the better, as far as Palmer was concerned.

He approached the junk yard slowly, made a right when he came to the corner and completely circumnavigated the block. Except for an empty truck parked in front of the main gate on the river side of the yard, there was no sign of traffic or action.

Palmer returned to the Clason Avenue side, drove to the center of the fence, then backed the Datsun around, so it was parked with its back to the junk yard at a slight angle. In this way, Palmer felt that he had his back protected and could command all approaches from one hundred and eighty degrees with the shotgun, which he had loaded with heavy deer shot.

He consulted his watch. It was five minutes to three. He was glad that he was there enough ahead of time to set up his own location. He flipped the switch on his CB transmitter. "This is me. You all set, Chris? Do you read me?"

There was a pause, then a static-y blare and Chris' tense voice. "I read you."

"You all set at the phone booth?"

"I'm about three blocks away on the other side of Hunts Point Road parked outside a pay booth."

"O.K., sit tight."

Palmer broke the shotgun open, checked that there was a shell in each barrel and flipped it closed again. Then he sat back waiting for the arrival of the three wise guys.

CHAPTER FIFTY-THREE

Another 747 roared overhead, swooping into La Guardia and the area settled again into silence. Behind him Palmer heard the grumble of some kind of motor starting up—not a car motor—a piece of machinery of some sort. From some where in the junk yard, there was a creaking of pulleys and the sound of clanging metal and straining cables.

Day Palmer assumed that there must be some sort of business going on in the junk yard, although it had looked almost deserted when he cruised past it a few minutes before. It was now one minute to three and still no sign of the wise guys.

Palmer began to wonder if this was all going to turn into a false alarm. Maybe they would hold back, until he left in disgust and then try to cut him off on one of the side roads. But then, such Machavellian double crossers as these mobsters were would want to be sure that he actually *had* the stocks first. They wouldn't take a chance that he was showing up empty-handed and had the stocks stashed somewhere else. Perhaps, that's what he *should* have done, but it would have been a very complicated deal to set up.

The whirring and clanging behind the Guccione fence grew louder now. There was a shadow overhead as though a small cloud was scudding by. What Palmer couldn't see from where he sat was the tall boom of a crane swinging around in the yard. Hooked to the end of the crane's cable was a huge, flat disc about six feet across, with lines radiating from the central core on the bottom surface. The whole thing looked like a giant inverted cast iron pie.

The crane swung the heavy iron disc high up in the air—and then swiveled and turned until the disc was suspended directly over the parked Datsun outside the fence. Gradually, slowly, delicately, the huge iron disc descended. The operator apparently was not anxious to actually crush the car by dropping the disc too suddenly. A few yards down, and on the inside of the fence, a pair of sleepy black eyes were watching the whole proceeding through a hole in the corrugated iron and directing the crane operator in the junk yard with hand motions.

The watcher, Home Run Pugliese, dropped his arm in the final signal. The crane operator in the yellow cab eased the gear forward very slowly and the huge iron disc dropped another six inches, and finally made jarring contact with the top of the Datsun, crushing its roof slightly but not enough to flatten the occupant. Day Palmer, inside the Datsun, suddenly felt himself bounced and shaken as though an enormous weight had fallen on top of the small sports car, which in fact it had.

Now, in the cab of the crane, the operator pushed a heavy knife-switch to the on position, at the same time pushing a lever to pull the round iron disc upward, the huge electromagnet swooped, sucked and grabbed the little Datsun, and the whole assemblage rose suddenly in the air on the straining cables at the end of the boom.

Palmer found himself swinging twenty-five feet in

the air, still seated in the Datsun, held by the giant crane-operated, electromagnet otherwise used to shift bundled bales of scrap iron around the Guccione yard. Now the giant boom swiveled, turned and lowered the swinging red Datsun about ten feet.

Palmer grabbed the shotgun and held it at the ready, but there wasn't much point in shooting at anything. The crane operator was well protected by his cab. A jump from this height would be extremely damaging, if not fatal; and then what?

Palmer looked out of the open window of the Datsun. About six men were standing there; several of them roaring with laughter. One was Pugliese, who was doing most of the laughing. He was dressed in chalk-striped pants and a sheepskin, surplus bomber jacket. Standing, in a more or less triangular arrangement under the suspended car, were three men who looked like junk yard workmen, in greasy work pants and tattered undershirts, their muscular shoulders tanned from working in the open yard and streaked with grease. But instead of acetylene torches, sledge hammers and giant prybars, the tools of their trade, each was carrying a different weapon.

To the north, a heavy-set worker with short cropped grey hair, was cradling an under-and-over shotgun. The man to the southwest had what appeared to be a standard army Thompson sub-machine gun with a drum magazine. And the fellow at the southeast corner was covering him with a Vietnam-style M 16 automatic carbine.

It appeared to Palmer at that moment that his chances of surviving without a piece of lead, or several of them, in his hitherto well-preserved body were close to zero.

In the background was a short, thick-set man wearing a white Fedora and an overcoat, though the day was warm. This Palmer assumed was Santini. Not far from him, a younger man, medium height in a yellow leather jacket stood toying with a large nickel-plated pistol.

"Hey, Pugliese," Palmer shouted from his perch above the yard. "What's the deal here? What is this? Some kind of a double cross?"

"Take it easy, Palmer," Pugliese said. "It's just our way of doing business. We don't want to take any chances. Where's the stocks?"

"Where's the money?" Palmer answered.

"We got it right here, see?" He held up a World War II surplus B 4 bag.

"O.K., put me down, let me have the money and I'll tell you where the stocks are."

"Oh, no, tell us where the stocks are first."

Palmer was stalling for time. If the wise guys moved as he expected them to, in a few minutes they'd know that the stocks were there in the Datsun's trunk and five minutes later Palmer would probably be dropped into the pit of the metal baler which he could now see from where he sat. It gaped beside a huge metal-eating alligator shears. In five minutes, he'd be an unrecognizable passenger inside a two-by-three foot cube of mashed iron.

This was definitely not one of the alternatives that Day Palmer had planned for himself.

Day gambled on the distance and difficult angle of view, and on his opponent's probable lack of technical expertise.

"You listening, Pugliese? Mr. Santini, are you listening?"

Pugliese's voice came back, low and harsh.

"What's on your mind, kid?"

Palmer took the small hand mike from the CB and turned it to broadcast, just in case Christina could pick up the conversation for whatever she could make out of it.

"You see this switch I'm holding?" he said, holding up the mike. "It's connected to a thermite bomb in the trunk of this car and the thermite bomb is right in the suitcase with the bonds. If I let go of this, the whole thing goes up. You got nothin' but a scorched sports car, a fried cop, and a bag of paper ashes."

"So it's like a Mexican stand-off, huh?" Pugliese's voice said from below.

"How about letting me see the money?" Palmer said, pretending for the moment that he believed them.

"Sure," Pugliese said. He zipped open a side pocket of the B-4 bag, reached in carefully and pulled out a wad of paper that looked like a pack of hundred dollar bills.

"Would you mind ruffling through that wad so I can see what's underneath that top bill?" Palmer said.

"What's the matter? Don't you trust me?" Pugliese said astonished.

"I wouldn't say that, Home Run. You've got a *terrific* business reputation. I'm just being cautious—like you guys were being with the goddamn crane."

Palmer was really beginning to feel stupid, looking down from this dangling position. Now he ducked back into the Datsun, out of sight and spoke into the microphone.

"Christina, I don't know what you made out of all that conversation, but you wouldn't believe this. They've got me hanging from an electromagnet from the end of a crane inside this junk yard. Do you read me?"

The speaker blared forth a burst of static and nothing else. Palmer repeated the question.

"Do you read me, Christina? Palmer speaking. Do you read me, Christina?"

Again nothing but static. Frantically he checked out all the connections. Everything was tight. There didn't seem to be anything wrong with the transmitter.

"Palmer to Christina. Do you read me?" Nothing. Hastily, Day scrambled around under his shirt trying to find the loose ends of the transmitter antenna and plug the jack back into the box strapped to his back. Reconnecting the Task Force transmitter had to be a calculated risk for Palmer. If he turned it on too soon, it would pick up the conversation with the wise guys

293

and reveal the fact that Palmer was not *buying* the stocks but, on the contrary, was *selling* them.

"Whad'ya doing up there?" Pugliese yelled. "We ain't got all day."

"I'm tying my shoelace," Palmer said.

"I think that termite bomb, you're talking about, is a lot of bullshit," Pugliese said.

"*Thermite*," Palmer said, "not *termite*. Why do you question me? Did I ever cross you before?"

"We never done no business on this scale of magnitude before," Pugliese said.

In the junk yard below, Home Run Pugliese was conferring with Benedetto and Santini. Apparently they were arguing over whether Palmer was going to burn up the stocks with his fire bomb, or whether they could move in on him before anything happened. Home Run came back and stood near the dangling Datsun.

"Hey, Palmer," he said, "turn off your termite bomb and we'll let you down, and you can get out of here with the money."

"You haven't *got* any money," Palmer said. "What's in it for me? You'll just take the stuff and rub me out. I might as well go down in flames."

"I give you my *woid*," Pugliese said hopelessly knowing that it wasn't much of an offer.

Ultimately, Palmer would have to take the risk of connecting the transmitter and getting the Task Force to Guccione's junk yard as quickly as possible. If not, he was certain, he wouldn't have to worry about his future anyway, since it would probably not extend beyond that afternoon.

Finally, he located the jack swinging in a difficult position behind his back and managed to reach up and plug it back into the black box.

"Palmer to Task Force," he said. "I am in a big jam here. I am at Guccione's junk yard, Clason Avenue off Hunts Point Road. Get here fast. Get whatever you can pull together. The boys here are not happy with me at all. If you could hear me, Sally, I really need you now."

Then to cover future explanations about the transmitter, he wiggled the antenna wire a few times.

"I think there's something wrong with the transmitter. Have you been picking up?" he said. "It seems to me that there's something wrong with the antenna wire."

Having said that, he pulled the wire loose again to keep from inadvertently broadcasting the details of his negotiation with Santini, Pugliese, Benedetto and company.

What could have happened to Christina? They had tried the CB transmitters out over and over again. It didn't seem possible that anything could have gone wrong with them.

From below, there was nothing but silence as the three men put their heads together again to come up with a plan. Peering out the windows of the Datsun, Palmer could see that there were only two ways to get into the yard—the front entrance, and a pair of large double gates on the North side.

How long would it take for the Feds to get there, he wondered. If they were waiting where he put them, if they were ready with the equipment, they should be there in minutes.

"I tell you what," Palmer shouted out the car window, "you send one of your guys under here where I can keep him in the sights of this shotgun." He poked the barrel out of the window.

"Hey, don't point that thing at me!" Pugliese said. "It could go off!"

Now, listening, Palmer heard over the sound of the calling sea gulls, incredibly, the squealing sounds of sirens in the distance. *Would they be dumb enough to use sirens?* Palmer thought. But the sounds were so far off and the men below were so focused on their own activities, no notice was taken. *Maybe they're just using sirens to clear the traffic, until they get near here,* Palmer hoped. Palmer instructed Pugliese with care, hoping he could time things so he hit the ground just as the raiding party arrived.

"Remember," Palmer said, "this thing is loaded with heavy deer shot. If anything funny starts to happen, I'm going to blow your fucking head right off."

"Listen," Pugliese said reasonably, "why me? I can't help it if *these* guys make a move. They wouldn't mind you blowing my head off for their cut of those hot stocks."

"That's *your* problem, isn't it?" Palmer said.

Now, he definitely heard the quiet sound of wheels rolling on pavement outside. At this point he had to play it just right. He had to be sure he was on the ground when the Task Force came in, because it would be very hard to explain his presence dangling at the end of the crane with all the bonds in the back of the Datsun, which was registered to the wise guys or possibly stolen.

"O.K., you guys win," Palmer said. "Let me down very slowly. Don't do anything suddenly, like dropping me, because I can get a shot off from this thing very fast and there's a shell in each chamber."

"Come on," Pugliese said. "What would we want to do a thing like that for?"

The crane operator in the cab looked toward Pugliese for a signal. Just before he moved, Palmer from his vantage point in the air could see what appeared to be the booms of a heavy duty police tow truck over the top of the fence at the rear of the yard. There were sounds at the front entrance, too. Benedetto apparently heard them also and began to turn around curiously. But before he said anything, Pugliese had given the signal to lower the electromagnet with the Datsun.

Now, the crane operator shifted his gears and Palmer felt himself being slowly lowered toward the scrap-littered ground.

"Hey, what's them noises? It sounds like a lot of cars out there?" Benedetto said. "Watch it, everybody! Something's happening here!"

Now the car itself was almost on the ground and Palmer had his hand on the door handle ready to go. Suddenly there was an enormous rending and crunching sound. And incredibly the fence on both sides of the yard began to topple over, pushed, it seemed, by two enormous Police Department tow-away trucks. Riding on the trucks were about fifteen cops and plain clothesmen armed with riot guns, tommy guns and pistols. At the top of the boom was De Groot, with a forty-five in one hand and a bull horn in the other.

"All right you men, Free . . ."

But before he could finish the sentence there was a blast from the shotgun in the hands of the crew-cut workman which blew the bull horn right out of the pudgy federal agent's hands.

Instinctively, De Groot leaned down to capture the tumbling electronic megaphone. As he did so there was a blast from the second barrel of the shotgun and a red patch as big as a cherry pie suddenly appeared in the trim striped fabric of the federal agent's Palm Beach suit.

The driver of the tow truck who had been standing on the ground in the shelter of the truck's body, reached up and grabbed the stricken slipping body, pulling it down onto the diamond-plate deck of the truck in the shelter of the big winch.

Now a feminine voice cut in with a bull horn on the other side. The operator, this time, was apparently in the cab of the truck.

"This is a federal raid. All you men throw down your arms and freeze."

It was Sally's voice. She may have been a woman, Palmer thought, but she sounded plenty businesslike at that moment.

However, the junk yard gang was in no mood to palaver. All three of the workmen and Benedetto began to open up on the two trucks which were now lumbering slowly into the yard. The police in plain-clothes leaped from the truck and scattered for cover among the crushed cars and baled iron. At least four heavy bullets, probably from the Thompson, struck the Datsun and started it spinning in its perch. Palmer hit the door, which he had half-open anyway, and leaped the short distance from the car to the ground.

Now, another shot hit the gas tank of the Datsun and fuel started pouring in a white stream from the ruptured tank. Palmer crouched low and ran for the shelter of the massive alligator shears.

Sally's voice was on the bull horn again talking in heavy measured tones.

"This place is completely surrounded by our cars. You men throw down your arms. There's no way out for you. Just throw down your arms."

Now, there was another burst of fire from the crane cab where one of the workers had taken shelter. The chubby one was swinging the automatic M 16 in a wild arc, spraying the area aimlessly. Several of the bullets struck the growing puddle of gas under the Datsun. Suddenly, there was a wooshing sound and the gasoline on the ground exploded, quickly igniting the tires and under-structure of the Datsun.

The operator in the cab crane reacting in panic, pushed the lever and dropped the iron electromagnet and the Datsun heavily to the ground, possibly thinking it would put out the fire. But it didn't. It simply flattened the Japanese sports car and caused it's trunk lid to pop open like the mouth of a pre-historic animal.

The raging gasoline flames spread quickly and the suitcase in the trunk began to burn with incandescent vigor, almost as though there really had been a fire bomb in there. The explosion and fire froze all hands for a fraction of a second as they stared fascinated at the flaming pyre.

Now, another harsh, heavier voice came in over the bull horn. "All right, you men, this is Captain Dreyfuss from the Four One Precinct. I think a couple of you men know me. You know I mean what I say. If you guys don't come out by the time I count ten, we're going to hose this whole place down with gasoline and torch it with you guys in it. And I'm one man who would be happy to see it happen. This is one rap you won't beat. ONE ... TWO ... THREE ..."

There was another puff and a minor explosion from the trunk of the squashed Datsun. And pieces of charred paper began to float all over the sky on the rising air convection currents generated by the flames.

Plainclothesmen began to make little darting jumps from their hiding places, trying to grab some of the fugitive flaming fragments.

"FIVE ... SIX ... SEVEN ..."

"O.K. O.K.," it was the low harsh voice of Santini who rose from behind the drum of copper lathe turnings where he had been crouched. The white hat was now smeared with black grease and cinders.

"All right, you guys, everybody come out and don't nobody say nothin' till we get a mouth piece," he shouted to his colleagues.

Slowly, one by one, the three workmen, the three hoods, and the crane operator surfaced from their iron foxholes.

CHAPTER FIFTY-FOUR

As the seven men emerged from their protective positions they were taken in hand and handcuffed by the uniformed officers of the Four One Precinct.

The federal agents and U.S. attorneys danced wildly about the yard trying to catch as many bits of charred ashes of municipal bonds that now were floating around in the stirring autumn breeze like a black snow fall. There didn't seem to be any piece bigger than an airmail stamp.

Sally emerged from the tow truck at the south part of the junk yard and came running up to Day Palmer, who was standing there watching the burning Datsun, his shoulders slumping with fatigue, his face grey with tension.

Half-sobbing, Sally Friedlander ran to Day and threw her arms briefly around his neck, kissing him wetly on the cheek and the ear.

"I'm glad you're o.k.," Sally said. "I really never thought it would get to this."

"I'm o.k., but you'd better check on your side kick. I think he caught a pretty bad shot gun blast there."

"De Groot. My God! I didn't even know. I was watching ..."

Their conversation was interrupted by the whoop-whoop-whoop sound of a Sydenham Hospital ambulance that slid to a stop by the south gate, its red emergency light flashing.

"They must have radioed for a meat wagon," Palmer said as they both started trotting across the cluttered cobblestone pavement of the scrap yard toward the tow truck blocking the north entrance. The driver of the tow truck, now stripped to the waist, had ripped off his cotton T-shirt and was holding it wadded into the huge wound ripped by the shotgun blast on De Groot's side.

De Groot lay there, his Palm Beach jacket still buttoned, the knot of his tie loosened only about an inch to allow for easier breathing. His face was the color of a slab of paraffin and his eyes were clouded with pain, but he recognized the slim, blonde frame of Sally Friedlander as she loped across the yard to his side.

"I'm sorry, Sally," he muttered. "I goofed up the whole detail. I should have just stayed down. I goofed up everything ..."

Then two ambulance aides in green tunics were by his side carrying a folded stretcher. With them was the third aide carrying a flask of plasma and a long tube with a needle which they quickly inserted in De Groot's arm after cutting their way through the thin fabric of the suit and the broadcloth shirt.

Day Palmer could see that De Groot was trying to protest over this damage to his wardrobe, but was too weak to make the gesture. Sally grabbed Day's hand and held it as the attendant started to move the wounded agent out to the ambulance. Her eyes were bright with tears, but Palmer thought the expression on her face was more of anger and exasperation than sorrow.

When the ambulance had whoop-whooped its way up into the far reaches of the East Bronx, Sally and Day Palmer turned and started back to the junk yard to wrap up all the many loose ends of the arrest. The air in the yard was still thick with floating cinders of charred paper.

"There goes my case," Sally said gesturing hopelessly toward the swirling black fragments.

"Not necessarily," Palmer said as they walked back toward the south end of the yard where the seven wise guys were being frisked and cuffed by the patrolmen of the Four One Precinct. The assistant U.S. attorney and Treasury Department officers of the Federal Task Force still chased aimlessly after the falling fragments of charred municipal bonds.

One of them had found a fire extinguisher in the office and was spraying at the trunk of the Datsun in hope of salvaging some of the valuable paper but he couldn't get close enough to the hot flames to do much good with the tiny chemical spray.

"I wouldn't say it was hopeless," Palmer argued. "You still got plenty on these guys. Conspiracy to commit murder on *me*, for one thing. You got them on weapons charges. Everyone of them was packing a rod, except maybe Santini."

"Look, Palmer, we made a deal based on a *major* collar," Sally said, stopping half way through the yard to remonstrate with him. "We were supposed to catch these guys with ten million dollars' worth of hot stock out of the mayor's office. How do you think we're going to look coming in with a couple of Sullivan Law raps which aren't even federal, anyway. And *conspiracy*, none of that is even in our department. I don't see how I can deliver any deal I promised you based on this."

Fred, the Treasury Department agent, waved to them from the doorway of the corrugated tin shack adjoining the big drive-in Fairbanks scale which served as the junk yard office. On a desk inside the shack, he had assembled whatever fragments he had been able to collect thus far of the burned bonds.

"We couldn't get much," he said. "And it's funny. It looks like a lot of these bigger pieces of paper are blank. Nothing on them at all. But there's one or two fairly good pieces. There's one here." He indicated a charred fragment about the size of a lottery ticket.

"You can see that the number 'five thousand dollars' is on it. Here's another piece that says 'Battery Park' something. And a couple of chunks that say 'New York.' Then there's a few bits of engraving and pictures of dead treasurers and presidents and so on. But I don't see how we can establish the quantity of this stuff or its origins.

"Also, some of this is definitely just some plain typing paper. Look at this piece that didn't get burned." He indicated a brown corner that was unburned at the edges. "That don't look like securities paper to me, it looks like plain typing paper. Maybe there was some other stuff in that trunk."

Palmer picked up the fragment and examined it carefully. A horrible thought was beginning to take place in his mind. Christina had had access to the suitcase full of bonds for at least an hour when she was driving the Mustang. And now Christina seemed to have disappeared. A weird scenario was forming in Palmer's head. One in which a man with a suitcase full of fake packs of money topped with a few real bills, was negotiating with another man who had a suitcase full of typing paper topped by a few real bonds. In this scenario, a beautiful, dark-skinned, black-haired girl was already on her way south, maybe to Atlanta, Georgia with a suitcase containing ten million dollars' worth of municipal bonds give or take a few thousand that had been used to cover the typing paper. It is not the ending Palmer would have chosen for this story. But he had to admit that he had let his infatuation blind him to what had been a fairly mercenary proposition in the first place. The fact that they had made beautiful love together did not wipe

out the fact that Christina had made it clear that
without the money there was no deal. She told him in
no uncertain words, that she had no interest in being
a cop's wife again.

But how would Christina sell the stocks? Probably
through Frazer Arnold. And now a few pieces more
of the scenario fell into place. It's funny how you
didn't notice things unless you were looking for them
specifically. Palmer had not been paying attention at
the right time.

Frazer Arnold was a brother to Christina only in
the sense of being a "soul" brother. That slipped out
when they each described a different father. It should
have had more meaning for him, but it seemed so
unimportant at the time. And now something else
came to him. That beautiful smell of hot house roses,
the smell he thought was an olfactory hallucination.
Actually, Christina herself had given him the clue
when she told him she could smell the perfumes of
different women on Pancho's clothes and body when
he returned after a date.

What he had smelled in Frazer Arnold's room was
attar of roses. That special perfume so identified with
only one woman—Christina. That would explain why
Frazer decided to go up to Pascag Island ahead of
time by chopper. Palmer had been so busy with the
complication of the dope and stock deal that he
hadn't noticed what was going on under his nose—the
beautiful smell that he had ignored.

What really hurt was the fact that Christina had
left him there in the hands of those murdering thugs,
knowing that there was an almost one hundred percent chance that he would be killed when they found
the suitcase contained nothing but Hammermill bond
instead of municipal bonds. In fact, there's no question that it was that that she must have counted on.
That he wouldn't be around to know what happened.
That he'd never even get the chance to put the finger
on Frazer Arnold for having ripped off the bonds.

But there was still a problem. If Frazer Arnold had

known how to convert those bonds into a considerable amount of cash, he would never have become involved in the deal with Palmer in the first place. Frazer would have the same problem that he himself had had in unloading the hot paper. Perhaps a *greater* problem was of his extreme high profile. A black to start with, and one associated with the city treasury. If he even started to go through the motions would probably bring on enough heat to queer the deal.

For a fleeting moment, Palmer wished they'd dropped the giant electromagnet on the Datsun with him still in it. But now he found himself charged with surging anger and for the second time, a deep compulsion to take that boojie nigger by the neck and throttle him till his eyes popped out like cue balls.

Glancing over to the table where the Treasury man was trying to hold down charred fragments of paper with a large piece of plastic, Palmer realized that he still had a way to get Frazer, though it wouldn't be quite as satisfying as throttling him with his own hands.

There was a small private office opening off the scale room. Palmer gestured to Sally Friedlander to follow him in there. He closed the door and sat down with his hip on the battered oak desk of the inner office.

"Suppose," he said, "I give you proof of *exactly* what is missing, how much and what the serial numbers are. You guys could probably find a few pieces that have at least enough of the serial numbers to link it to my evidence and then you'll have a good case, right?"

"I don't even know if municipal bonds qualify for a federal case. But there should be some angle."

"There is," Palmer said. "They were stolen from a shipment in interstate travel, between a printing plant in Philadelphia and New York. Does tht give you a federal angle?"

"I guess so," Sally said. "But what's the scoop?"

Palmer pulled a black police notebook from his hip pocket.

"There's a vault on the eighth floor of the municipal building in the controller's office. In that vault, they keep most of the bonds that the city is planning to sell, also, securities posted by contractors as guarantees, treasury certificates and stocks. As you may have read recently, there has been in the past a pretty sloppy control over the checking in and checking out of those securities. If you look on the shelf that contains the Battery Park Municipal Bonds, you will find in going through the serial numbers that there is a discrepancy ..." He referred to the notebook. "Between number H 243742 and H 245742. That discrepancy accounts for two thousand bonds in five thousand dollar denominations, amounting to ten million dollars. You'll find when you collect enough chunks of these ashes, that what's floating around in this yard are the remains of that missing ten million dollars' worth of bonds. Can you make a case out of that?"

Sally shrugged. "Maybe. As far as I can see most of the stuff in that car is plain blank paper."

"How do you know that?" Palmer said. "Who can tell how much went up in flames? You found *some* of the pieces and when you find that gap you'll know how much is missing exactly."

"And who do we nail on the charge of stealing the stuff?"

"There's a lot of people that can walk in and out of that office and into the vault," Palmer said. "And as you can see, ten million dollars' worth of bonds in five thousand dollar denominations doesn't take up that much room. Any one of a number of guys could have carried it out a million at a time, stuffed in his shirt. The stuff could have been ripped off in the printing plant also. Or in the delivery process between the plant and Philadelphia and here."

"But there's one guy who had the job of checking out the bonds when they came in who would know if they were stolen earlier. He's a guy that if you run a check on him, you'll find that his style of living indicates an income of maybe triple what his salary is—$27,500 dollars a year. His name is Frazer Arnold and you'll find him tomorrow, right in his office in City Hall—I hope. But you'll have to put a complete lid of security on this case. In fact, you'll have to put out the word that I'm dead."

CHAPTER FIFTY-FIVE

"I had a call just before I left the office this morning," Sally said. "It was from the Joint Task Force. It seems as though your old partners down in Narcotics South had a terrific collar last night, up in the two-six in Harlem."

"No kidding?" Palmer said, his eyes widening with interest. "What happened?"

"They had a raid on this soul food restaurant on Lennox Avenue. Somebody phoned in an anonymous tip. There was a big cutting lab in the back of the place. They snatched everything—the works, the junk, the scales ..."

"Any trouble?" Palmer asked.

"You said it! There was a big shootout. Your pal Rogers is in Bellevue with a slug in his lungs. It looks like he's headed for early retirement." (*Good! Palmer thought. If that sonovabitch has to live on his pension, he'll cut his throat.*) "The owner of the joint, some big spade basketball player named Haynes, got a superficial wound in the cheek. He's out now on $500,000 cash bail."

Palmer whistled appreciatively.

"That's heavy, isn't it? How much stuff did they get?"

"It was a big one, all right," Sally agreed. "They got twenty-five pounds of pure white heroin. It tests out at eighty percent. Nobody's seen that kind of stuff around since the French Connection bust."

Palmer pursed his lips appreciatively. As far as he could tell there was no irony in Sally's smooth features.

"Twenty-five pounds, that's a big haul all right; but nowhere as *big* as the French Connection take, is it? You remember that's what attracted our attention to that bunch of pirates you used to work with in the first place. Anyway on this caper we're pretty sure we got it all."

"Right," Palmer said.

It's fantastic, he thought. That pile of skaq will just keep going round and round in ever-diminishing quantities, corrupting everyone it touches, as it dwindles gradually to nothing. It all reminded him of the story of the Killy-Loo bird that flew in ever-decreasing concentric circles until it flew up it's own asshole.

"I got a funny feeling about that whole deal," Sally said, eying him shrewdly. "It seems like quite a coincidence that that raid would take place last night, just when all this deal that you set up here was about to go down. But I can't really make the connection. And another thing. How come the only transmissions we could pick up from your wire was the one where you called for help?"

Palmer shrugged. "You know these transmitters have a very limited range and they could be blocked out by almost anything. It's probably all this iron around here that blocked out the transmission. And before that, I was too far away. Besides, I don't think the thing is working quite right.

309

Sally still looked skeptical. "And what about this business of reporting you dead?"

"If Arnold thinks I'm dead he'll probably stay put and you could nab him. Maybe you can watch him for a while and find out how much other stuff he's gotten away with. But if he knows I'm alive, he's gonna take it on the lam."

"I don't know if we could get away with it. The only hope we have is that since this whole thing took place in this God forsaken part of the Bronx, the news guys may not get hold of it right away. But we won't be able to keep a cover story like that up for long. And the reasons you give don't exactly add up as far as I'm concerned."

"You want the collar, don't you? You realize what this will do for you? This guy Arnold is number two in the controller's office. This is gonna shake up the whole city."

"And what are you getting out of all this?"

"The same thing I dealt for in the first place. A clean record and a new job."

"That's a lot to ask for—a guy in your spot. First the tapping charges and now all this funny business you've been up to in the last couple of weeks. They could really wipe me out if they knew what I let you get away with. Not to mention the highly questionable ethics involved here."

"I suppose *you* never bent the code a little bit? You're Ms. Clean."

"I try to be," Sally said.

"Don't make me laugh. What about that scene back in the hotel—between the two of us?"

Sally's face flushed with anger. "That was personal. It had nothing to do with professional ethics."

"And what about you and Pancho? Was that strictly personal too?"

"*I'm* asking the questions," Sally said, cutting in on his speculations.

"O.K. for now, Sally," Palmer said. "But I want to

come back to that later. Now what's bothering you about this case?"

"For one thing, the fact that you were in that Datsun when we got here, along with the bonds. If, in fact, there *were* any bonds. I'd like to know how you'd explain that."

"It was all part of the deal," Palmer said. "I had a B4 bag full of newspaper clippings with a couple of hundred dollar bills on the outside. You'll find that out in the yard here somewhere."

"O.K., what next?"

"I had Christina Navarro drive me here in my car. At their instructions, she left me at a certain corner in this neighborhood. At the corner of Hunt's Point and Clason Avenue, Home Run Pugliese picked me up in the Datsun. I think you'll find it either a stolen car or registered to someone in the Santini family. You'll find their prints all over it and—mine, of course."

Palmer was doing some heavy thinking; although he had already been over the ground in his own mind. He laid in the details very carefully.

"When we drove into the yard, the other guys were there waiting. I knew that the minute they got a look inside my suitcase and saw that the money was phony, it would be the end for me. So I pulled a gun on Pugliese and made him get out of the car, stalling for time. And before I knew it, while we were talking, they moved the big crane over me and picked me up with that big magnet."

Sally sounded doubtful. "I suppose there *are* people who would buy that. It's all certainly a very cute explanation."

Their exchange was interrupted by the sudden harsh jangling of the phone. Palmer reached it before Sally. He held his hands over his lips. "Guccione's junk yard," he said, trying to sound as workmanlike as possible. There was a pause. A woman's voice said, "Is Mr. Pugliese there?"

"Just a minute," Palmer said. He covered the

311

mouthpiece. "It's for Home Run Pugliese. Do you want to put him on?"

"Sure," Sally said. "We may be able to pick up something. But I doubt that he's gonna really talk in front of us."

"You're holding a pretty big rap over his head. Maybe he'll play ball. I'm sure you know how to handle that kind of thing."

"You may be right," she said and went into the other room to call Pugliese in from the yard where he was still being held with the other prisoners.

When she was gone, Palmer fingered the button on the telephone receiver for a moment trying to decide whether to cut the call off or not. He had recognized the woman's voice on the other end of the line. It was Christina. He picked up the receiver and listened. In the distance there was a sound of Latin music. It sounded as though she were in a bar someplace. Probably not far away. He tried to picture her in the booth filling the close quarters with her sweet rosebud smell. He thought about just shouting into the phone, "Bitch, I'm alive. How's that grab you? I'm alive!" . . . I'm alive!"

Somewhere that tall tawny bitch is riding around with a satchel full of hot bonds. She's a smart dame. I wonder if she'll ever find a way to unload it? Or will it be jinxed the way everything tied to the French Connection dope had been from the start?

He was almost sure that he could hear the sound of her breathing coming over the line. Looking through the window, he could see Sally returning now leading the handcuffed loan shark to the weigh-in shack.

He wasn't sure exactly what Christina would have to say. She hadn't known about the transmitter, of course, the one that the Task Force had taped to his chest. She would have assumed that by now Palmer was dead. And now, no doubt, she was gonna try to close the deal herself.

Palmer would have given his trigger finger to sit in on a phone call where she made her rendezvous to

312

dump the bonds. But he was afraid that the conversation might reveal too much about his own part in trying to sell them. Slowly, regretfully, he pressed his finger down on the receiver button breaking the contact.

Sally had just come into the office. She put her head around the corner.

"I got Pugliese in here," she said. "You think I should put him on now?"

"Too late. The person on the other end hung up," Palmer said.

"Goddamn it," Sally said angrily. "Can't anything go right here today? O.K. Pugliese, you can go back and join your friends." She signaled to one of the precinct cops lounging in a chair by the scale and had him return the loan shark to the waiting group of prisoners.

The strain of the day was beginning to take its toll. Tension was making little worry lines blossom on a usually smooth brow. And her immaculate blonde hair was now speckled with black cinders from the fire.

"You've got grease on your nose," Palmer said. "I guess a junk yard isn't exactly the cleanest place to work."

Sally came back into the office, snapped open her big saddle leather shoulder bag and reached in to search around for a Kleenex. "Which side is it on?"

"The left side," Palmer said. But he was looking into the open maw of the shoulder bag. Something he saw there jogged a vague memory in his mind.

It was a shiny, nickel-plated Walther PPK. He reached into the bag and picked out the small automatic.

"This sure is a beauty," Palmer said hefting the piece. "I suppose it's only reasonable that you carry some kind of protection in your work."

"It's not a bad idea," Sally Friedlander said.

"Did you buy this one yourself?"

313

Sally looked at him curiously. "No, it was ... a gift ... from a friend ..."

"... named Pancho Navarro."

"Right."

Sally held his eyes in a steady gaze. But Palmer was sure he saw a current of uneasiness beneath her cool appraising stare.

He sank into the battered swivel chair behind the junk yard desk, leaned back and pressed his hands together, watching the tall blonde U.S. attorney speculatively. He could never go to court with what he suspected. But it would help to know the truth.

"How close are you to De Groot? It seemed to me that he always looks at you as though you were a lamb chop and he was a hungry Great Dane."

Sally shrugged. "He has a crush on me, I guess. He's always after me to go out with him after work."

"Did you ever?"

"Maybe a few times, so what?"

"There really wasn't any need for him to be up on the boom of that tow truck this afternoon, was there? I mean he came riding in there like Lochinvar out of the West. Why would you say that was?"

Sally turned and looked out at the tangled metallic debris of Guccione's yard. The view was murky and distorted through the streaked and battered iron casement window.

"I suppose he was trying ... he was trying to make an impression on me. He is always trying to do that."

Their conversation was interrupted again by the jangling of the phone. Palmer grabbed the receiver before Sally could get to it, worried that it might be Christina on the line again, but it was a man's voice.

"Sgt. Shiblansky of the Four One. Is Miss Friedlander there?"

"It's for you," Palmer said handing her the receiver.

"Friedlander here," Sally said. "What's the problem?"

There was a suppressed squeaking and crackling

314

from the other end of the receiver. Sally's face suddenly lost all of its hard efficient lines. Her eyes brightened for a moment with tears and she bit her lips nervously.

"I see, Sergeant," she said. "Thank you," and hung up. She leaned with both hands on the receiver, biting her lip to hold back the tears. "De Groot," she said finally. "He died in the Intensive Care Unit five minutes ago."

"I'm sorry," Palmer said.

Sally's voice broke. "He just ... had lost too much blood. He was trying very hard, you see ..." She was rapidly losing control of her voice. Finally she whispered her last words softly into the tissue she was still holding in her hand, "He could be so stupid," she said. "He didn't have to ... have to ..."

"And now," Palmer said, "you don't have to cover up for him any more."

He'd been doing a lot of thinking about De Groot that afternoon. "But maybe we now can just close out the case of Pancho Navarro."

Sally looked up at him now, her eyes red rimmed from crying. "What are you talking about?"

"I don't know why I didn't get it earlier. I should have got the picture that time in the hotel room. I finally figured out from Frank's phone book that you were seeing each other pretty regularly. You were crazy about him, weren't you?"

Sally set her lips tightly together and looked to the window. She didn't answer the question.

"You had something on Pancho the way you had something on me. You caught him up to some of his monkey business. Pinching a piece of skag or something like that, and you were using him to get the French Connection dope. He must have asked for a deal something like the one I asked for. He would have had to go under cover. Once he ratted on his pals on the Narcotics Squad, he was a dead man for sure.

"The Feds would have sent him away where you would never see him again. Protecting a federal wit-

315

ness. Except that you were planning to go away also, following him along a little afterwards.

"De Groot knew all about the deal, right? About Pancho being a federal witness. And the other part, what was going on in between you and Pancho, he probably had no trouble guessing either. But he couldn't stand the thought of you going away like that. He was a little, no-talent boob, but being with you made him feel important."

"Mmmph." Sally made a sound that might have been a grunt or a sob.

"He's a member of the Joint Task Force. It was a cinch for him to set up a meet with Pancho in East Harlem. He just took the panel wagon out of the Task Force Motor Pool, parked it up the block, and waited. The suicide note was ready typed. There was nothing to it. They used the same office. Half the time they shared the typewriter.

"He pulled his service pistol on Pancho and made him hand over the Walther. Pancho had never registered it. He always figured he could use it as a throw-away piece. He told me that himself. It came from a shipment stolen from the docks down in the Red Hook District.

"You know, Pancho was like that. He played it pretty straight but he'd always hold out a few things for himself. After that it was simple. De Groot just took the Walther and blew him away. At that range, even a pea shooter like that can rip you up pretty good."

Now the sounds were clear. Sally was standing there staring out the window, her shoulders shaking, trying to suppress the croaking sobs. "Deep down, I think you really knew about it, didn't you, Sally? But there was no way that you could make it right without involving yourself in a really messy scene."

He was standing close behind her now and she turned and leaned her tear-streaked face against his chest.

"I couldn't ... I couldn't open up the case. Nobody

316

wanted it. And for me it would have been the end. The end of the job, the end of my ambition of getting anywhere in the Attorney General's office. Pancho was gone and there was nothing I could do about that."

She leaned back and looked up at Day's face now. Her lashes were gummed together in a little starry pattern by tears. "You're the only one that knows, I suppose. All those guys on the Narcotics Squad probably suspect one another of having done it. It makes a kind of bond between them, doesn't it?"

"Kind of," Palmer said.

She held his eyes in a long serious stare and Palmer was positive she was measuring him to fit in Pancho Navarro's shoes. He took her by the shoulder and bent his head toward her and she turned her face up to meet his, her eyes closed now, her mouth half parted. Gently he placed a very chaste kiss right at the point where blonde hair met her smudged brow.

"You've got *your* ambition, sweetheart, and I've got mine, and right now, what I want is to get as far from you and any other woman as I can get."

There was a long pause. Sally turned her back to him again, her arms folded her head bent in thought.

"It would work, you know, you and me."

"Maybe," Palmer said, "but I just don't think so. I just can't see myself as the husband of the Attorney General.